BEAT THE REAPER

JOSH BAZELL has a BA in English literature and writing from
Brown University and an MD from Columbia University.
He is currently a resident at the University of California,
San Francisco, and is working on his second novel.

BEAT THE REAPER

A NOVEL

JOSH BAZELL

WILLIAM HEINEMANN: LONDON

Published by William Heinemann 2009

2 4 6 8 10 9 7 5 3 1

First published in the United States in 2009 by Little, Brown and Company,
a division of Hachette Book Group, Inc.

First published in Great Britain in 2009 by
William Heinemann
Random House, 20 Vauxhall Bridge Road,
London SW1V 2SA

www.rbooks.co.uk

Addresses for companies within The Random House Group Limited
can be found at: www.randomhouse.co.uk/offices.htm

The Random House Group Limited Reg. No. 954009

A CIP catalogue record for this book
is available from the British Library

ISBN 9780434019236

The Random House Group Limited supports The Forest Stewardship
Council (FSC), the leading international forest certification organisation.
All our titles that are printed on Greenpeace approved FSC certified paper
carry the FSC logo. Our paper procurement policy can be found at:
www.rbooks.co.uk/environment

Reaper designs by Rebecca Bazell

Printed and bound in Great Britain by
CPI Mackays, Chatham, ME5 8TD

In Memoriam
Stanley Tanz, MD
1911–1996

If Nietzsche is correct, that to shame a man is to kill him,

then any honest attempt at autobiography will be an act of self-destruction.

— Camus

BEAT THE REAPER

1

So I'm on my way to work and I stop to watch a pigeon fight a rat in the snow, and some fuckhead tries to mug me! Naturally there's a gun. He comes up behind me and sticks it into the base of my skull. It's cold, and it actually feels sort of good, in an acupressure kind of way. "Take it easy, Doc," he says.

Which explains that, at least. Even at five in the morning, I'm not the kind of guy you mug. I look like an Easter Island sculpture of a longshoreman. But the fuckhead can see the blue scrub pants under my overcoat, and the ventilated green plastic clogs, so he thinks I've got drugs and money on me. And maybe that

I've taken some kind of oath not to kick his fuckhead ass for trying to mug me.

I barely have enough drugs and money to get me through the day. And the only oath I took, as I recall, was to *first* do no harm. I'm thinking we're past that point.

"Okay," I say, raising my hands.

The rat and the pigeon run away. Chickenshits.

I turn around, which rolls the gun off my skull and leaves my raised right hand above the fuckhead's arm. I wrap his elbow and jerk upwards, causing the ligaments to pop like champagne corks.

Let's take a moment to smell the rose known as the elbow.

The two bones of the forearm, the ulna and the radius, move independently of each other, and also rotate. You can see this by turning your hand from palm up, in which position the ulna and radius are parallel, to palm down, where they're crossed into an "X."* They therefore require a complicated anchoring system at the elbow, with the ligaments wrapping the various bone ends in spoolable and unspoolable ribbons that look like the tape on the handle of a tennis racket. It's a shame to tear these ligaments apart.

But the fuckhead and I have a worse problem right now. Namely that while my right hand has been fucking up his elbow,

---

* And you can compare this to your lower leg, where the same setup is vestigial. The two bones of the lower leg, the tibia and fibula, are locked in place. The outer one, the fibula, doesn't even support weight. In fact you can take most of it out—to use as a graft or whatever—and as long as you don't fuck up the ankle or the knee, it won't affect the patient's ability to walk.

my left, having somehow come into position by my right ear, is now hooking toward his throat in a knife-edge.

If it hits, it will crush the fragile rings of cartilage that keep his trachea open against the vacuum of breathing in. Next time he tries, his windpipe will clench shut like an anus, leaving him at ReaperTime minus maybe six minutes. Even if I ruin my Propulsatil pen trying to trache him.

So I beg and plead, and coax the trajectory of my hand upwards. Past the point where it's aiming for his chin, or even his mouth—which would have been disgusting—to where it's aiming for his nose.

Which caves in like wet clay. Wet clay with twigs in it. The fuckhead crashes to the pavement, unconscious.

I check to make sure I'm calm—I am, I'm just annoyed—before getting heavily to my knees down next to him. In this kind of work, as in every kind of work, probably, planning and composure are worth a lot more than speed.

Not that this particular situation requires much planning or composure. I roll the fuckhead onto his side so he won't choke to death, and bend the arm that isn't broken under his head to keep his face off the frozen sidewalk. Then I check to make sure he's still breathing. He is, in fact with a bubbly *joie de vivre*. Also the pulses at his wrists and ankles are reasonably strong.

So, as is usual in these situations, I imagine asking the Great One—Prof. Marmoset—whether I can leave now.

And, as is also usual in these situations, I imagine Prof. Marmoset saying *No*, and *What would you do if he was your brother?*

I sigh. I don't have a brother. But I know what he's getting at.

I put my knee into the guy's fucked-up elbow and pull the bones as far apart as the tendons feel likely to bear, then let them come slowly back together into their positions of least resistance. It makes the fuckhead groan in pain in his sleep, but whatever: they'd just do the same to him in the ER, only by then he'd be awake.

I frisk him for a cell phone. No such luck, of course, and I'm not about to use my own. If I did have a brother, would he want me getting hassled by the cops?

So instead I pick the fuckhead up and fold him over my shoulder. He's light and stinky, like a urine-logged towel.

And, before I stand, I pick up his handgun.

The gun is a real piece of shit. Two pieces of pressed sheet-metal—no grips, even—and a slightly off-center cylinder. It looks like something that began life as a starter pistol at a track meet. For a second it makes me feel better about there being 350 million handguns in the United States. Then I see the bright brass ends of the bullets and am reminded how little it takes to kill someone.

I should throw it out. Bend the barrel and drop it down a storm drain.

Instead, I slip it into the back pocket of my scrub pants.

Old habits die harder than that.

In the elevator up to Medicine there's a small blond drug rep in a black party dress, with a roller bag. She's got a flat chest, and the arch of her back boosts her ass, so she's shaped like a sexy, slender kidney bean. She's twenty-six after a bit too much sun exposure,* and her nose is the kind that looks like a nose job but isn't. Freckles, I shit you not. Her teeth are the cleanest things in the hospital.

"Hi," she says like she's from Oklahoma. "Do I know you?"

"Not yet, no," I say. Thinking: *Because you're new on this job, or you wouldn't have such shitty hours.*

"Are you an orderly?" she asks.

"I'm an intern in Internal Medicine."

An intern is a first-year resident, one year out of medical school, so typically about six years younger than I am. I don't know what an orderly is. It sounds like someone who works in an insane asylum, if there are still insane asylums.

"Wow," the drug rep says. "You're cute for a doctor."

If by "cute" she means brutal and stupid-looking, which in my experience most women do, she's right. My scrub shirt is so tight you can see the tattoos on my shoulders.

Snake staff on the left, Star of David on the right.†

"You're from Oklahoma?" I ask her.

"Well yes I am."

"You're twenty-two?"

"I wish. Twenty-four."

---

* Doctors always know how old you are. We use it to tell whether you're lying to us. There are various formulas for it—compare the creases of the neck to the veins on the backs of the hands and so on—but they're not really necessary. If you met thirty people a day and asked them how old they were, you'd get good at it too.

† The tattoo on my left shoulder—winged staff, two snakes—turns out to actually be the symbol of Hermes, and therefore of commerce. The symbol of Asclepius, and therefore of medicine, is a nonwinged staff with one snake. Who knew?

"You took a couple of years off."

"Yes, but oh my God that is a boring story."

"It's okay so far. What's your name?"

"St*aaaaa*cey," she says, stepping closer with her arms behind her back.

I should say here that being chronically sleep-deprived is so demonstrably similar to being drunk that hospitals often feel like giant, ceaseless office Christmas parties. Except that at a Christmas party the schmuck standing next to you isn't about to fillet your pancreas with something called a "hot knife."

I should also maybe say that drug reps, of whom there is one for every seven physicians in the U.S., get paid to be flirtatious. Or else to actually fuck you—I've never been quite clear on that.

"What company do you work for?" I ask.

"Martin-Whiting Aldomed," she says.

"Got any Moxfane?"

Moxfane is the drug they give to bomber pilots who need to take off from Michigan, bomb Iraq, then fly back to Michigan without stopping. You can swallow it or use it to run the engine.

"Well yes I do. But what are you gonna give me in return?"

"What do you want?" I say.

She's right up under me. "What do I *want?* If I start thinking about that, I'll start crying. Don't tell me you want to see that."

"Beats going to work."

She gives me the play slap and leans over to unzip her bag. If she's wearing underwear, it's not of any technology I'm familiar with. "Anyway," she says, "it's just things like a *career*. Or not having three roommates. Or not having parents who think I should have stayed in Oklahoma. I don't know that you can help me with that."

She stands up with a sample pack of Moxfane and a pair of Dermagels, the Martin-Whiting Aldomed eighteen-dollar rubber gloves. She says, "In the meantime, I might settle for showing you our new gloves."

"I've tried them," I say.

"Have you ever tried kissing someone through them?"

"No."

"Neither have I. And I've kind of been dying to."

She hip-checks the elevator "stop" button. "Oops," she says.

She bites the cuff of one of the gloves to tear it open, and I laugh. You know that feeling where you're not sure whether you're being hustled or in the presence of an actual human being?

I love that feeling.

"The ward is a fucking nightmare," Akfal, the other intern on my service, says when I finally show up to relieve him. What "Hello" is to civilians, "The ward is a fucking nightmare" is to interns.

Akfal is a J-Card from Egypt. J-Cards are graduates of foreign medical schools whose visas can be rescinded if they don't keep their residency directors happy. Another good word for them would be "slaves." He hands me a printout of current patients—he's got one too, though his is marked up and heavily creased—and talks me through it. Blah blah Room 809 South. Blah blah colostomy infection. Blah thirty-seven-year-old woman for regularly scheduled chemotherablah. Blah blah blah blah blah. It's impossible to follow, even if you wanted to.

Instead I'm leaning back against the nursing station desk, which is reminding me that I'm still carrying a handgun in the inside pocket of my scrub pants.*

I need to stash the gun somewhere, but the locker room is four floors away. Maybe I should hide it behind some textbooks in the nurses' lounge. Or under the bed in the call room. It doesn't really matter, as long as I can focus enough to remember where I put it later.

Eventually Akfal stops talking. "Got it?" he asks me.

"Yeah," I say. "Go home and get some sleep."

"Thanks," Akfal says.

Akfal will neither go home nor get some sleep. Akfal will go do insurance paperwork for our residency director, Dr. Nordenskirk, for at least the next four hours.

It's just that "Go home and get some sleep" is intern for "Goodbye."

Rounding on patients at five thirty in the morning usually turns up at least a handful of people who tell you they'd feel fine if only you assholes would stop waking them up every four hours to ask them how they're feeling. Other people will keep this observa-

---

* Scrub suits are reversible, with pockets on both sides, in case you need to run anesthesia or whatever but are too tired to put your pants on correctly.

tion to themselves, and bitch instead about how someone keeps stealing their mp3 player or medications or whatever. Either way, you give the patient the once-over, keeping a particularly sharp lookout for "iatrogenic" (physician caused) and "nosocomial" (hospital caused) illnesses, which together are the eighth leading cause of death in the United States. Then you flee.

The other thing that sometimes happens when you round early on patients is that none of them complain at all.

Which is never a good sign.

The fifth or sixth room I enter is that of Duke Mosby, easily the patient I currently hate least. He's a ninety-year-old black male in for diabetes complications that now include gangrene of both feet. He was one of ten black Americans who served in Special Forces in World War II, and in 1944 he escaped from Colditz. Two weeks ago he escaped from this very room at Manhattan Catholic Hospital. In his underpants. In January. Hence the gangrene. Diabetes fucks your circulation even if you wear, say, shoes. Thankfully, Akfal was on shift at the time.

"What's going on, Doc?" he says to me.

"Not much, sir," I tell him.

"Don't call me sir. I work for a living," he says. He always says this. It's some kind of army joke, about how he wasn't a commissioned officer or something. "Just give me some news, Doc."

He doesn't mean about his health, which rarely seems to interest him, so I make up some shit about the government. He'll never find out differently.

As I start bandaging his reeking feet, I say, "Also, I saw a rat fighting a pigeon on my way to work this morning."

"Yeah? Who won?"

"The rat," I tell him. "It wasn't even close."

"Guess it figures a rat could take a pigeon."

I say, "The weird thing was that the pigeon kept trying, though. It had its feathers all puffed out and it was covered with blood. Every time it attacked, the rat would just bite it once and throw it onto its back. Go mammals, I guess, but it was pretty disgusting." I put my stethoscope on his chest.

Mosby's voice booms in through the earpieces. "That rat must have done something pretty bad to that pigeon to make it keep on like that."

"Doubtless," I say. I push his abdomen around, trying to elicit pain. Mosby doesn't seem to notice. "Seen any of the nurses this morning?" I ask him.

"Sure. They been in and out all the time."

"Any of the ones in the little white skirts, with the hats?"

"Many times."

Uh huh. You see a woman dressed like that, it's not a nurse, it's a strip-o-gram. I feel the glands around Mosby's neck.

"I got a joke for you, Doc," Mosby says.

"Yeah? What's that?"

"Doctor says to a guy, 'I got two pieces of bad news for you. First one is, you got cancer.' Man says, 'Lordy! What's the second one?' Doctor says, 'You got Alzheimer's.' Man says, 'Well, at least I don't have cancer!' "

I laugh.

Like I always do when he tells me that joke.

In the bed by the door of Mosby's room—the bed Mosby had until the ward clerk decided he'd be less likely to escape if he was five feet farther from the door—there's a fat white guy I don't know with a short blond beard and a mullet. Forty-five years old. Lying on his side with the light on, awake. When I checked the computer earlier, his "Chief Complaint"—the line that quotes the patient directly, thereby making him look like an idiot—just said "Ass pain."

"You got ass pain?" I say to him.

"Yeah." He's gritting his teeth. "And now I got shoulder pain too."

"Let's start with the ass. When did that start?"

"I've already been through this. It's in the chart."

It probably is. In the *paper* chart, anyway. But since the paper chart is the one the patient can request, and that a judge can subpoena, there's not much incentive to make it legible. Ass-man's looks like a child's drawing of some waves.

As for his *computer* chart—which is off the record, and would contain any information anyone actually felt like giving me—the only thing written besides "*CC: Ass pain*" is "*Nuts? Sciatica?*" I don't even know if "nuts" means "testicles" or "crazy."

"I know," I say. "But sometimes it helps if you tell it again."

He doesn't buy it, but what's he going to do?

"My ass started to hurt," he starts up, all resentful. "More and more for about two weeks. Finally I came to the emergency room."

"You came to the emergency room because your ass hurt? It must really hurt."

"It is fucking killing me."

"Even now?" I look at the guy's painkiller drip. That much Dilaudid, he should be able to skin his own hand with a carrot peeler.

"Even now. And no, I'm not some kind of drug addict. And now it's in my fucking shoulder, too."

"Where?"

He points to a spot about midway along his right collarbone. Not what I'd call the shoulder, but whatever.

Nothing's visible. "Does this hurt?" I say, poking the spot lightly. The man screams.

"Who's there!?" Duke Mosby demands from the other bed.

I pull the curtain aside so Mosby can see me. "Just me, sir."

"Don't call me sir—" he says. I let the curtain fall back.

I look down at Assman's vitals sheet. Temp 98.6, Blood Pressure 120/80, Respiratory Rate 18, Pulse 60. All totally normal. And all the same as on Mosby's chart, and on the vitals sheets of every other patient I've seen on the ward this morning. I feel Assman's forehead like I'm his mother. It's blazing.

Fuck.

"I'm ordering you some CT scans," I tell him. "Seen any nurses around here lately?"

"Not since last night," he says.

"Fuck," I say out loud.

Sure enough, a woman five doors down is flat-out dead, with a look of screaming horror on her face and a vitals sheet that reads "Temp 98.6, Blood Pressure 120/80, Respiratory Rate 18, Pulse 60." Even though her blood's so settled at the bottom of her body that it looks like she's been lying in a two-inch pool of blue ink.

To calm myself down I go start a fight with the two charge nurses. One's an obese Jamaican woman busy writing some checks. The other's an Irish crone cruising the Internet. I know and like both of them—the Jamaican one because she sometimes brings in food, and the Irish one because she has a full-on beard she keeps shaved into a goatee. If there's a better *Fuck You* to the world than that, I don't know what it is.

"Not our problem," the Irish one says, after I've run out of things to complain about. "And nothing to do about it. We had that pack of Latvian cuntheads on the overnight. Probably out selling the lady's cell phone by now."

"So fire them," I say.

It makes both nurses laugh. "There's a bit of a nursing shortage on," the Jamaican one says. "Case you haven't been noticing."

I have been noticing. Apparently we've used up every nurse in the Caribbean, the Philippines, and Southeast Asia, and now we're most of the way through Eastern Europe. When the white supremacist cult Nietzsche's sister's founded in Paraguay re-emerges from the jungle, at least its members will be able to find work.

"Well I'm not filling out the certificate," I say.

"Sterling. And fuck the Pakistani, eh?" the Irish one says. Her face is remarkably close to the computer screen.

"Akfal's Egyptian," I say. "And no, I'm not leaving it for him. I'm leaving it for your Latvian shitheels. Stat."

The Jamaican one shakes her head sadly. "Won't bring the lady back," she says. "You ask them to do the certificate, they're just going to call a code."*

"I don't give a fuck."

"Párnela?" the Jamaican one says.

"I neither," the Irish one says. "Dim bitch," she adds, sort of under her breath.

You can tell by the way the Jamaican one reacts to this that she knows the Irish one is talking about me, not her.

"Just tell them to do it," I say, leaving.

I feel better already.

But even after that I have to take a slight break. The Moxfane I chewed up half an hour ago, along with some Dexedrine I found in an envelope in my lab coat and ate in case the Moxfane took too long to kick in, is making it hard for me to concentrate. I'm peaking a little too sharply.

I love Dexedrine. It's shield-shaped, with a vertical line down the middle so it looks like some vulvae.† But even on its own,

---

* "Stat" is short, though not very, for *statim*. "Calling a code" is what you do when you want to pretend you don't know someone's already dead.
† In fact, the medical word for pubic hair, "escutcheon," *means* "shield," although in free-range humans only women's pubic hair is shield-shaped. Men's is naturally diamond-shaped, pointing up toward the navel as well as

Dexedrine can sometimes make things too slippy to focus on, or even look at. On top of a Moxfane it can make things start to blur.

So I go to the medicine residents' call room to chill out, and maybe take some benzodiazapines I've got hidden in the bed frame.

The second I open the door, though, I know there's someone in there in the darkness. The room stinks like bad breath and body odor.

"Akfal?" I say, though I know it can't be Akfal. Akfal's aroma I will take to my grave. This is worse. It's worse than Duke Mosby's feet.

"No, man," comes a weak voice from the corner with the bunk bed.

"Then who the fuck are you?" I snarl.

"Surgery ghost,"* the voice says.

"Why are you in the Medicine call room?"

"I . . . I needed a place to sleep, man."

He means, "Where no one would look for me."

Great. Not only is the guy stenching up the call room, he's using the only available bunk, since the upper one is covered by a complete run of *Oui* magazine from 1978 to 1986, which I know from experience is too much of a pain in the ass to move.

I consider just letting him stay. The room smells unusable for the foreseeable future anyway. But I've got that Moxfane Edge,™ and there's always deterrence to think about.

---

down toward the groin. Which is why women who shave their pubic hair into a diamond shape subconsciously skeeze you out.

* This is an actual job, though it's not interesting enough to go into.

"I'll give you five minutes to get the fuck out," I tell him. "After that I'm dumping a bottle of urine on your head."

I turn the lights on as I go.

I'm feeling slightly more focused now, but still not focused enough to talk to patients, so I go and check labs on the computer. Akfal has already copied most of them into the charts. But there's a pathology report on a patient of Dr. Nordenskirk's who actually has insurance, so Akfal hasn't touched it. Dr. Nordenskirk doesn't let anyone who's not white or Asian interact with patients with insurance.

So I scan the report on-screen. It's a bunch of bad news for a man named Nicholas LoBrutto. The Italian name alarm in my head goes off, but I'm pretty sure I've never heard of this guy. And anyway mobsters—like most people with options—don't come to Manhattan Catholic. It's why I'm allowed to work here.

The key phrase in the pathology report is "positive for signet cells." A signet cell is a cell that looks like a ring with a diamond (or a signet, if you're still sealing your letters with wax) on it, because its nucleus, which is supposed to be in the center, has been pushed to the wall by all the proteins the cell can't stop making because it's cancer. Specifically, either stomach cancer or cancer that *was* stomach cancer and has now metastasized, like to your brain, or your lungs.

All stomach cancers suck, but signet cell is the worst. Where most stomach cancers just drill a hole through your stomach wall, so you can have half your stomach cut out and conceivably live, just not be able to shit solid, signet cell cancer infiltrates the stomach along the surface, producing a condition known as "leather bottle stomach." The whole organ has to go. And even then, by the time you're diagnosed it's usually too late.

The CT scan of Nicholas LoBrutto's abdomen is inconclusive about whether his cancer has spread or not. (Although, helpfully, he now has a 1 in 1200 chance of contracting some other form of cancer just from the radiation of the scan. He should live so long.) Only surgery will say for sure.

And in the meantime, at six thirty in the morning, I get to go tell him all of this.

Mr. LoBrutto? There's a call for you on line one. He didn't say, but it sounded like the Reaper.

Even for me, it's early to be wanting a drink.

LoBrutto is bedded down in the Anadale Wing, the tiny deluxe ward of the hospital. The Anadale Wing tries to look like a hotel. Its reception area has wood-patterned linoleum and a schmuck in a tuxedo playing a piano.

If it really were a hotel, though, you'd get better healthcare.* The Anadale Wing actually does have hot 1960s nurses. I don't mean they're hot now. I mean they were hot in the 1960s, when they first started working at Manhattan Catholic. Now they're mostly bitter and demented.

One of them shouts out to ask where the hell I'm going as I

---

* Think more money can't buy you worse healthcare? Forget the endless studies showing that the U.S. spends twice as much per capita as any other country, with results outside the top thirty-six. Take a look at Michael Jackson.

pass the charge desk, but I ignore her on my way to LoBrutto's "suite."

When I open the door I have to admit it's pretty nice for a hospital room. It's got an accordioning wall, now mostly retracted, that divides it into a "living room"—where your family can come eat dinner with you at an octagonal table covered with vinyl that looks easy to clean vomit off of—and a "bedroom" with the actual hospital bed. The whole thing has floor-to-ceiling windows, with a view, at the moment, of the Hudson River just starting to catch light from the east.

It's dazzling. They're the first windows I've looked out since I got to work. And they backlight LoBrutto in his bed, so he recognizes me before I recognize him.

"Holy shit!" he says, trying to crawl away from me up the bed, but held back by all his IV and monitor lines. "It's the Bearclaw! They sent you to kill me!"

2

One summer when I was in college I went to El Salvador to help register indigenous tribes to vote. A kid in one of the villages I was visiting got his arm pulled off by an alligator while he was fishing with a hand line, and would have died in front of me if it hadn't been for one of the other American volunteers, who was a doctor. Right then and there I decided to go to medical school.

This never actually happened, thank the Christ, and in fact I barely went to college, but it's the kind of thing they tell you to say when you apply to med school. That or how you had some disease growing up that was so brilliantly cured you can now work 120 hours a week and be happy about it.

What they tell you *not* to say is that you want to be a doctor because your grandfather was a doctor and you always looked up to him. I'm not sure why this is so. I can think of worse reasons. Plus, my own grandfather was a doctor, and I did look up to him. As far as I could tell, he and my grandmother had one of the great romances of the twentieth century, and were also the last truly decent people on earth. They had a humorless dignity I've never managed to come close to, and an endless concern for the downtrodden that I can barely stand to think about. They also had good posture, and what appeared to be a sincere enjoyment of Scrabble, public television, and the reading of large and improving books. They even dressed formally. And although they were citizens of a vanished type, they showed forgiveness toward people who weren't. For example, when my stoned-out mother gave birth to me, on an ashram in India in 1977, then wanted to go on to Rome with her boyfriend (my father), my grandparents flew over and took me back to New Jersey, where they raised me.

Still, it would be dishonest to place the origins of my becoming a doctor in my love and respect for my grandparents, since I don't believe I even considered going to medical school until eight years after they were murdered.

They were killed on October 10, 1991. I was fourteen, four months away from being fifteen. I came home from a friend's house around six thirty at night, which in West Orange in October is late enough that you need the lights on. The lights weren't on.

At the time, my grandfather was doing mostly nonsurgical, though medical, volunteer work, and my grandmother was volunteering at the West Orange Public Library, so they both should have been home by then. Also, the glass pane next to the front door—the kind of glass they call "pebbled"—was broken, like someone had smashed it to reach in and open the lock.

If this ever happens to you, leave and call 911. There could be someone still in the house. I went in, because I was afraid someone would hurt my grandparents if I didn't. You'll probably go in too.

They were on the border between the living room and dining room. Specifically my grandmother, who had been shot through the chest, was on her back in the living room, and my grandfather, who had doubled forward after being shot in the abdomen and hence was face down, was in the dining room. My grandfather had his hand on my grandmother's arm.

They'd been dead for a while. The blood in the carpet sucked at my shoes, and later, when I was lying down in it, at my face. I called 911 before I went and put my head down between theirs.

In my memory the whole thing is in vivid color, which is interesting, because I now know that we don't actually see color in low-light situations. Our minds imagine it for us and paint it in.

I know I put my fingers in their gray hair and pulled us all together. When the EMTs finally got there, the only thing for them to do was pull me off so that the cops could photograph the crime scene and let City Services remove the bodies.

The particular irony of my grandparents' story is that they had survived a much more elaborate attempt to murder them fifty years earlier. They had met, legendarily, in the Białowieża Forest in Poland in the winter of 1943, when they were fifteen, barely older than I was when I found them dead. They and a bunch of other newly feral teenagers were hiding out in the snow and trying to kill off enough of the local Jew-hunting parties so that the Poles would leave them alone. What this precisely involved they never told me, but it must have been pretty ferocious, because in 1943 Hermann Göring had a lodge at the southern end of Białowieża where he and his guests dressed as Roman senators, and he must have been aware of the situation. There's also the question of a straggler platoon of Hitler's Sixth Army that disappeared in Białowieża that winter en route to Stalingrad. Where, to be fair, it would have been wiped out anyway.

What finally got my grandparents caught was a scam. They got word from a man in Kraków named Władysław Budek that my grandmother's brother, who had been working in Kraków as a spy for the Bishop of Berlin,* had been captured and sent to the Podgorze "Ghetto," which was a holding pen on the rails to the Camps. Budek claimed he could get my mother's brother out for 18,000 zlotys, or whatever the fuck money they were using then. Since my grandparents had no money, and were suspicious any-

---

* This was Konrad Preysing, aka "The One Good German." Preysing made thirteen separate presentations of Holocaust evidence to Pope Pius XII, who in 1941 announced that Nazi policies did not conflict with Catholic teachings. When Pius gets sanctified, I hope they cite that as his miracle.

way, they went to Kraków themselves to check things out. Budek called the police and sold them into Auschwitz.

It was typical of my grandparents that they later described being sent to Auschwitz as a stroke of luck, since not only was it better than being shot by Polish crackers in some forest, it was better than being sent to a death camp.* At Auschwitz they were able to contact each other twice through smuggled notes—which, to hear them tell it, made surviving until liberation easy.

Their funeral was near my Uncle Barry's place. This was my mother's brother, who had freaked out and become an Orthodox Jew. My grandparents had certainly considered themselves Jewish—they had visited and supported Israel, for example, and were dismayed by the world's quick demonization of it—but to them being Jewish meant they had certain moral and intellectual responsibilities, not that religion was anything other than a bloodstained hoax. My mother had burned through every traditional form of rebellion before Barry could even get started, though, so dressing like a shtetl dweller in 1840s Poland was probably his only recourse.

My mother attended the funeral and asked me if I needed her to stay in the U.S., and whether I wanted to move to Rome. My father did me the favor of not pretending: he just sent me a rambling, slightly touching letter about his relationship with his

---

* Auschwitz *had* a death camp—Birkenau—but it also had Monowitz, which was a slave labor camp. That made odds of survival at Auschwitz 1 in 500, which is why you've even heard of Auschwitz. Odds of survival in the death camps were 1 in 75,000.

own grandparents and how as you go through life you never really feel any older.*

Barry adopted me to keep Child Protective Services off my back, but it was easy to convince him to let me stay in my grandparents' house. At fourteen I was physically enormous and had the mannerisms of an elderly Polish Jewish doctor. I liked to play bridge. Plus, Barry and his wife weren't crazy about exposing their own four kids to someone who'd been abandoned at birth and then come home one day to find his foster parents dead by violence. What if I became dangerous?

What indeed. Smart move, Barry and Mrs. Barry!

I sought out the dangerousness and refined it. As any other American child would, I picked Batman and Charles Bronson in *Death Wish* as role models. I didn't have their resources, but I didn't have much in the way of expenses, either. I hadn't even had the carpets changed.

I felt I had no choice but to take on the case myself. I still feel that way, really.

I know from experience, for instance, that if you go into the woods and shoot a handful of survivalist pedophile pimps—men who have destroyed the lives of literally *hundreds* of children—then the police will go apeshit trying to find you.

---

* My parents had long since gotten divorced. My mother had become a real estate agent, and my father, who was Italian—but not, I should say, Sicilian—had moved to Riverside, Florida. Last I heard he ran an upscale franchise restaurant I won't name. They both have different names now, and I am not in contact with either of them.

They will check the drains in case you washed your hands after running them through your hair. They will cast for tire tracks.

But if the two people you care about most get brutally murdered by some scumbag who rifles a couple of cabinets and takes the VCR, it will all be a fucking mystery.

Did they have any enemies?

Any enemies who needed a VCR?

It was probably a crackhead.

A crackhead with transportation, and gloves, and a fuck of a lot of luck not to be seen by anybody.

We'll ask around.

We'll let you know.

And it will be obvious to you just how justice will get served: by you or by nobody.

What kind of choice is that?

The different martial arts all share an interesting gimmick. (I went from *tae kwon do* to *sho ryu karate* to *kempo,* one foot-smelling dojo much like another, as I followed the traditional Japanese directive to spend more time training than sleeping.) You're supposed to act like an animal. I don't mean in the abstract: you're supposed to model your strategies on those of real, specific creatures. Using "crane style" for precise, fast, distance attacks, for instance, or "tiger style" for aggressive, in-close slashing. The underlying idea is that the last animal you'd want to emulate in a violent situation is a human being.

This turns out to be true, by the way. Most humans are instinctively terrible fighters. They flinch, they flail, they turn away.

Most of us are so bad at fighting that it has actually been an evolutionary advantage, since before the mass production of weapons people had to think to truly hurt each other, so the smart had a fighting chance. A Neanderthal would kick your ass and then eat it, but try finding one to test this.

Alternately, consider the shark. Most species of shark hatch live inside their mothers and start killing each other right then and there. The result is that their brains have stayed the same for 60 million years, while ours kept increasing in complexity until 150,000 years ago, at which point we became able to speak, and therefore human, and our evolution became technological instead of biological.

There are two ways of looking at this. One is that sharks are vastly evolutionarily superior to humans, since if you think we'll last 60 million years, you're insane. The other is that we're superior to sharks, because they'll almost certainly be extinct before we will, and their demise, like ours, will be thanks to us. These days a human's a lot more likely to eat a shark than vice versa.

On the tiebreaker, though, sharks win. Because while we humans have our minds and our ability to transmit the contents of them down through the generations, and sharks have their big ol' teeth and the means to use them, sharks don't appear to agonize about the situation. And humans sure as hell do.

Humans *hate* being mentally strong and physically weak. The fact that we get to take this planet down with us when we go brings us no joy whatsoever. Instead we admire athletes and the physically violent, and we *loathe* intellectuals. A bunch of nerds build a rocket to the fucking *moon,* and who do they send? A blond man named *Arm*strong, who can't even say the line right when he lands.

It's a weird curse, when you think about it. We're built for thought, and civilization, more than any other creature we've found. And all we really want to be is killers.

Meanwhile, around Thanksgiving of '91 I started fucking Officer Mary-Beth Brennan of the West Orange Police Department. In her Crown Victoria, since she was married and cops don't like to leave their "cruisers" when they're on duty. Hers was infested with not just roaches but rats, because the fuckheads on the other shifts kept shoving the bones from their fried chicken down between the hard leather seats. The thing was a fucking habitrail.

I don't mean to say I didn't appreciate the sex. I'd never had sex with anyone before, and it was a nice relief from that. And I had no reason to think sex could be better, since it was already so different from anything I'd seen in a movie or read in a book.

But I did realize there had to be more to it than smacking your head on a radio while someone who seemed impossibly soft and old (she was younger than I am now, and all breasts turn out to be soft, but who knew?) squirms on you with her uniform shoved past her knees, and all the time you're wondering how much harder you can push her to get some real, usable information from the Detective Grade 3's and 4's who must know *something* about who killed your grandparents. Plus it's winter, so everything outside of her is freezing.

What Officer Brennan eventually found out for me was this:

The detectives didn't think it was Nazis, neo or otherwise, since those people tend to target Hasidim. Nor was it much of a robbery, since so little was taken, and burglars avoid old people on the grounds that they're home all the time and don't tend to keep cash in the house anyway. The few things that *were* stolen, like the VCR, probably constituted either impulse shopping or a calculated attempt at misdirection.

"So who?" I asked Mary-Beth Brennan.

"He didn't say."

"You're lying," I said.

"I just don't want you to get hurt."

"Fuck that."

She told me. The murders had probably been the point of the whole event. Old people may not make great burglary victims, but they're fantastic homicide targets. They move slowly, they have a better chance of lying around for days before they get discovered, and, like I say, they're usually at home. Anyone determined to commit murder who doesn't care who the victim is wants someone like my grandparents. And that kind of person falls into one of two categories: serial killers and auditioning mobsters.

In West Orange, New Jersey, in early 1992, you'd be a jackass to bet on serial killers.

So most likely this was someone looking to prove he could kill, and to give the mob leverage over him as an initiation fee. Or rather it was two people, since there was a victim for each, and my grandparents had been shot with bullets from different guns.

According to one of the detectives Officer Brennan hit up for me, this meant there was a good chance that eventually these guys would be caught. Mob *omertà* bullshit runs both ways—the old guys blackmail the new guys, and the new guys finger the old guys. So eventually the police would hear about two particular fuckheads who'd gotten made at the same time, and they'd have their suspects.

But that might be decades from now, and there might or might not still be evidence, or interest, by then. And it assumed that these guys actually managed to get "made," and didn't get rejected, or choose to just go back to their jobs at Best Buy or whatever.

The whole thing was weak. It was thin. Maybe it had been a serial killer after all. Or some junkies.

But the hounds don't shun the fox for being mangy. The mob theory was all I had to go on, so I chased it.

And nothing else was coming. I'd pushed Mary-Beth too hard one day, and she had cried on my chest and said she worried that I didn't really love her.

When you grow up in northern New Jersey you hear a lot of bullshit about the mafia and whose fathers are in it. But you also hear about a military academy day school in Suffern, where every time you meet someone who goes there he's some smug dipshit with an Iroc-Z and a gold necklace that looks like it's going to break his cocaine mirror. And where, when you look up luminaries of the Five Families in *Who's Who in New Jersey,* a fuck of a lot of them turn out to have gone to school.

I won't name it. Suffice to say it has the same name as one of the more famous military academies in England, despite having been founded 150 years after the Revolutionary War.

I'd been expecting a Catholic school, but it didn't make much difference. I was already doing the push-ups.

I transferred over the summer. The school was expensive, but I still had money from the wills and the insurance settlement. And, like I say, I didn't have too many other needs.

As a military school it was a hoax. Reveille at "07:30" and "14:30," forty minutes a day of parade class, parade show once a month. There was a core of dipshits who took it all seriously, and went out for the sports teams and so on, but everyone else smoked pot in the bathrooms and snuck out to the Pizza Hut on the highway to hook up with the girls from the girls' school, which was on the other side of the tennis courts and the woods. The bathrooms at the Pizza Hut were coed.

You had to wait in line.

I chose Adam Locano to make friends with because he was so popular, not because of his mafia connections. I wasn't even sure those existed until later, when I asked him how he got his nickname, which was "Skinflick."

I'd heard it was because he'd made a porn movie with his babysitter when he was twelve.

"I wish," he told me. "It was a hooker in Atlantic City. Dude,

I don't even remember it, I was so drunk. Then some asshole from my dad's social club stole the tape and made copies for everyone. It sucked."

Bells went off, and I knew I'd stepped knee-deep into mafia. But before then I couldn't be sure, because Locano was different from the other mob kids.

Like me, he was fifteen. Unlike me, he was pudgy, with puffy, diagonally creased nipples and a Droopy Dawg face with jowls and eye bags. His lower lip was too fleshy. Also unlike me, he was *cool*. He made looking like he did a point of pride, managing to appear—even in the dumbass uniforms we had to wear on parade—like he'd been out all night drinking. In Las Vegas. In 1960.

Another part of his charm (and another part I could only wonder at) was that he seemed to speak his mind with absolute freedom. He'd talk casually about whacking off or taking a crap, or about how he was in love with his first cousin, Denise. The second he got angry or frustrated he said so—including, inevitably, when he was annoyed at how much better I was at sports or fighting than he was.

I did my best to avoid those kinds of situations, but, being kids, and particularly kids at a so-called military academy, they came up. And I was permanently impressed by how gracefully Skinflick dealt with them. He would bellow in rage, then laugh, and you knew he'd been honest in both responses. On top of which, despite the way he acted, and his claim that he had read only one book cover to cover in his life, he was the smartest kid I'd ever met.

He was also self-assured enough to be friendly with all kinds of people—geeks, cafeteria workers, everybody—and this made it possible to get close to him.

Not that I didn't have to work for it. I cut down on the Old Europe mannerisms and started dressing shaggy-preppy, with Vuarnets and a coral necklace. I slowed my speech down and lowered it, and spoke as seldom as possible. Every loner high school kid should be given a deadly serious incentive to fit in. It cools you up fast.

I also started dealing drugs. I had a connection through a nerd I'd known at my old high school, before my grandparents were killed and all my friends had stopped speaking to me because they didn't know what to say. The nerd's older brother was making a business of it, and got me eight-ounce bags of weed and full-on ounces of cocaine for a good rate. I think the two of them thought I was self-medicating.

I ended up having to sell for below cost anyway—it turns out buying friends is not the world's most unique idea—but it worked. It was through pot that Skinflick and I met.

He passed me a note in class one day that said, "Brother, can you spare a dime?"

I am surely God's original asshole—a monkey in the Mayan ruins, shitting on what I can't understand, worse than a Neanderthal. But of all the shameful things I've done, the easiest for me to understand is falling in love with Adam Locano and his family when I was fifteen years old.

Years later, the Feds tried to break me down with it: with how only a complete dipshit could go from finding his grandparents killed by mob scumbags to living with mob scumbags, and working for them, and sucking up to them, and needing them. But the reasons were obvious.

There are cops who go bad for 70,000 dollars and half a kilo of cocaine. The Locanos took me into their *family*. Their literal family, not some mafia movie bullshit. They took me *skiing*, for fuck's sake. They took me to *Paris*, and afterwards Skinflick and I went to Amsterdam on the train. They were not fundamentally kind people, but they did have empathy toward others, and they were remarkably kind to me. Besides Skinflick and his parents, there were two younger brothers. And no one in that family had haunted looks, or a constant awareness of mass murder. They all seemed to face forward, into a world of life, instead of backwards into a deathtrap they couldn't explain. And they seemed like they wanted to take me with them.

I wasn't even close to strong enough to pass it up.

David Locano, Skinflick's father, was a lawyer at a four-partner law firm near Wall Street. I later learned he was the only partner who did mob work, though he was also the one who kept the firm afloat. He wore sloppy expensive suits and had black hair that winged down off the back of his head. He never managed to fully hide how sharp and competent he was, but around his family he seemed mainly befuddled, and in awe. Any time he needed to know something—about a computer, or whether he should take up squash or go on the Zone diet or whatever—he would ask *us*.

Skinflick's mother, Barbara, was thin and humorous. She made appetizers frequently and either actually cared about professional sports or did a reasonable job of pretending to. *"Oh please,"* she liked to say. Like *"Oh please, Pietro—now* you're *calling him Skinflick?"*

(Pietro was my actual name, by the way. Pietro Brnwa, pronounced "Browna.")

And then there was Skinflick. Hanging out with him was not exactly like being brainwashed, in that brainwashing usually tries to get you to accept as desirable a reality that is, in fact, shitty, whereas hanging out with Skinflick was *fun*. But it had the same effect.

Tell me this, for example:

What is the value of one night at a bonfire party on the beach? How about if you get to be sixteen years old at the time? And you can feel the fire on one side of your face and the wind on the other, and the cold sand on your ankles and through the butt of your jeans, but the mouth of the girl you're kissing and can barely see is hot and wet and tastes like tequila, and you feel like you're communicating with her telepathically, and furthermore you have no regrets or disappointments in life, because for all you know the future's going to rock, and you've had losses, sure, but it seems only right to expect to gain just as much as time goes on?

What are you supposed to give up for that? And how do you weigh it against your obligation to the dead?

It isn't complicated: you take one look and walk away. You shake your head and go back to being a giant, lonely geek whose grandparents are dead. You be happy you've kept your soul.

I didn't do that. I stayed with the Locanos long after I'd gotten what I'd set out to get from them, until my life became a mockery of my original mission. I could say being raised by my grandparents had given me lousy defenses against people for whom lying and manipulation were ways of life and forms of entertainment. But I could also say that being with the Locanos made me sick with happiness, and I didn't want it to end.

And the truth is, I've done plenty of worse things since.

3

The man in the bed in the Anadale Wing is a guy I used to know as Eddy Squillante, aka Eddy Consol.

"What the *fuck?*" I snarl, grabbing up a fistful of the front of his gown. I double-check his chart. "It says your name's LoBrutto!"

He looks confused. "It is LoBrutto."

"I thought it was Squillante."

"Squillante's just a nickname."

"*Squillante?* What kind of nickname is *Squillante?*"

"It's from Jimmy Squillante."

"That shitbag from the garbage industry?"

"The man who *reinvigorated* the garbage industry. And watch your mouth. He was a pal to me."

"Wait a minute," I say. "You're called Squillante because Jimmy Squillante was a *pal* to you?"

"Yeah. Though his real name was Vincent."

"*What the fuck are you talking about?* I knew a girl named Barbara once—I don't ask people to call me Babs."

"Probably wise."

"What about 'Eddy Consol'?"

"That's another nickname of mine. From 'Consolidated.'" He chuckles. "You think somebody's real name is 'Consolidated'?"

I let go of him. "No, I got that part, thanks."

He rubs his chest. "Jesus, Bearclaw—"

"Don't call me that."

"Okay . . ." He trails off. "Wait a minute. If you didn't know I was Squillante, how'd you find me?"

"I didn't find you."

"What do you mean?"

"You're a patient in a hospital. I'm a doctor."

"You're dressed as a doctor."

"No. I *am* a doctor."

We stare at each other.

Then he says, "Get the fuck outta here!"

I find myself waving it off. "It's not that big a deal."

"Bullshit! Mazel Tov, kiddo!" He shakes his head. "You fuckin Jews. What, they don't let wiseguys become lawyers?"

"I was never a wiseguy."

"I'm sorry about that."

"I'm not asking you to apologize."

"It was an oversight. No insult intended."

I've forgotten that mob guys talk like that—like there was some unified and democratic meeting they all attended. "Don't worry about it," I say. "Half the guys I shot for David Locano were wiseguys."

He swallows, which isn't that easy when you're getting all your fluids through your arm. "You gonna kill *me*, Bearclaw?"

"I don't know yet," I tell him.

His eyes shoot to his IV bag.

"If I do, I'm not going to put air in your IV tube," I say.

If getting a small amount of air in your IV tube really killed you, half the patients at Manhattan Catholic would already be dead. In real life the LD_{50} of air—the dose that will be lethal in 50 percent of people—is two cubic centimeters for every kilogram of weight. For LoBrutto, or whatever his name is, that would be about ten syringes.*

Maybe I should stick a cork down his throat. Light woods are invisible on X-ray, and no pathologist at Manhattan Catholic is going to go to the trouble of dissecting Squillante's voice box. But where am I going to find a cork?

"Stop thinking about it!" he says.

"Relax," I say. "Right now I'm not even sure I'm going to kill you."

---

* The actual amount that will stroke out any particular person is highly variable, because 30 percent of people have a hole in the wall between the right and left sides of their heart capable of sending a bubble that would otherwise go to their lungs (and from there into the atmosphere) directly into their brain. But most pieces of IV equipment are a lot harder to clear than a syringe, so nobody bothers to do it.

A moment later I realize this is true, because I've figured out how to do it if I have to.

I'll just jack him with potassium. If I do it slowly enough, it will stop his heart without spiking his EKG,* and after he's dead so many of his cells will burst that his whole body will be flooded with potassium.

"Jesus," he says. "For all I know I have cancer anyway."

"You do have cancer," I say.

"What do you mean?"

"I just read your biopsy results."

"Jesus! Is it bad?"

"No, it's fantastic. That's why everybody wants it."

Squillante, with tears in his eyes, shakes his head. "Such a fuckin smartass. From the time you were a kid." He grabs my ID badge. "What are they calling you these days, anyway?"

When he reads it he boggles. " 'Peter Brown'? Like in the Beatles song?"

"Yeah," I say, impressed.†

"They changed your name from Pietro Brnwa to *Peter Brown?* How stupid do they think we are?"

"Pretty fuckin stupid, apparently."

An announcement comes out of the PA in the ceiling: *"Code*

---

* Electrocardiograms are abbreviated "EKG" because "ECG" sounds too much like "EEG," which is an electroencephalogram. Or maybe Willem Einthoven, who invented them, called them "electrokardiograms."

† *The Ballad of John and Yoko*: "Peter Brown called to say / You can make it O.K. / You can get married in Gibraltar near Spain." Peter Brown was the longest-serving roadie for the Beatles.

Blue. All available medical staff to 815 South." It repeats a couple of times.

Squillante realizes what's up. "I won't say shit, Bearclaw," he says. "I promise."

"If you do, I'll come back and kill you now. Are you capeesh-ing that, you dickhead?"

He nods.

I grab the phone cord and rip it out of the wall on my way out.

I reach the code. The hallway outside of it, anyway.

All the world loves a code, because you get to act like you're on television. Even if you don't get to yell "Clear!" with the defi-brillator paddles, you might get to squeeze the respirator bag, or inject drugs handed to you by nurses from out of the crash cart. Also, people come from all over the hospital—not just from Medicine, for whom it's mandatory—so it's a great opportunity to socialize. And if the person who called the code did it because the patient is actually crashing, you might even save someone's life, and justify your awful career choice.

This is not one of those times, however, I remember as soon as I get there. This is one of those times when the patient's been dead for hours, and some nurse is trying to cover his Latvian ass.

"Who's got time?" I say.

A nurse named Lainie turns around with a stopwatch and a checklist of who's required to be there. "Yo hi, Dr. Brown," she says. She winks. "I already put you down."

"Thanks," I say. Lainie's foxy, but she's married. Granted, to a man who looks twelve and wears a basketball jersey long enough to be a cocktail dress, but homey don't play that.

What homey *do* play is getting back to Squillante's room. And either killing him or figuring out what to do about him instead.

There doesn't seem to be an obvious choice. If I let him live, and he tells David Locano where I am, I'm either dead or on the run. On the other hand, supposedly I work at a hospital to *make up* for killing people.

Or something along those lines.

"Sir?" It's a small voice behind me. I turn.

My medical students. Two cups of human misery in short white coats. One is male and the other one female, and they both have names. That's all I can ever remember about them.

"Good morning, sir."

"Don't call me sir. I work for a living," I say. "Go check labs."

This mostly confuses them, but one of them says, "We already did."

"Then just stay here."

"But—"

"Sorry, kids. I'll teach you something later.* And I'll see you at Attending Rounds at seven thirty."

Of course, ten feet farther on I get beeped by Akfal, who's in

---

* This basic interaction—Good morning, sir/Sorry, kids. I'll teach you something later—is the primary activity of the last two years of medical school. The primary activity of the first two years is a PowerPoint presentation by whatever bitter, unpaid PhD was too slow to avoid getting tapped by the dean that morning.

the Intensive Care Unit. "You got a minute?" he says when I phone him back.

Instead of "No," I say, "Is it serious?" Which is a stupid question, since Akfal wouldn't page me if it wasn't. He doesn't have that kind of time.

"I need your help on a thoracostomy."

Fuck. "I'll be right there," I tell him.

I turn back to my med students. "Change of plans, kids," I tell them. "Uncle Akfal's got a procedure for us."

As we head toward the fire stairs, one of the med students nods nervously back toward the code. "Isn't that our patient, sir?"

"She's God's patient now."

Thoracostomy is just sticking a sharpened tube through someone's chest wall. You do it when the amount of blood—or pus, or air, or whatever—in their thorax is starting to compress one or both lungs, making it difficult for the person to breathe. You have to avoid the key organs—lungs, spleen, liver—and the undersides of the ribs, since the undersides are where the vein, artery, and nerve run. (You can see this on a rack of ribs, even after it's been cooked. Then you can go yack.) But otherwise placing a chest tube is simple, as long as the patient's holding still.

Which is never. That's where I come in. Though it gives me no joy to admit it, the medical task I perform nearest to perfection is holding people down. My med students are about to get a rare glimpse of genius.

So I'm surprised when we get to the Intensive Care Unit to

find the patient canted over on his side, with his eyes open and his tongue hanging out. In fact I'm worried he died while Akfal was phoning me, but then I feel the patient's carotid and it's pulsing fine, though there's no indication he can feel me checking. "Was he like this before?" I ask.

Akfal's setting up a procedure table, using all Martin-Whiting Aldomed materials. "Apparently he's always like this. Massive CVA* six years ago."

"So what do you need us for?"

"Chart says he's capable of sudden violent movements."

I tap the guy's eyeball. No response. "Somebody's bullshitting you. The guy's a lawsuit Barbie."

"Probably." He opens a pack of Dermagels onto the blue paper tablecloth he's set up, then pulls them on one at a time, touching only the insides with his skin. "Ready," he says.

I crank the bed up, and each med student takes a leg. I untie the guy's gown and let it drop to his waist. The guy is saggy with coma fat.

Akfal iodine-sponges a patch on the lower left ribcage, then picks up the tube. I throw an arm across the top of the guy's chest and arms.

Akfal jabs. The patient screams and boots both med students off his legs so hard they hit the walls. One of them also knocks over some kind of monitor.

---

* "CVA" stands for "cerebrovascular accident," or stroke. A brain artery either getting jammed (usually by a clot, usually from your heart) or outright exploding. Meet the Reaper: it's the number two cause of death in the United States.

But the tube is in. In *what* is up for debate, since the fluid that sprays out—and across Akfal's chest and face before he can grab up a bedpan to deflect it—looks like dark, ropy blood. After a couple of moments it begins to pulse out normally.

The patient sighs and relaxes again in my arms. "Kids, you all right?" I say.

"Yes, sir," they both say, shaky.

"Akfal?"

"Lovely. Watch out: there's blood on the floor."

Later, when the students and I emerge from the ICU, we get stopped by a guy who looks just like a younger, less zombified version of the patient.

"How's my dad?" he says.

"He's doing great," I tell him.

In the fire stairs, headed back up, I say:

"What's the lesson, kids?"

"DNR," they say in unison.

"Damn straight."

The Do Not Resuscitate order. The *for-Christ's-sake-let-me-die* request.

Which, if doctors explained it to their patients and patients signed it, might rescue a U.S. healthcare system that now spends 60 percent of its funds on people who will never see the outside of a hospital.

Think that's doing the Reaper's work? Newsflash: by that point, the Reaper's work is done. "Brain death" doesn't mean the brain is dead, although it is. It means the brain's so gone that the *body* is effectively dead. The patient's beating heart might as well be in a vat.

Speaking of not doing the Reaper's work, I decide to head back to Squillante's room, certain now that I will do everything possible to scare him into silence before I even think about killing him.

Pretty certain, anyway. I send the kids ahead to Attending Rounds—an event so loathsome that even under the circumstances I feel guilty for not getting them out of it—just in case.

Sure enough, though, when I get there, Squillante's talking on a cell phone.

"I'll be off in a minute," he says to me, covering the mouthpiece. "What am I, a fuckin dinosaur, I don't know how to use a cell phone?"

Then he holds up a finger and talks into the phone again. "Jimmy," he says. "I gotta call you back. The Bearclaw's here right now."

In movies hitmen always use a silenced .22, which they drop at the scene. Dropping your gun at the scene I understood, since Michael drops his gun at the scene in *The Godfather,* a movie from the 1970s about the 1950s that mob guys model their lives on to this day.* When I first started thinking about it, though, using a .22 seemed idiotic.

---

* Michael drops the gun after shooting the cop in *The Godfather* because the kid drops the gun after shooting the cop in *Battle for Algiers*. Where it at least makes sense, since during the Algerian Revolution the French had check-points every other block.

Obviously, smaller bullets tend to go faster, and speed is the primary component of kinetic energy, and hence of the shock waves that a well-placed bullet will send through your body fluids until the walls meant to keep them apart dissolve. But the amount of kinetic energy that actually gets transferred from a bullet to a body is difficult to calculate, since it relies on things like rotational speed and "impulse," which is what physicists call the amount of time two objects actually spend in contact.

Conservation of *momentum,* on the other hand, is easy to do the math on. For example, if a bullet weighing 230 grains (15 grams, the weight of a .45 bullet, which is 45 percent of an inch across) goes from the speed of sound (slow for a bullet) to a complete stop inside your body (much easier to achieve with a big bullet than a small one), then 15 grams of your body has to accelerate to the speed of sound to make up for it. Or 150 grams of your body to one-tenth the speed of sound, and so on. It's much less demanding to think about.

I told the geek at the Nassau Coliseum Gun Show, which I'd read about in *Shoot the Jew Weekly,* or *Blow Your Own Brains Out* or whatever, that I wanted twin .45 automatics.

That was the easy part. The guns I ended up buying looked cheesy—they had walnut grips and barrels so shiny they looked mirrored—but they were solid, with clean actions, and I figured I could always paint them later. Plus, wooden grips supposedly absorb some recoil.

The hard part was buying the silencers.

Just possessing a silencer has been a felony since the Vietnam War. I'm not sure why this is so. True, silencers are only used to kill people, but you could say the same thing about assault rifles, and the NRA keeps *them* cheap and easy. At the gun show I had to walk around for hours after I'd bought the guns before anyone took the bait.

This was a white-haired guy with glasses and a polyester shirt. Not survivalist-looking in the least, though he had all the signs out on his table: memoirs of high-ranking Nazis, weird guns and knives. I asked him if he had any suppressors.

A suppressor is a half-assed version of a silencer you use on your assault rifle, so you don't go deaf when you're gunning down your classmates or whatever.

"Suppressors for what?" he said. When he stopped talking his tongue, which was gray, rested on his lower lip.

"Sidearm," I said.

"Sidearm? You don't suppress a sidearm."

"I'm looking for some very *strong* suppressors," I said.

"Very strong suppressors."

"Very *quiet* suppressors," I said.

He looked annoyed. "I look like a Fed to you?" he said.

"No."

"Then speak your mind. What kind of ammo you lookin to use?"

"Magnum load hollow-points."

"For serious?"

"Yeah."

"Them the guns?"

"Yeah." I handed over the shopping bag I was carrying. He pulled the two pistols out and laid them on a copy of *The Protocols of the Elders of Zion.* For a moment he just stared at them. "Hmm," he finally said. "That's not so easy. But come around back."

I went around the table to where there was an extra folding chair. The gun maniac picked a fishing-tackle box up off the floor and opened it under the skirt of the tablecloth. It was packed with silencers.

"Hmm," he said, digging through them. "You need one for each?"

"Yes."

He pulled a couple out. "Don't know how good these are," he said.

They were long—easily a foot, with six inches of thick tube attached to six inches of thin tube. "What is that?" I said, pointing to the thin part.

"It's a barrel. Watch this." In about ten seconds, entirely out of sight, he stripped one of my automatics down and built it back up. Only, instead of the original barrel, which he left lying on the table, the barrel that was part of the silencer was now integrated into the gun. "That way you can swap out and they can't match the bullets," he said. "Course, you want to make the *shells* impossible to trace, you got to switch out the breechblock. Sand it down, at least."

"Huh," I said.

"Keep the original in the weapon when you're not using it, case the Feds come. And keep it loaded, too, case they come all hinky." He winked, though that may have been a tic. "You hear me?"

"Yes," I said.

"Good. That'll be four hundred dollars."

Around the middle of December 1992, Mrs. Locano said, "Pietro, what do you want for Christmas?" and I decided to make my move. We were all at dinner.

"I'm Jewish," I said.

"Oh please."

"The only thing I ever think about wanting," I said, staring at David Locano, "is to know who killed my grandparents."

Everyone fell silent. I thought: *All this. And I've fucked it up.*

And when it seemed to just blow over, I was grateful.

But a few days later David Locano called me and asked if I would come with him to Big 5 Sporting Goods to find a Christmas present for Skinflick. He'd come pick me up.

We went. He got Skinflick a speed bag, which was ridiculous—Skinflick couldn't hold his hands above his head for ten minutes *without* having to punch something at the same time—but Locano didn't really seem to want my advice.

In the car on the way home, he said, "How serious are you about getting the scumbags who killed your grandparents?"

It surprised the shit out of me so badly I couldn't say anything for about a minute.

"That's pretty much why I'm alive," I finally said.

"That is so fucking stupid," he said. "I know it's why you went to Sandhurst,* and why you became friends with Adam. But it's

* Oops, I said it.

bullshit. You can back off of it. You *should* back off it. And I know you want to."

"What happens to me if I don't?"

Locano swerved to the side of the street we were on and slammed on the brakes.

"Cut the tough guy crap," he said. "I don't threaten people. I'm a lawyer, for fuck's sake. And if I did threaten people, I wouldn't threaten you."

"Okay," I said.

"I'm just telling you—you've got a lot to live for. And to stay out of trouble for. Adam loves you. He respects you. You should listen to that."

"Thank you."

"Are you hearing me?"

"Yes."

I was, but I was still stunned.

"And you're stuck to this thing?"

"Yes."

He sighed. Nodded. "All right, then." He reached into his jacket.

I almost stopped him. I was thirteen months into eight hours a day of martial arts training. It would have been easy to block his gun arm, push his chin till his neck broke.

"Relax yourself," he said. He pulled out his appointment book and a pen. "I'm gonna see if I can get you a contract."

"What do you mean?"

"I'll see if I can hook it up for someone to pay you to do this."

"I won't take money for it."

He looked at me. "Yes you will. Otherwise you're a rogue, and they'll put you down like a dog. We'll start a rumor that whoever these scumbags are, they're talking too much—bringing down more heat than they're worth. Maybe they're someone's nephew's nephews or something, but it shouldn't take too much. Are you understanding this?"

"Yes," I said.

"Good. Are you gonna need a gun?"

They were brothers. Joe and Mike Virzi. Like the cops had thought, they'd done it to get jumped into the mob.

I didn't just take Locano's word for it. For one thing I followed them, for weeks.

The Virzi brothers were a pair of violent dicks who got crazed with boredom pretty much nightly, then took it out on whoever they could find. They'd pull some poor schmuck out of a nightclub or a pool hall or whatever by the hair, telling everybody else to shut the fuck up, this was mob business, then leave the guy in a puddle of teeth and blood out in the alley. Sometimes they'd beat the guy to the point where it looked like he was going to get maimed or killed, or they'd pick a woman, and I'd have to anonymously call the cops.

Here's the weird part: *I watched them get made.* I was following them pretty much every night, but it still surprised me when it happened.

It was in a Temple of St. Anthony, in the basement of the activities building attached to a church in Paramus. You could see in through the bars of the sunken window, which was open to let the heat out. There were three shitty buffet tables set up in a "U," with old mobsters seated around it and Joe and Mike Virzi standing in the center naked, repeating after the geezer in the middle.

I couldn't hear too much of it, but there were parts in Italian, Latin, and English, and the Virzis kept promising to go to hell if they betrayed the mafia. At one point a couple of geezers from the ends of the table, looking particularly ridiculous with medallions and felt hats on, set slips of paper on fire and dropped them onto the Virzis' palms. I tried this at home later. It didn't hurt at all.

The squalidness of the whole thing enraged me. I couldn't believe my grandparents had died for this bullshit. I left before it ended to go drive by the Virzis' house.

It was a little one-story with an attached garage. As usual when they were out, the garage door was open.

Cause who was gonna rob them?

The next morning before school—it was early March, and it was freezing out—I went into the woods near Saddle River to practice shooting, and found out why hitmen use .22's.

The first shot out of each gun sounded like someone slamming a stapler closed. The second sounded like the warning bark of a dog. The sixth and seventh sounded like low-flying jets, and by that time the insides of both silencers were actually on fire, with black smoke and blue flames coming out of the barrels. The paint on the barrels was bubbling.

Still, the work those bullets did was intriguing. The one time

I managed to land shots from both my right hand and my left hand on a single tree trunk—not so easy when the kick made it feel like I was hauling myself up a swimming pool ladder every time I pulled the triggers—there were four-inch chips in the bark where the bullets had gone in.

And two-foot satellite dishes of sawdust out back.

I chose a weekend right before spring break of my junior year.

I'd rebuilt my silencers. I'm not particularly anxious to divulge how to do this, but suffice to say that it helps to already have the metal cylinders, as well as some fiberglass insulation and a stack of full-inch washers. And that, even in the days before the Internet, it wasn't too hard to find instructions.

I knew the Virzis never locked the door between their garage and their kitchen. I'd been through it a dozen times, been through the whole scumbag house, with all its Cindy Crawford posters and prints by that guy who did the covers of the Duran Duran albums.

On the night I'd decided to kill them I followed them to a club, then went to their house and locked the kitchen door. Then I stood to one side of the open garage door and waited for them to come home.

A professor of mine in med school claimed that the sweat glands of your armpits and the sweat glands of your groin are controlled by entirely separate parts of your nervous system, so that it's nervousness that makes your armpits sweat, while it's heat that makes your groin sweat. I don't know if this is true or not, but I can tell you that standing waiting for the Virzis to get back I dropped enough sweat from both my groin and my armpits to fill my shoes. My entire body was slick inside my stifling overcoat. The heat and the nervousness were hard to tell apart.

Eventually there was a bang on the sidewalk and the Virzis' racing-stripe Mustang heaved into the garage beside me, putting out a wave of hot exhaust and rubber.

They got out loud and clumsy, the one in the driver's seat pressing the remote on his visor so the garage door started closing. The one from the passenger's seat stomped up the two steps to the door to the kitchen and tried the doorknob, then shook it.

"What the fuck?" he shouted over the noise of the garage door.

"What?" the other one said.

"Door's fuckin locked."

The garage door came to a stop.

"Bullshit."

"It is!"

"So fuckin open it."

"Dick, I don't have a key!"

"How about just turning around?" I said. "Slowly." My voice sounded distant even to myself. Something—the exhaust, the stress—had made me light-headed, and I was worried I would fall.

They turned around. They didn't look scared. Just stupid.

One of them said, *"What?"*

The other one said, "Who the fuck are you?"

"Cooperate and you won't get hurt," I said.

For a second no one said anything. Then the first one said *"What?"* and they both started laughing.

"Fucker," the other one said, "you are fucking with the wrong two guys."

"I don't think so," I said.

"Cooperate?" the first one said.

"You knocked over a house in West Orange, a year ago October," I said. "Killed a couple of geezers. All I want is the tape that was in the VCR you took."

They looked at each other. Shook their heads in disbelief.

The first one said, "Asshole, if we took a VCR from those poor fucks, we sure as hell didn't keep the tape."

I took a breath so I wouldn't have to for a while. Then I started pulling the triggers.

Let me tell you about revenge. Particularly murderous revenge.

It's a bad idea. For one thing, it doesn't last. The reason they tell you revenge is best served cold is not so you'll take the time to get it right, but so you'll spend longer on the fun part, which is the planning and the expectation.

For another thing, even if you get away with it, murdering someone is bad for you. It murders something in yourself, and has all kinds of other consequences you can't possibly foresee. By way of example: eight years after I shot the Virzi brothers,

Skinflick completely destroyed my life, and I threw him headfirst out a six-story window.

But on that night in early 1993, all I could feel was the joy.

Shooting the Virzi brothers with my silenced .45's was like holding a photograph of them, then tearing it in half.

5

I take Squillante's cell phone from his hands and twist it into pieces.

"Talk, asshole," I tell him.

He shrugs. "What's to say? As long as I stay alive, my guy Jimmy won't call Brooklyn."

"Won't call who in Brooklyn?"

"A guy of David Locano's who can get word to him in Beaumont."

I make a fist.

"Relax!" Squillante says. "It's only in the event of my death!"

I jerk him up off the bed by the loose skin where his jaw meets his neck. It's dry, like that of a lizard.

"In the event of your *death?*" I say. "Are you fucking *insane?* You have a terminal illness! You're already dead!"

"Les ho I'n ot," he drools.

"Hope won't get either of us shit!"

He mumbles something. I let his head drop back.

"What?" I say.

"Dr. Friendly's going to operate. He says we might be able to beat this thing."

"Who the fuck is Dr. Friendly?"

"He's a famous surgeon!"

"And he operates at Manhattan Catholic?"

"He operates all over town. He brings his own OR staff."

My beeper goes off. I hit the "kill" button.

"Him and me are gonna beat this together," Squillante says.

I slap him. Lightly.

"Can the shit," I say. "Just because you're dying doesn't mean you get to take me with you. Call off your connection to Locano."

"No," he says quietly.

I slap him a little harder. "Listen, dumbfuck," I say. "Your chances of living suck as it is. Don't make me kill you now."

"You can't."

"Why not, if it doesn't make a difference?"

He starts to say something, then blinks instead. Starts again. Then begins to cry. He turns his head away and pulls up into as much of a fetal position as his various inputs and outputs will allow.

"I don't wanna die, Bearclaw," he says through the tears.

"Yeah, well, no one's asking for your permission. So snap out of it."

"Dr. Friendly says I have a chance."

"That's surgeon talk for 'I need a slightly longer Chris-Craft.' "

My beeper goes off again. I kill it again. Squillante grabs my forearm with his chimplike hand. "Help me, Bearclaw."

"I will if I can," I tell him. "Call off your guy."

"Just get me through the surgery."

"I said, I will if I can. Call him off."

"If I can just make it through the surgery and get out of here, I promise I will. I'll take it to my grave. I don't need to live forever."

"Hey there! What kind of talk is that?" a voice says behind me.

I turn to see a couple of doctors entering the room. One's a gangly, exhausted-looking resident in scrubs, the other's a fat cat who's fifty-five years old. I don't know either of them. The fat cat's ruddy, with a truly audacious comb-over—a comb-around-and-around, to be more accurate. But that's not what's interesting.

What's interesting is the guy's thigh-length white lab coat. It's covered with drug-name patches, like something out of NAS-CAR. And it's *leather.* Better still, the patches are over the parts of the body each particular drug works on: *Xoxoxoxox* (pronounced "zoZOXazox") over the heart, *Rectilify* over the sigmoid colon, and so on. Over the crotch—cut in half because the coat is open—is the familiar logo of the erection drug *Propulsatil.*

"That's an amazing coat," I say. The guy looks at me, trying to decide whether I'm being sarcastic, but I don't know myself, so he can't tell.

So he just says, "Are you the Medicine team?"

"Yeah."

"I'm Dr. Friendly."

Great. I wouldn't trust this guy to work on my car.

"I'm taking this patient to the OR this morning," he says. "Make sure he's ready."

"He is ready," I say. "He doesn't want a DNR."

Dr. Friendly drops a hand on my shoulder. Nice manicure, at least. "Of course he doesn't," he says. "And don't kiss my ass. I get enough of that from my resident."

I just look at him.

"If I need to talk to you, I'll have you paged," he says.

I try to think of an excuse to stay, but I can't. I'm distracted—first by the fact that Dr. Friendly's coat has *Marinir* patches over the kidneys when he turns his back on me, and then by the smell of his resident.

Which, suddenly, I recognize. The resident's dark-circled, bloodshot eyes stare back at me as I turn.

"Surgery ghost?" I ask him.

"Yeah," he says. "Thanks for letting me sleep." His breath is still utterly rank.

I turn back to Squillante as I leave. "Try to stay alive till I get back," I say.

As I leave the Anadale Wing there's a high-pitched whine in my left ear.

I try to imagine what Prof. Marmoset—the Great One—would tell me to do. I ask him, almost out loud: *Professor Marmoset!!! What the fuck should I do???*

I imagine him shaking his head. *Beats the fuck out of me, Ishmael.**

Fuck it. I pull out my cell phone. Say "Marmoset" into it and press "dial."

A nurse walking past me says "You can't use a cell phone in here."

"Yeah," I say to her.

On the phone, a ridiculously breathy and sexual female voice says, *"Hi. I'm Firefly, the automated answering service. For whom are you looking?"* It's like speech from a vagina.

"Marmoset."

"Professor Marmoset is not answering his phone right now. Would you like me to go look for him?"

"Yes," I tell the fucking thing.

"Please state your name."

"Ishmael."

"One moment, please," Firefly says. *"Would you like music while you wait?"*

"Eat shit," I say.

But the joke's on me. A song by Sting comes on.

"I was unable to locate him," Firefly finally says. *"Would you like to leave a message?"*

---

* Ishmael was my code name inside WITSEC, though no one except Prof. Marmoset ever actually called me that. WITSEC is the abbreviation the Feds use, helpfully, for the Federal Witness Protection Program.

"Yes," I say, fighting tears of bitterness at having to converse with this monstrosity.

"You're welcome. You may begin your message now."

"Professor Marmoset—" I begin. There's a beep.

Then silence. I wait for a few seconds. Nothing happens.

"Professor Marmoset," I say. "It just beeped. I don't know if that means it just started recording or that it stopped recording. It's Ishmael. I really need to talk to you. Please call me or page me."

I leave both numbers, even though I have to read the one for my cell phone off the name tag on my stethoscope. I can't remember the last time I gave it out to anyone.

Then I consider trying to call Sam Freed, who brought me into WITSEC in the first place. Freed's retired, though, and I have no idea how to reach him. And I am nowhere near ready to talk to whoever's doing his job now.

When my pager goes off again, I look at it in case it's Marmoset. But it's just an alphanumeric reminder that, as bad as things are, they can always get worse:

"WHERE R U? ATTNDG RNDS IF NOT COEM NOW U R FIRED."

Even on a good day I would prefer talking to an insurance company employee to having to sit through Attending Rounds. Now, when some fuckhead I haven't even thought about in years has a good shot at getting me either killed or back on the run, it's galling.

Because, *COEM NOW* or not, odds are I am *FCKD.*

6

Here's a fun thing to do next time you're in Sicily: Get the fuck out. Run.

The place has been a shithole since the Romans burned its forests and razed its hills so they could have a wheat farm near the Italian peninsula but too far off shore for the locusts to reach it. Even Garibaldi's Redshirts, when they liberated Italy, left Sicily in chains. It was too valuable to give up.

The Sicilians themselves, over the centuries, got compacted into three distinct classes. There were the serfs, about whom what can you say, really. There were the landowners, who had mansions on the island but visited as seldom as possible. And there were the overseers—a leech class who, if they kept production up, were allowed to do anything to the serfs they wanted to.

The overseers lived in the owners' mansions when the owners were away. During the Ottoman years they were called *mayvah*, which meant "swaggerers." The word later became *mafia*.

When Sicilians began to immigrate to the U.S. in the early twentieth century, mostly to work picking paper out of the trash on the Lower East Side of Manhattan, the mafia followed to keep sucking their blood. During Prohibition the mob did something arguably socially useful, but when that ended they returned to blackmailing people with the threat of violence full-time. A Roman history fetishist named Sal "Little Caesar" Manzaro even started a private army, using Italianized Roman rank names like *capodecini* and *consiglieri*, and life in New York got so bad the Feds finally became interested. The only thing that saved the mafia at that point was the garbage business.

For reasons that remain unclear, but probably have to do with it being easier for private companies than public ones to illegally dump trash across state lines, in 1957 New York City stopped collecting garbage for commercial businesses. Stopped for *every* commercial business, overnight. For the first time in a hundred years. Suddenly every company in the city was in the export business, with a massive, rotting product that could only be moved with trucks.

The mafia knew trucks from the paper-hauling days, and liked them. Trucks are slow and easy to find, and their crews are small and easy to fuck up. By the mid-1960s the mob routinely had the garbage workers' unions, which it controlled, go on strike against the garbage companies, which it owned, then watched as the mayor jumped to raise collection rates to stop the resulting rat and disease epidemic.

This happened into the 1990s. You hear a lot about Armani suits, and "Dapper Dons," and *respect,* and how *Ha-ha, Tony Soprano pretends to be in the garbage business* and so on, but for years it was garbage that kept the Five Families alive. Drugs, murder, hookers—even gambling, before the Indian thing—were just sidelines.

Eventually, though, Rudy Giuliani decided enough was enough and brought in Waste Management, a multinational corporation so scary it made the mafia look like little girls in those competitions JonBenet Ramsey used to enter. Waste Management's own crimes were severe enough to ultimately force changes in the SEC, among other things, but its appearance on the New York garbage scene inspired another round of funeral announcements for the mafia.

Once again, though, the actual death was averted by legislation. This time at the state level.

For a number of years the mob had been running a scam where they opened gas stations using dummy owners, then closed them when the state tax bill came due. Since the state tax was over twenty-five cents a gallon, this meant they were able to drive every honest competitor out of business, which was lucrative but involved a lot of downtime, since each gas station had to stay closed for a minimum of three months between bankruptcies. Then the state changed the law, requiring gasoline wholesalers instead of retailers to pay the gas tax.

The idea was to kill the Gas Tax Scam, but the result was the much more lucrative New Gas Tax Scam—which, if you believe it, was invented by Lawrence Iorizzo and the Russian mobster "Little" Igor Roizman simultaneously, like Newton and Leibniz inventing the calculus.

In the New Gas Tax Scam you opened and closed sham *wholesalers,* and kept the gas stations open all year round, which was a bonanza. It sounds obvious and ridiculous, but by the end of 1995 the Sicilians and the Russians had used it to steal a combined four hundred million dollars from New York and New Jersey alone.

Ultimately, though, for the Sicilians to be in the same business as the Russians was a very bad idea. The Sicilians, after two thousand years of jackal vs. carrion culture, had become as lazy as the British, with the same dreams of living in a castle and being waited on by serfs. The Russians, who had recently had every illusion about organized society stripped from them, may have wanted the same thing, but they were willing to work their asses off for it.

You could see where this was headed. The Russians would eventually own the New Gas Tax Scam, just as they would own Coney Island, another disputed possession. It was only a question of when, how smoothly, and how profitably for the Sicilians.

Those Sicilians who saw things clearly realized that sooner was better, since a negotiated retreat while they still had power left from the garbage years was preferable to a rout.

Those Sicilians who failed to understand this, though, had a harder time saying goodbye, and caused problems. And the Russians had their own share of troublemakers. So as the sale of organized crime in New York worked its way to completion, there were always corners needing to be smoothed.

Smoothing out the corners was David Locano's job.

I finished out my junior year of high school expecting to be arrested for the murder of the Virzi brothers. That was part of the reason I decided not to go to college, although more of it was just laziness. The way I saw it, I was too old and worldly to sit around a dorm room reading Faulkner while some dipshit played acoustic guitar. And while I knew that stopping my education would have scandalized my grandparents, I was also aware, constantly, that they weren't around to feel scandalized by anything anymore.

I took a very brief break from the Locanos. I didn't go with them to Aruba, for example, though I wanted to, and I stayed at my grandparents' house while they were gone. And I made other brief and weak attempts to examine and justify continuing to spend time with them.

For example, once when Skinflick and I were high I asked him if he was planning to join the mafia himself. We were walking to Jack in the Box, since Skinflick and I both had an easy susceptibility to what potheads call "the munchies."*

"No fuckin way, dude," he said. "And even if I wanted to, my father would kill me."

---

* Expand the mind, and the body will follow, you might say, but it never seemed to make me fat, and Skinflick was fat already.

"Huh," I said. "By the way, who did your father kill to get into the mafia?"

"No one. He got a dispensation cause he was a lawyer."

"You believe that?"

He belched. "Absolutely. The guy doesn't lie to me."

Skinflick did seem to have an incredibly smooth relationship with his father, although the one book he claimed he'd ever read in its entirety was *The Golden Bough*, by James Fraser. Which, aside from being a weird choice for the only book you've ever read, is essentially about patricide, and how the origins of civilization lie in intergenerational struggle. The golden bough is what young slaves in a primitive society Fraser discusses pluck when they want to challenge the king to a duel to the death, with the winner keeping the crown.

Skinflick denied that this showed any hostility toward his father, though. He said he'd only picked up *The Golden Bough* because Kurtz is reading it in *Apocalypse Now,* and had stuck with it because its ideas about freedom and modernity appealed to him.

"For instance," he once said, coincidentally while he and I were riding with his father in his father's car, "people are always bitching about how their primitive fight-or-flight instincts are being repressed, and how they're depressed because of it. But I can shoot a *shotgun* while I'm driving down the *freeway*. No one in history has been that free."

"You can't shoot a shotgun standing still," his father said.

72

My own relationship with David Locano seemed unreal. He had insisted on giving me forty thousand dollars for killing the Virzis—"Throw it out if you want," he had said—then never mentioned the incident again, even when we were alone.

Once, though, when I came over and Skinflick was out renting a movie, and Mrs. Locano was out doing whatever, he and I sat at the kitchen table and he asked me if I wanted another job.

"No thanks," I said. "I think I'm done with that line of work."

"This isn't that line of work."

"What is it?"

"It's just talk."

I didn't stop him.

"Paranoid Russians won't talk on the telephone," he went on. "I need you to go to find some guy in Brighton Beach and ask him what it is he wants to say to me."

"I don't know Brighton Beach at all," I said.

"It's easy," Locano said. "Particularly if you're not me. It's tiny. You go down to Ocean Avenue, ask in a bar called the Shamrock, they'll know the guy. He's a big deal guy."

"Is it dangerous?"

"Probably not as dangerous as driving there."

"Huh," I said.

I should back off for a moment and note that there's a concept many criminals become obsessed with, which is the idea of *turning out*.

The template for it is the classic aspiring pimp who needs to find a woman to work for him. No professional will do it, because they all have pimps already. So he picks a girl from the neighborhood, as sheltered and unworldly as possible, and courts her. Plays up a big romance, then one day tells her he's in big trouble if he can't get some money fast, and that a friend of his is willing to pay a hundred dollars to screw her once. After she does it, he acts disgusted with her, and beats her and degrades her, then gives her narcotics for the pain. Once she's hooked and working steadily, i.e., has been "turned out," he moves on to Bachelorette #2. Lovely species we belong to.

Today the turnout can be found in any number of situations. The most literal is prison, where the idea is to progress as quickly as possible from lending your cellmate a cigarette to hiring him out to large groups in return for a double-A battery or some smack. Most instances of it are more subtle, though, and have to do with the many ways in which people enter into, or are led into, or believe they are led into, lives of criminality.

I knew all this. I'd read *Daddy Cool*. I knew that what David Locano was doing was turning me out. And that even if the job I'd just accepted didn't require violence, taking it meant I was willing to get violent later on.

I just allowed myself to ignore those things.

I drove to Coney on a sunny Saturday. Put one of my silver, wood-handled .45's, unsilenced, in the inside pocket of my anorak and took my grandparents' Nissan across the George Washington Bridge into Manhattan then over the Manhattan Bridge out of it. Took the highway all the way down through Brooklyn. I was able to park at the Aquarium, midway along the Island, just by dropping David Locano's name. They didn't even check a list.

I'd been to the Aquarium as a kid, and also west along the boardwalk to the old amusement park. Eastwards, into Brighton, was a mystery.

It was jammed. Gangster-looking young blond guys in fluorescent sweat suits so bright they stung your eyes, and old people on the benches with bathing suits and socks on, with towels over their shoulders even though they were two hundred yards from the water. Also huge families of Hispanic people dressed for summer and Orthodox Jews dressed for winter. Everywhere you looked someone was beating a child.

The beach curved away as I entered Little Odessa. The buildings looked like sets from a tenement movie. Elevated subway tracks above Ocean Avenue, and in the shadows down below ancient storefronts with either their original signs or new wooden ones in Cyrillic. I found the Shamrock within a couple blocks. It had a neon sign of a clover leaf, with the power off. I went in.

The Shamrock had a cedar bar, splintered floor, and barfed-up beer smell that were probably from back when it was actually Irish, but it was better lit than you'd expect, and the small square tables had laminated red gingham tablecloths. Two tables were taken, one by a man and a woman and one by two men.

The bar started by the door. Leaning against the wall behind it there was a young blond woman who didn't look much older than I was. She had dark circles under her eyes and a thinness like maybe she'd missed out on a few key years of nutrition back in the Old Country.

Her English was good, though.

"If you want food you can sit at a table."

"Just a club soda," I told her. "I'm looking for Nick Dzelany."

She came off the wall, toward me. "Who?"

"Nick Dzelany," I said, this time accentuating the "D." I felt myself blushing. "Dzelany" is hard enough to say when you think you're doing it right.

"I don't know him," she said. After a moment: "Do you still want a club soda?"

"Yeah, sure," I said. "Is there another bar around here called the Shamrock?"

"I don't know."

When she brought my drink, in a ridiculously narrow glass, I said, "Is there anyone you can ask?"

"Ask about what?"

"Nick Dzelany." I said it loud enough to be heard at the tables, in case those people knew him. "I was told people here knew him."

The bartender seemed to think, then she went and got a pen off the register. She brought it back with a napkin. "Spell, please."

I did. I was pretty sure I got it how David Locano had showed it to me, but I wasn't completely sure, and I was getting less sure by the moment. Maybe Locano had gotten it wrong himself.

She took the name over to a phone at the far end of the bar and made a call. It went on for minutes, in Russian. At one point she got strident, then apologetic. Not once did she look at me.

She came back over. "Okay, I found out who he is. I am supposed to take you. Even though I am working."

"Sorry," I said. I got off the stool. "What do I owe you?"

"Four fifty."

Whatever. It was Virzi money. I left a ten. The bartender didn't look at it, just lifted the gateway and came around the bar.

"This way," she said, leading me toward the back.

We passed through a tiny kitchen where a fat blond woman was sitting on an upside-down plastic bucket, smoking and reading a hardcover book in Cyrillic. She didn't look up. The bartender undid the three locks on the door on the other side and led me out into the alley.

Almost immediately she tripped on a pothole and went down, squealing and grabbing her ankle. I went down with her, catching her. Thinking, but not fast enough.

There was a noise behind me, and something tore into the back of my head. I managed to twist as I tripped forward over the bartender, and jammed myself to a stop on one leg.

But there were three guys facing me, and one was already hitting me again with brass knuckles.

I blacked out so fast I barely felt the hit of the opposite wall.

I blinked awake and my eyes filled with water even though I had tunnel vision. I felt like I was suspended face down by my arms and legs. I was incredibly thirsty. I also felt like there was someone standing on my head, trying to kick the back of my skull off.

The only parts that turned out to be true were the headache and the thirst. As I blew snot out my nose and squeezed my eyes clear, I could see I was on the ground floor of a burned out building, with the whole wall in front of me blasted away. I was overlooking a wasteland of dunes of loose bricks and broken concrete, hot in the light from the blue sky.

And I wasn't suspended, though my upper body was hanging forward. I was in a wooden chair, with my arms and legs bound with gaffer's tape.

I heard some words in Russian, and someone smacked me in the torn up mess at the back of my skull. Stupid pain—stupid because I knew it was just surface, but it made me cry out anyway—ran down to my right ankle and also around my head into my right eye socket. There were more words in Russian.

They stepped into my field of view. The three guys from the alley—one still holding the brass knuckles with bits of my scalp on it—plus a new guy.

The new guy in particular had that look of foreignness that makes you wonder whether your face gets changed by speaking a different language, or by drinking water with too much cadmium in it or something. He had a pointy chin and a broad, high forehead, so that his face was a downward-pointing triangle.*

When my eyes adjusted to his blocking out the light I could see that his face also had deep lines in it for an otherwise young-looking guy. It was part of a generalized runtiness.

"Hello to you," he said. "Are you looking for me?"

I leaned back to look up at him. The chair creaked and shifted beneath my weight, and I suddenly felt a whole lot better.

"I was looking for a guy named Nick Dzelany," I said.

"I am that guy."

"Is there something you wanted to tell David Locano?"

---

* Like a woman's escutcheon, if you've been paying attention.

"David Locano?"

"Yes."

Dzelany looked around at the others and laughed.

"Tell him to go fuck himself," he said to me. "Actually, I'll tell him myself, by sending him your head. That's something I like to do. Did he tell you that?"

"No, he didn't." Nor had I noticed, somehow, until that moment, that Dzelany was holding a machete. Slapping its blade against his thigh. He slowly raised it and put the flat of it against the side of my neck.

This is what happened next:

I thought, *I should do something.*

I felt the thought race down my spine. I tried to pull it back. I wasn't ready. Then I realized that it was too late to pull it back, and that trying to pull it back would just fuck it up. So I went with it.

I stood up out of the chair, fragmenting it by jamming my arms forward and my legs backward. Dzelany was right in front of me, the top of his head just below my sternum. I triple-slapped him.

The triple-slap is from that lovely martial art called *kempo.* You bring your hands together like you're clapping, but with the right slightly higher than the left, and slightly faster. So that an instant after you slap Dzelany on one cheek with your right hand, you slap him on the other cheek with your left. Then you bring your right hand back across, slapping him again with the back of it. The speed of the three strikes is disorienting: it's too much to think about, like when you hold all four legs of a chair out toward a lion and its brain shuts down.

I didn't really triple-slap Dzelany, though. After I'd slapped him twice I back-handed him not with my open right hand, against his cheek, but with my closed right fist, against his temple. Never do this. It's guaranteed to take someone down, and might even kill him. It got Dzelany right out of my way.

So I jumped straight forward, toward the man with the brass knuckles. I was still in a hammering mood, and brought my right fist down toward his face.

He flinched back, but that's the beauty of a hammering strike: if your target tries to get out of range, your fist (or foot, or whatever) keeps going forward as well as down, so you still eventually hit something. In this case it was the guy's right collarbone, which didn't even bend, just spat its middle third downwards into his chest, collapsing him.

Strategically I could have done this better, since there was now someone to my left and someone else to my right, and neither one of them was all that close. But the mere fact that there were two of them was an advantage. People who aren't trained in coordinated combat almost always fight worse when they're in a group, because they tend to stand back and wait for their friend to do the hard part.

I turned to the one on my left. Jumped backwards away from him over the wreckage of the chair and horse-kicked the guy behind me in the solar plexus,* aiming for the wall two feet past him.

The guy I was still facing started to pull a gun, and got it out

* For those following along in their *Gray's Anatomy*, in medicine the solar plexus has been called the celiac plexus for the last few decades. About as long as it's been since anyone read *Gray's Anatomy*.

of his leather blazer just as I jammed my forearm, with the arm of the chair still taped to it, into his throat, carrying both of us to the wall behind him. When I let him go, he fell to his knees and made some awful noises, but not for very long.

I picked up his gun, a fancy Glock, and, after I realized it didn't have a safety, shot each one of those four assholes in the head. I took their wallets so I'd know who they were, and as I was searching them I found my .45 on the guy with the brass knuckles. Which figured. Nothing that ugly stays lost.

It took me longer to get the tape and wood off of me than it had to triple the number of people I'd killed.

At four PM I rang the doorbell of the Locanos. Mrs. Locano answered it and screamed. I knew why from looking in the rearview mirror as I'd driven there, after I'd walked back to the Aquarium from the Flatbush Flatlands, staying off the boardwalk. I looked like I'd been ax-murdered.

"Oh my God, Pietro! Come in!"

"I don't want to get blood on anything."

"Who cares about that!"

David Locano came into sight. "Jesus, buddy!" he said. "What happened?"

Together they helped me into the house, which I appreciated because it kept me from touching the walls.

"What happened?" Locano repeated.

I looked at Mrs. Locano.

Locano said, "Honey, excuse us."

"I'm going to call an ambulance," she said.

"Don't," Locano and I said together.

"He needs a doctor!"

"I'll get Dr. Campbell to come to the house. Go get some stuff set up in the bedroom."

"What kind of stuff?"

"I don't know, honey. Towels and shit. Please."

She left. David Locano pulled over a chair from a wooden desk they kept mail on in the hallway, so I wouldn't have to sit on the living room furniture.

He crouched beside me and whispered. "What the hell happened?"

"I asked for Dzelany. They set me up. Three guys plus him. I got their wallets."

"You got their—?"

"I killed them."

Locano looked at me a moment, then hugged me gingerly.

"Pietro, I am so sorry. I am so sorry." He backed off to look me in the eye. "But you did good."

"I know," I said.

"I promise you'll get paid for this."

"I don't care about that."

"You did good," he said. "Jesus. I think you might be really fucking good at this."

This was an interesting moment in my life. The moment when I should have said, "I'm out of here," or "I'm scared shitless," and "I'm never doing that again." But when I chose to instead express my pathetic need for the Locanos, and my rapid-onset addiction to bloodshed.

"Never lie to me again," I said.

"I didn't—" Locano said.

"Fuck you. And if you do, and I end up killing an innocent, I'm coming after you next."

"Of course," he said.

We were already negotiating.

7

At seven forty-two AM I fall asleep in my armchair again and my head hits the wall. Proving, interestingly, that no amount of stress on earth can keep you awake through Attending Rounds.

Attending Rounds is when a large group of people convenes in one of the ward lounges and goes through the patient list to "make sure we're on the same page" and satisfy the legal requirement that someone actually qualified to be making patient-care decisions at least hears about these decisions after they've been made.

This person is the Attending Physician, a real-world doctor

who comes in and supervises the ward for one hour a day for one month each year, in return for which he gets to call himself a professor at a prestigious New York medical school that, as far as I can tell, has no other connection with Manhattan Catholic whatsoever. In keeping with the clarity goals of healthcare terminology, the Attending is the person present on the ward least.

This particular Attending is one I know. He's sixty. He always has superbly expensive-looking shoes, but what has truly earned him my admiration is that his usual answer to my asking him how he's doing in the morning is "Terrific. I'm on the nine a.m. back to Bridgeport."

Right now he's supporting his head with one hand, which his jowls overhang like the corners of a tablecloth. He has his eyes closed.

The other people in the room are: an intern who's one of the counterparts to Akfal and me but for the ward at the other end of the building (she's a young Chinese woman named Zhing Zhing, who sometimes gets so depressed she needs you to unbend her limbs for her), our combined four medical students, and our Chief Resident. We have the lounge to ourselves, because we kicked out the herd of bathrobed patients who were watching TV in the hopes of dying somewhere outside of their hospital beds. Sorry, folks. There's always the hall.

But Jesus fucking Christ am I tired.

One of the medical students — not even one of mine, one of Zhing Zhing's — is reading an incredibly long list of obscure liver function test results, verbatim. These tests should not have been ordered in the first place. The patient has heart failure. And since they've all come back normal, you would think the med student would at least spare us having to hear them.

And yet, no one screams.

I have a waking hallucination that there's moss growing up one of the walls, then I feel myself falling asleep again. So I try the trick where you keep one eye open—the one the Chief Resident can see—and hope that means half my brain is getting some rest. My head bangs off the wall again. I must have drifted off.

Now it's seven forty-four.

"Are we boring you, Dr. Brown?" the Chief Resident asks.

The Chief Resident has finished her residency but has chosen to stay on at ManCat for an extra year, in a manifestation of what I believe is still called "Stockholm Syndrome." She's wearing a fairly hot skirt suit under her white coat, but also her usual facial expression, which would go well with her saying "You took a *shit* on my *shoes?*"

"No more than usual," I say, trying to rub my face into wakefulness. I notice there actually is moss growing up one of the walls, though my double vision is exaggerating it.

"Maybe you'd like to tell us about Mr. Villanova."

"Sure. What would you like to know?" I say, wondering who Mr. Villanova is. For a moment I worry it might be another of Squillante's nicknames.

"Apparently you ordered stat CT scans of his chest and buttocks."

"Oh, right. Assman. I'd better go check those."

"Do it later."

I sit back down. Wipe my nose with my left hand to cover the slow movement of my right hand toward my beeper. "Guy's got some right buttock and subclavicular pain OUO despite PCA,"* I say. "Looks like a fever, too."

"His vitals were normal."

"Yeah, I noticed that."

My right thumb flicks the test button on my beeper so quickly I wouldn't have seen it either. When the glorious alarm goes off, I glance at the LCD and jump to my feet.

"Shit. I gotta go."

"Please stay till the end of rounds," the Chief Resident says.

"I can't. Patient," I say. Which is not so much a lie as a non sequitur.

To my med students I say, "One of you look up the statistics on gastrectomy for signet cell cancer. I'll catch up to you later."

And, just like that, I'm free.

I'm thinking too slowly to deal with the Squillante problem, though, so I crush a Moxfane with my fingertips and snort it out of the declivity you can make at the end of your wrist by sticking your thumb out as far from your hand as it will go.

It makes my nostrils burn crazily, and my vision goes out for a second. What brings me back is my stomach, which is making a series of accelerating metallic spring noises.

I need to eat something. Martin-Whiting Aldomed is probably hosting a free breakfast somewhere in the hospital, but no way do I have time for that.

---

* Like you care what this means.

In the rack of used trays by the service elevator I find an un-opened plastic bowl of Corn Flakes and a reasonably clean spoon. There's no milk, but there's a half-full four-ounce bottle of Milk of Magnesia. Which, I'm sorry to tell you, under certain circumstances is as good or better.

I take the whole thing into a room with an empty door-side bed, and sit on the edge of the piss-stained mattress to eat.

I've just dug in when a female voice from the other side of the curtain says, "Who's there, please?"

I finish first—it takes about four seconds—then chew an-other Moxfane and stand and walk around to the other bed.

There's a young woman in it. Pretty, twenty-one years old.

Pretty is rare in a hospital. So is young.

But that's not what stops me.

"Fuck," I say. "You look like someone I used to know."

"Girlfriend?"

"Yeah."

The resemblance is slight—it's the dark vixen eyes or some-thing—but in my current condition it rocks me.

"Bad breakup?" the woman asks.

"She's dead," I say.

For some reason she thinks I'm kidding. It's the Moxfane fucking with my facial expressions or something. She says, "So now you work in a hospital to save people?"

I shrug.

"That's pretty corny," she says.

"Not if you've killed as many people as I have," I say. Think-ing, *Huh. Maybe I should leave the room and let the drugs do* all *the talking.*

JOSH BAZELL

"Medical mistakes, or is it more of a serial killer thing?"

"Probably a little of both."

"Are you a nurse?"

"I'm a doctor."

"You don't look like a doctor."

"You don't look like a patient," I say.

Which is true. Visibly, at least, she's pure health.

"I will soon."

"Why's that?"

"You're not my doctor?"

"No. I'm just curious."

She looks away. "They're cutting off my leg this afternoon."

I think about this for a moment. Then I say, "Donating it, huh?"

She laughs, harshly. "Yeah, to a trash can."

"What's wrong with your leg?"

"I have bone cancer."

"Where?"

"Knee."

Prime osteosarcoma territory. "Can I see it?"

She flips back the covers. They take the corner of her gown with them, giving me a glistening beaver shot. The modern type: Mexican hairless beaver. I can see her blue tampon string. I quickly pull the covers back over her crotch.

Look at her knees. The right one's noticeably swollen, more so at the back. Soggy when I feel it.

"Yuck," I say.

"Tell me about it."

"When was the last time someone biopsied it?"

"Yesterday."

"What'd they find?"

"They called it 'Bleeding amorphous glandular tissue.' "

Double yuck. "How long have you had it?"

"This time?"

"What do you mean?" I say.

"The first time I had it was for maybe ten days. But that was three months ago."

"I don't understand. It went away?"

"Yeah. Till about a week ago. Then it came back."

"Huh," I say. "I've never seen that before."

"They did say it was pretty rare."

"But they don't want to see if it goes away again?"

"The kind of cancer it is is too dangerous."

"Osteosarcoma?"

"Yeah."

"That's true."

If it *is* osteosarcoma.

Though what the fuck do I know?

"I'll look it up," I tell her.

"You don't have to. It'll only be around for a couple of hours."

"I will, though. Do you need anything else?"

"No." She pauses. "Not unless you want to give me a foot massage."

"I can give you a foot massage."

She blushes like a police siren, but keeps her eyes on mine. "Really?"

"Why not?" I sit down on the edge of the bed and take her

foot. Start pushing the ligament of her arch around with the edge of my thumb.

"Oh, fuck," she says. She closes her eyes, and tears come out of them.

"Sorry," I say.

"Don't stop."

I keep going. After a while she says, barely loud enough to hear, "Will you lick it?"

I look up at her. "Lick what?"

"My foot, you pervert," she says, still not opening her eyes.

So I lift her foot to my mouth and lick along the arch.

"And my leg," she says.

I sigh. I lick up the inside of her leg, almost to her crotch.

Then I stand up. Wondering, briefly, what my life as a doctor might look like if I ever behaved like a professional.

"Are you all right?" I say.

She's crying. "No," she says. "They're cutting my fucking leg off."

"I'm sorry. Do you want me to check on you later?"

"Yes."

"I will, then."

I consider adding "if I'm still around," but decide against it.

I don't want to bum anybody out.

8

In the winter of 1994 the Locanos went skiing again, this time at Beaver Creek or something in Colorado, and invited me to go with them. I said no, and went to Poland instead. But I swear to God I did not go to Poland to kill Władysław Budek, the man who sold my grandparents into Auschwitz.

I went for a far worse reason. I went because I believed there was an entity called "Fate," and that if I did as little planning as possible, Fate would either place Budek in my sights or not, and thereby show me whether I should become an off-the-books hit-man for David Locano. Somebody he could use to take out both

Italians and Russians, and also be sort of a bodyguard for Skinflick. And in the meantime I could use one turned-down ski trip
to prove to myself I wasn't closer to the Locanos than I had been
to my grandparents.

Speaking medically, the strange thing about my decision to
let a fictional, supernatural agency choose the course of my
life—as if the universe had some sort of consciousness, or
agency—is that it doesn't qualify me as having been insane. The
Diagnostic and Statistical Manual, which seeks to sort out the va-
garies of psychiatric malfunction to the point where you can bill
for them, is clear on this. It says that for a belief to be delusional
it must be "based on incorrect inference about external reality
that is firmly sustained *despite what almost everyone else believes*
and despite what constitutes incontrovertible and obvious proof
or evidence to the contrary." And given the number of people
who buy lottery tickets, knock on wood to avoid jinxing themselves, or feel that everything happens for a reason, it's hard to
label *any* mystical belief as pathological.

Of course, the *DSM* doesn't even attempt to define "stupid."
My own feeling is that there are eleven or so different kinds of
intelligence, and at least forty different kinds of stupidity.

Most of which I've experienced firsthand.

Since it seemed unlikely I would even be able to find Władysław
Budek, I decided to at least see the sights. I made my first desti-
nation the primeval forest my grandparents had been hiding in
when Budek contacted them. I flew to Warsaw, stayed a night in

the ex-Communist *shithotel* in Old Town (it's literally called Old Town, like it's the capital of Old Country), ate some weird-shaped tubes of breakfast meat in the restaurant there, then took a train to Lublin. From there I got on a bus with a bunch of zit-faced sixteen-year-old Catholic school girls, who talked about blow-jobs the whole trip. My vocabulary in Polish—which was crap, though my pronunciation was okay—picked up a bit.

Meanwhile, every place we passed through was mostly fac-tories and train tracks. If I was Polish, I might try: *"Of course I didn't know the Holocaust was happening! The whole fucking country looks like a concentration camp!"*

Like I would care, if I was Polish.

Finally we reached a town so rural it only had four factories, and I got off the bus. There was a plowed access road that ran out of town and along the front of the woods. I double-checked the return schedule, left my backpack with the woman at the sta-tion, and started down the road.

Did I mention how fucking, fucking cold it was in Poland? It was really fucking cold. The kind where your eyes gush water to keep from freezing and your cheeks clench up and pull your lips back, and the only thing keeping you warm is the image of Hit-ler's Sixth Army's hobnailed boots conducting their body heat into the ground. The air was almost too cold to breathe.

I chose a random departure point from the road and climbed up into a snowdrift so deep and soft that moving through it felt like swimming. The surface had a glassy coat of ice that cracked and slid away in tectonic sheets as I pushed my way into the woods.

Fifty yards in, my eyes adapted to the gloom. The noise and wind were gone. Weird giant trees I couldn't identify (not that I could identify, say, an oak) had branches going out in all directions. The lowest-lying ones snagged my feet beneath the snow.

It took so much attention just to pick my way forward that I didn't notice the ravens until one dropped to a branch right above and in front of me. Another two stayed higher up and watched me. I lay back against the snow and stared at them. They were the largest wild birds I'd ever seen. After a while they started cleaning themselves like cats.

I breathed the clean sharp air and wondered whether ravens could live as long as parrots, and if so whether these ones had been here during World War II. Or World War I, for that matter. I wondered if my grandparents had ever tried to eat them.

If they hadn't tried to eat them, what *had* they tried to eat? How did you even get around in a place like this? How did you do laundry, let alone fight off Nazis? The place was like some kind of afterlife.

Eventually one of the ravens screamed, and all three flew away. Shortly after, I heard machine noises.

The obvious thing to do was go back to the road, since the snow was starting to work into my boots. But I was curious—not just about the source of the noise, but about how quickly you could get someplace through these woods if you had someplace you needed to go. So I followed the noise, and went farther into the woods.

As the noise got louder, other mechanical sounds joined it.

Soon I could see the tops of cranes. Soon after that I stumbled out through another wall of snow and rolled to my feet in a clearing.

It was a clearing in the sense of "just recently cleared." The ground was scraped perfectly flat for maybe a hundred acres, and men in parkas and primary-colored hardhats were using giant machinery to clear more trees from the edges, whacking them down and cutting them into lengths that could be lifted onto flatbeds. Black exhaust from half a dozen sources smudged into the otherwise white sky.

I tried to talk to one of the workers. I think he said he was from *Veerk*, the Finnish lumber company, but we didn't seem to have a common language, so in the end we both just shrugged and laughed, since what the fuck else can you do.

It wasn't very funny, though. Białowieża is the last remains of a forest that once covered eighty percent of Europe. Seeing another chunk of it mowed down was like watching the navel of the world sanded off. It left one less point of entrance to the past— my grandparents' or anyone else's. One less sign that we'd been human to begin with.

And one more piece of history as vapor, in which you could see anything you wanted, or nothing at all.

I backed up to Lublin and headed south for the main event. Took the Iron Curtain Express down to Kraków by sleeper car, something I'd never done before and probably won't do again, though it wasn't a bad time. In my upper bunk I ditched the blanket, which appeared to have an inordinate amount of pubic hair woven into it, and lay on the sheets in my overcoat, reading by the bare bulb near my head.

I'd bought a stack of books in Lublin. The Communist-era stuff was funny but shallow. (*"Visitors are invited to inspect the Lenin Steel Works, the Czyżyny cigarette factory, and the Bonarka artificial fertilizer plant!"*) Most of the modern Polish stuff was stupid and hateful, with hundreds of pages on how Lech Wałesa was a saint, and none on how he should be eating shit like the pig-faced bitch that he is.* And the stuff that seemed accurate was just depressing.

Jews blamed for fire! Jews blamed for plague! Jews blamed for all of Europe being ruled by Jew-hating fucks!

Jews making up a third of Kraków's population in 1800, a quarter in 1900, and none at all in 1945.

In the morning, on my way from the train station to my hotel, I stopped and bought my bus ticket to Auschwitz.

I'll spare you most of it.

Auschwitz when it was up and running was really three different camps: the death camp (Birkenau, also known as "Auschwitz II"); the I. G. Farben factory camp ("Auschwitz III," or Monowitz) where the slaves worked, and the combination holding and extermination camp that lay between them ("Auschwitz

---

* My favorite Lech Wałesa story is from shortly before I went to Poland. Realizing he was about to lose the presidency, Wałesa announced that his opponent was secretly Jewish. He then denied he was a bigot, saying, "Actually I wish I was Jewish myself. Because then I would have a lot more money." Funny guy!

I," or simply Auschwitz). Since the Germans bombed Birkenau as they fled—proving Plato's claim that human shame arises solely from the threat of discovery—and then the Poles scavenged the ruins for bricks, the main museum is at Auschwitz I.

To get there you take one of those buses that, through some kind of historical leapfrogging, are more modern than any in the United States. The Poles call the neighborhood *Oświęcim*—you never see a sign that says "Auschwitz." The area is fully industrialized and occupied, with apartment buildings across the street from the concentration camp entrance, although the tour guide tells you in Polish that they would have been knocked down to build a supermarket by now if it hadn't been for militant international Jews making too much trouble. You look around to see who's taking offense at this, but the only people grinding their teeth are the Hasidic family at the back of the bus.

You cross an outer courtyard. The Nazis kept expanding the camp as long as they were able to, so to get to the famous *"Arbeit Macht Frei"* gates you have to go through a building with a snack bar, a film kiosk, and a ticket counter. This was previously the building where the inmates were tattooed and got their heads shaved, and where the Nazis kept the Jewish sex slaves. It smells like sewage because they don't clean the bathrooms, and in the pictures the tattoos don't even look like the ones your grandparents had.

Inside the gates themselves, there's a sixty-foot wooden cross with a bunch of nuns and skinheads around it handing out pamphlets about how hysterical international Jews are trying to forbid Catholic services at Auschwitz, which is in a Catholic country. It makes your hands itch, and you wonder if twisting a skinhead's neck would satisfy Freud's dictum that the only thing that can ever make us happy is the fulfillment of childhood desires.

But you do what you're there to do. You look at the razor-wire bunkhouses, the gallows, the random-death guard towers. The medical experimentation building. The crematoria. You ask yourself the questions: Would I clean out the gas chambers to keep myself alive for one more month? Would I pack the ovens?

You feel fucking awful.

Eventually you start to wonder why there's a bunkhouse dedicated to the victims of every nationality you've ever heard of — Slovenians, for example — but Jews aren't mentioned anywhere. You ask a guard. He points you across the street.

You find Bunk 37, and realize the guard was half right. It's a combo bunk, the only one at Auschwitz: Slovakians (the original exhibit; you can tell from the signs) and now also Jews. Though the whole thing is closed, with a chain around the doorknob. Later you find out that this particular bunk has been closed more often than it's been open, for example not opening once between 1967 and 1978. The Hasidic family from the bus stands looking at the chain forlornly.

Naturally you stomp the fucking padlock off and push the doors open, letting the Hasidic family go first.

Inside, you see a lot of bad shit. So many Jews died at Auschwitz that the things they left behind — the hair, the wooden legs of the veterans who had fought for Poland in the First World War, the children's shoes, and so on — fill whole glassed-off rooms, in which they rot and stink. Compared to these, the casually evil museum plaques—on which "Polish" has been scratched off "Polish Jews," and the National Socialists are said to have been "reacting to an overrepresentation of Jews in business and the government"—barely get to you. Even though the "over-representation" line is your favorite Jew-hater stereotype, because every time someone kills off half the Jews on earth, like they did in WWII, the survivors are suddenly twice as "over-represented."

Eventually you get back on the bus and go to Birkenau, the death camp. (Sorry—*Brzezinka*. In Poland "Birkenau" doesn't appear in print either.) There, in the vast Roman-bath ruins of the death factory, even the Europeans cry. The sadness over that place is practically something you can hear, a scraping feeling that comes in through your ears.

Finally the tour guide finds each one of you and taps you on the shoulder, and says softly that you're going back to Kraków.

"But we're stopping at Monowitz?" you say.

She says she's not familiar with "Monowitz."

"*Monowice*," you say. "*Dwory*. The I. G. Farben camp. Auschwitz III."

"Oh. We do not go there," she says.

"Why not?" you say. Half the people who survived Auschwitz were enslaved at Monowitz. Not just your grandparents: people like Primo Levi and Eli Wiesel.

"I'm just the tour guide," she says.

Ultimately you threaten to walk if they won't drop you off, and she takes you up on it. You find the road and follow it for half an hour. You reach a barbed-wire gate—a new one, with actual guards with machine guns. One of them tells you that visiting is by "special permission only."

Looking past him, you see why. Monowitz is pumping soot into the sky *right now*. It's still operating, and has never been shut down.*

After talking with the laughing guards at the gates, you walk back to Auschwitz to get a cab, with your nails cutting the skin of your palms.

Back in Kraków—*Holy shit! The Smurfs built a medieval village on a hill! And it still looks great, as finely detailed as a clock, because the Nazi governor of Poland lived in the castle and protected the buildings!*—I had dinner in a Kommunist-era Koffee House with a wood-burning stove, then went to the back to read through the giant, ancient phone book.

Every customer in the place seemed to have prehensile lips and a conspicuous lack of teeth, and the ones I could overhear were complaining about things it looked like they had good reason to complain about. I realized with a start that I might have just passed Władysław Budek.

* I. G. Farben, the chemical company that ran the labor camp at Auschwitz— it isn't named after a person, it's short for "International Dye Company" in German—stayed in business after the war by claiming it needed to pay reparations to its former slaves, of whom it had used 83,000 at any one time. It then went on to portray itself for decades as being unfairly hounded by greedy, vengeful Jews. In 2003 it found itself on the verge of being forced to actually pay out two hundred and fifty thousand dollars (total, not per person), and declared bankruptcy instead. But not until it had spun off Agfa, BASF, Bayer, and Hoechst (now half of pharmaceutical giant Aventis), all of which prosper to this day.

I'd always pictured Budek as an aged Claus von Bülow: a smirking, unrepentant lion with a Luger in the pocket of his smoking jacket. But what if he was just some shuffling dipshit, with his bottom eyelids hanging inside out and a plastic pillbox with the days of the week written on its different compartments? What if he was too deaf and senile to even understand what I'd be accusing him of?

What was I going to do, shout *"YOU WERE AN EVIL FUCK FIFTY YEARS AGO"*? Or *"YOU PROBABLY STILL ARE, THOUGH IT LOOKS LIKE YOU DON'T HAVE THE ENERGY TO DO ANYTHING ABOUT IT"*?

Well, I was about to find out. I felt the spark in my fingers before my eyes even processed the image: Budek's address was listed, six blocks away.

It was the top floor of a townhouse in a row of townhouses that backed onto a long narrow park with a private gate. I considered entering through the park and going in through the back, but before I knew it I was up the steps and had rung the twist-type bell.

Sweat appeared all over me, like all the water in my body was trying to form a shadow version of me and run off. I told myself to calm down, then gave up on that. Why bother?

The door opened. A wizened face. Female. Or at least the housecoat was pink.

"Yes?" she said, in Polish.

"I'm looking for Władysław Budek."

"He isn't here."

"Slowly, please," I said. "My Polish is bad. When do you expect him?"

She studied me. "Who are you?" she said.

"I'm an American. My grandparents knew him."

"Your grandparents know Władys?"

"Yes. They did. They're dead now."

"Who were they?"

"Stefan Brnwa and Anna Maisel."

"Maisel? That sounds Jewish."

"It is."

"You don't look Jewish."

I had the feeling I was supposed to say "Thank you." I said, "Are you Mrs. Budek?"

"No. I am Władys's sister, Blancha Przedmieście."

Things became suddenly surreal. I had heard about this woman from my grandparents. Legend had it she had spent the war simultaneously fucking a Nazi and a man whose wife had connections to the Jewish underground, and had thereby made her brother's scheme possible.

She said something I didn't understand. "Excuse me?" I said.

"I am very well known to the police," she repeated, more slowly.

"Why would you need the police?"

"I don't know. You are American."

Good answer. "Can I come in?" I said.

"Why?"

"Just to ask you some questions about your brother," I said. "If you don't like them, you can call whoever you want."

She considered. Jew-hating may be a primordial cracker urge, but loneliness goes back to the amoeba. "Fine," she finally said. "But I won't feed you. And don't touch anything."

Inside, the apartment was musty but uncluttered, with boxy sixties furniture and a television with a bulging screen. A couple of side tables held framed photographs.

One was of two young people in front of an ivy-covered stone wall: a woman who might have been this one and a bleak-looking black-haired man. "Is this him?" I asked.

"No. That is my husband. He died when the Germans invaded." Using a series of words and hand gestures she indicated that this was because her husband had been in the horse-drawn artillery, and the Germans had used airplanes. "Władys is here," she said, pointing.

This one was a flip-looking blond man on skis on a mountaintop, laughing bucktoothed in the sunshine. "He was a beautiful man." She seemed to be daring me to contradict her.

"You say 'He was.' Is he dead?"

"He died in 1944."

"In 1944?"

"Yes."

"What happened?"

She smiled bitterly. "Some Jews killed him. They came in through the window. They had guns."

It took me a while to understand what she said next. Apparently the Jews she was referring to had tied her up in the kitchen and shot her brother in the living room, near where I was standing at the end of the couch. They had used a pillow so no one would hear.

"But the police were already on their way," she said, "and they caught them going out."

"Wow," I said.

So someone had gotten here first. By a fairly healthy margin.

"It was a boy and a girl," she said. "Teenagers."

"Excuse me?" I said.

She repeated it.

"Are you joking?"

"What do you mean?" she said.

I felt nauseated. I sat down on the couch in case it showed and she tried to throw me out.

I needed more information. "What did they look like?" I said.

She shrugged. "Like Jews."

I tried another tack. "Why were the police on their way?"

"What do you mean?" She sat down on the armchair, but on the edge of its cushion, with good posture, like she was prepared to lunge for the phone at any moment.

"How did the police know there was going to be trouble?"

"I don't know, Władys had already called them."

"Before the boy and girl came in?" I said.

"Yes."

"But how did he know they were going to come in?"

"I have no idea. Perhaps he heard them. It was a long time ago."

"You don't remember?"

"No. I don't."

"Two Jews came in through the window and tied you up, and you don't remember how your brother knew they were coming?"

"No."

"Was it because you and he had taken money from them by claiming you could save their relatives?"

She grew very still. "Why are you asking me these questions?"

"Because I want to know what happened."

"Why should I discuss this with you?"

I thought about it. "Because you and I are the only two people on earth who care, and you don't look like you're going to be around much longer."

She said something along the lines of "Bite your tongue."

"Just tell me what happened. Please."

She was going from pale to red. "We sold the Jews hope. God knows they could afford it."

"Did you save any of them?"

"It was impossible to save Jews during the War. Even if you wanted to."

"And if they looked at you too closely, you had them killed."

She turned away at this. "Leave now," she said.

"Why did you hate them so much?" I asked.

"They controlled the whole country," she said. "Just like they control America. Get out of my house."

"I will," I said. "If you tell me the names of the Jews."

"I have no idea!" she said. "Get out!"

I stood. I knew I was as sure as I ever would be.

I went to the door. Freezing wind came in when I opened it.

"Wait," she said. "Tell me the names of your grandparents again."

I turned back. "I don't think I will," I said. "I'm just wondering why they let you live."

She stared at me. "I've always wondered that," she said.

I left and pulled the door shut after me.

For the record, what I decided was this:

No female targets (which was obvious), but also no targets whose misdeeds were solely in the past. Only ongoing threats. I had no way of knowing why my grandparents had let Blancha Przedmieście live, but she was a woman, and killing her brother had been enough to shut down their operation. So there you had it.

Meanwhile, if David Locano wanted to sic me on killers whose deaths would improve the world, I would verify his information and then feel free—obligated, even—to hunt them down and kill them.

Not once did I think that maybe, if my grandparents would have approved of this course of action, they would have preached to me less about peace and tolerance and told me more about their mission to assassinate Budek. I felt no need to consider such things. Fate itself had told me what to do.

Ah, youth. It's like heroin you've smoked instead of snorted. Gone so fast you can't believe you still have to pay for it.

9

I'm on my way to catheterize a couple of people when my med students find me. "Survival five years status post gastrectomy is ten percent,"* one of them says. "But only fifty percent survive the operation."

"Huh," I say.

The upside of this information is that if Squillante *does* live through his surgery, his odds of surviving another five years are

---

* "*Status post*," abbreviated "s/p," is a common medical term meaning "after" and implying "but not necessarily caused by." It's Latin for "Try suing me now, Fucker."

actually more like twenty percent than ten, because the ten percent figure presumably includes people who die during the operation. The downside is that Squillante has fifty-fifty odds of dying *today*, on the table. And calling David Locano down on me if he does.

The elevator doors open in front of us: Assman, getting returned to the floor in his stretcher-bed. Mostly to make it look like I'm doing something, I fall in beside him.

"How are you feeling?" I say.

He's still lying on his side. "I'm fuckin dying, you fuckin asshole," he says. Or something like that. His teeth are chattering too hard to be sure.

It gets my attention. He certainly looks like he's dying. "Allergic to any medications?" I ask him.

"No."

"Good. Hang in there."

"Fuck you."

I follow him back to his unit and quickly write orders for a whole collage of antibiotics and antivirals, putting "STAT" on every one of them. Thinking: *Should I go threaten Squillante some more? With what, and to what end?* Then I go pull Assman's CT scan up on a computer screen.

It's calming, in a way. If you know what you're doing, trackballing through a CT is beautiful. Probably even if you don't. You rise or fall through the hundreds of horizontal cross sections, and the various ovals—chest, lungs, heart chambers, aorta— expand and contract like roiling weather patterns, passing through each other and tapering at different levels. But even then you always know where you are, because the inside of a human being has practically no two cubic inches that are identical. This is true even on a left-right basis. Your heart and spleen are on the left while your liver and gallbladder are on the right. Your left lung has two lobes while your right has three. Your left and right colon are different widths and follow differently shaped paths. The vein of your right gonad drains directly toward your heart, while the vein of the left joins the vein of your left kidney. If you're male, your left gonad even hangs lower than your right, to accommodate the scissor motion of your legs.

So the two golf ball–sized abscesses on Assman's CT are immediately noticeable, one behind his right collarbone and the other in his right buttock. On closer inspection they might have some sort of fuzz around the edges—a fungus or something. They look like what alcoholics get when they pass out and inhale their own vomit, then grow colonies from it in their lungs. I'm pretty sure I've never seen anything like it in muscle before.

I send my med students off to page Pathology. It tends to be difficult to pry those people out of their nasty little lairs, which are lined with bottles of human organs like the homes of the serial killers they chase on TV, but Assman is going to need a biopsy. I tell them to page Infectious Disease while they're at it, since odds are neither service will answer us.

And once they're out of sight I close out the CT screen on the computer and Google Squillante's surgeon, John Friendly, MD, just to take one more depth reading on the shit I'm in.

But surprise: the word is positive. My man Friendly has either banded or reduced the stomach of every obese celebrity I've ever heard of. In fact, *New York* magazine—which should know, since its primary function is to transfer pathogens between the hands of people in waiting rooms—names him as one of the five best GI surgeons in the city. Friendly even has a book that's doing not too sucky on Amazon: *Eye of the Needle: Cooking for the Surgically Altered Digestive Tract.*

I keep searching until I find a picture that confirms these people are really talking about the guy I met earlier, since it's been that kind of morning. Along the way I find more happy articles. Apparently Friendly just did the colostomy on the guy who played the dad on *Virtual Dad.*

Like that guy must have said: what a fucking relief.

I try to figure out just how much of a relief. Does this mean Squillante actually has a seventy-five percent chance of surviving the operation? If so, what are the odds he keeps his word and doesn't rat me out if he lives? I get a page from a room where I don't currently have any patients.

I stare at the number on my pager screen and wonder if it's the new patient Akfal said something about to me three hours earlier. Then I realize it's the room with Osteosarcoma Girl in it, and run to take the fire stairs.

The first thing I realize when I see her again is that, although she's beautiful, her eyes really don't look like those of my lost Magdalena at all. Then I feel embarrassed to be so disappointed.

"What's up?" I say.

"What do you mean?"

"I got paged."

She stops biting her thumbnail to point toward the side of

the room where the door is. "I think it was the new girl," she says.

Oh right. That curtain's now drawn, and there are voices coming through. I pat Osteosarcoma Girl on her nondiseased leg, then knock on the wall and pull the curtain aside.

Three nurses are still setting up a new patient in the bed that was empty before.

It's another young woman, though it's hard to tell her age precisely because her head is shaved and bandaged, and the front left quarter of it is missing. Where it should be, there's just an indentation in gauze.

Below it she looks at me with wild blue eyes.

"Who's this?" I ask.

"New patient, Dr. Brown," the senior nurse says. "She's in from Neurosurgery."

"Hi," I say to the patient. "I'm Dr. Brown."

"Ay a ly ly ly," she says.

Naturally. In all right-handed people, and most left-handed ones, the front left lobe is where the personality is. Or was. The bandage over the missing part of her head starts pulsating from the effort of speaking.

"Just relax. I'll go read your chart," I tell her, and leave before she can answer.

Or respond to stimulus, or whatever you want to call it.

Head Girl's chart is brief: it says she's "*s/p craniectomy for septic meningeal abscess s/p lingual abscess s/p elective cosmetic procedure + s/p laparotomy for calvarium placement.*"

In other words, she got her tongue pierced and the infection ran to her brain. Then they cut her head open to get to it, and afterwards took the chunk of skull they'd removed and implanted it under the skin of her abdomen to keep it alive while they waited to see if the infection came back.

Calling a tongue piercing "cosmetic" is a bit of a stretch, since you don't get one because it makes you look better. You get one because you're so desperate for affection that you're willing to gruesomely harm yourself to advertise how well you suck dick.

Christ, I think: *I am in one bad mood.*

Just to complete my research into the house of mirth that is Room 808W, I call up Osteosarcoma Girl's chart.

Not much to learn there: a lot of "atypical" this and "high likelihood of" that. Her right femur sometimes bleeds, just above the knee. Other times it doesn't. And she's due to get the whole thing removed at the hip in a few hours.

The weirdest, worst shit happens to people.

I do Head Girl's admission paperwork without looking at it, but before I'm done I get another page, this one to the room shared by Duke Mosby and Assman.

The deal, by the way, is this: Akfal and I are required to admit thirty new patients to the ward each week. How long we keep these people in the hospital is up to us. Obviously we have an incentive to get them out fast, so we don't have to take care of them. But on the other hand, if they come back to the emergency room less than forty-eight hours after we've discharged them, we have to take them back onto our service. Whereas if they

come back, say, forty-*nine* hours after discharge, they get as-
signed randomly, as if it were their first visit, and odds are five to
one they'll be someone else's problem.

The art is in spotting the exact moment when a patient is suf-
ficiently well to survive a full forty-nine hours outside, then flush-
ing them. It sounds harsh—actually, it is harsh—but the second
Akfal and I stop doing it, our job will become impossible.

It's almost impossible already. Some insurance executive
long ago found the precise line past which it won't pay to push
us—our own forty-nine-hour mark, if you will—and is doing an
expert job of keeping us there. Between admitting new patients
and discharging old ones, both of which are paperwork night-
mares, we barely have time to manage the patients who are staying around.

This means that checking on any one of the patients we've
already seen for the day—like Assman and Duke Mosby—is a
pure waste of time. Unless the patient is in immediate, fixable
trouble.

Which is always an outside possibility, and in this case sends
me back to the fire stairs, then running down the hall to their
room.

There's a crowd just inside: the Attending Physician from rounds
(of all people), Zhing Zhing, our four med students, and the Chief
Resident. There are also two male residents I don't recognize.
One, who's darkly handsome but also crazed-looking, has a giant
syringe in his hand. The other one is birdlike and looks annoyed.

"No way," the Chief Resident is saying to the one with the syringe. "Unh uh, Doctor." She's standing between him and the bed.

I say, "Hi," and hold a fist out for Assman to knock with his knuckles, but he just glares at me. "Who are you guys?" I say to the residents.

"ID," says the one with the hypodermic. Infectious Disease.

"Pathology," says the other one. "Did you page me?"

"Maybe an hour ago," I say. "Did you page *me?*"

"I did, sir," one of the medical students says.

"This guy wants to biopsy the lesions," the Chief Resident says to me, meaning the ID guy.*

"Okay," I say.

"*Okay?*" the Chief Resident says. "This patient has an unknown pathogen that's *spreading,* and you want to risk disseminating it farther?"

"I want to find out what it is," I say.

"Did you think about informing the CDC?"

"No," I say.

Which is true.

"It's already gone from his glute to his upper thorax," the ID guy says. "How much farther can it disseminate?"

"How about through my whole fucking hospital ward?" the Chief Resident says.

The birdlike Pathology guy breaks in. "Why did you page *me?*" he says.

---

* "Lesion" is a nonspecific but extremely useful (because it sounds like a crater of pus) term for any abnormality.

The Chief Resident ignores him and turns to the Attending. "What do you think?"

The Attending looks at his watch and shrugs.

"I'm going in," the ID guy says.

The Chief Resident says, "Wait—"

But the ID guy gets an elbow around her and moves in with the needle. Taps twice on Assman's upper chest, raising a scream with the second tap. ID keeps his finger there and sinks the needle in right next to it, then quickly tugs at the plunger. Assman's howl rises in pitch, and the chamber of the hypodermic fills with blood swirled with yellow fluid.

"God damn you!" the Chief Resident shouts.

The ID guy yanks the needle out and turns to her, smug, but overestimates the distance between them. Actually there is no distance between them. As the Chief Resident gets knocked backwards, she and ID guy flail into a tangle and start to fall together.

Right toward me.

I shift sideways, but there's a med student under me, yapping beneath one of my clogs. I jam into the wall, and all I can do to protect my face is raise a forearm. Which the hypodermic hits, sinking up to the plastic.

There's a pause.

Then people start to get up, backing away from me. I stand too. Look down at my arm. The hypodermic's sticking out of it, empty, plunger all the way down. Starting to give me that pain any large shot will give you, because it separates the planes of tissue. I twist the syringe out of my arm.

I snap the needle off and drop it into the drawer of a sharps box on the wall behind me. Then I take hold of the front of the ID guy's scrub shirt and drop the hypo chamber into his pocket. "Scrape what you can out of this and analyze it," I tell him. "Take the Path guy with you."

"I don't even know what I'm doing here," the Path guy whines.

"Don't make me hurt you," I tell him.

"Dr. Brown," the Attending says.

"Yes, sir?" I say, still looking at the ID guy.

"Give me a five-minute head start?"

"You left ten minutes ago," I tell him.

"You're a mensch, kid. Cheers," he says as he leaves.

Everyone else stands frozen.

"Stat, you fucking assholes!" I tell them.

I'm almost out of the room when I realize something's wrong. Something else, I mean.

Duke Mosby's bed is empty. "Where's Mosby?" I say.

"Maybe he went for a walk," one of the med students says, behind me.

"Mosby's got bilateral pedal gangrene," I say. "The guy can't even hobble."

But apparently he can run.

10

I believe I've already mentioned that Skinflick was in love with his first cousin, Denise. He always had been.

She was two years younger. Skinflick talked about her all the time, often in the context of his *Golden Bough* bullshit. About how unfair it was that he and Denise couldn't be together just because of some stupid American prejudice that had no basis in scientific or even historical reality, and how the Sicilians had an expression, "cousins are for cousins," that was not only more accurate historically but also an excellent piece of advice.* "Every other fucking thing rednecks do, Americans love," he used to complain.

After Skinflick and I finished high school we drove across the country to Palos Verdes, south of LA, to visit her.

Denise's father, Roger, was Skinflick's mother's brother. He was suspicious the moment we got there, and it didn't help that Skinflick and Denise took every possible opportunity to sneak off—or out, or upstairs—and fuck.

Denise's mother, Shirl, was less of a problem, at least in that way. But in regard to hitting on *me,* and to getting turned on by the constant humping of her daughter by her nephew, she was a lot more of a problem. Not that I was exactly a saint.

Thankfully, it was Skinflick and Denise who Roger caught in the guesthouse, not me and Shirl. Roger exiled Skinflick from the house. Denise sobbed. In a sordid way it was romantic.

Skinflick and I backed off all the way to Florida, as if the point of our trip had been time on the beach. We had dinner with my father for a couple of nights running, which was pleasant enough. Silvio was selling boats and real estate at the time, and was in a phase of his life where he kept smiling and spreading his hands and saying, "Who can know about these things? Tell me that."

---

* Medically it's not all that clear. A woman who mates with her first cousin adds about 2 percent to her chance of having a kid with a birth defect. (For comparison, a woman who conceives at age forty has a 10 percent chance that the fetus will have Down's Syndrome.) On the other hand, offspring of cousins may benefit from an increased chance of family stability. Either way, the human genome is already far more "conserved," i.e., inbred, than that of any other known mammal, so we've already done a lot more cousin-jumping than, say, the rat.

He may still be in that phase. Last time I spoke to him was when he came to visit me in jail during my trial.*

Skinflick, meanwhile, continued to bitch and moan about Denise for the rest of the summer—even, charmingly, while we were out with other women.

He also continued to fail to progress athletically. His father kept urging me to teach him to fight, but Skinflick was naturally terrible at combat sports. He would try to protect his face and stomach by twisting away, which exposed his spine, his kidneys, and the back of his skull. His reflexes were good, but without willpower they just made him flinchy.

Skinflick and I had changed our minds about continuing with school by then and enrolled at Northern New Jersey Community College. We were living in a condo together in Bergen County. We both continued to laugh off Skinflick's klutziness, since at that point I still respected him for other reasons.

I saw Denise three more times. Once was in the lobby of a hotel in midtown Manhattan before she and Skinflick went upstairs to fuck. I don't remember what year that was. The second and third times were in August of 1999, on the night before and then the night of her wedding.

This was four and a half years after I had gone to Poland. In

---

* I should admit here that my failure to communicate with my parents has been more than just a WITSEC formality. You're allowed to exchange messages and even talk on the phone with your family through the Virginia clearinghouse, and if you do this often enough the agents will eventually "slip up" and give your family your direct contact information. I just never tried.

the meantime I had finished my two-year degree at Northern New Jersey Community College (which Skinflick had left after one year), helped Skinflick run a "record label" (paid for by David Locano) into the ground (it was called Rap Sheet Records, good luck finding anything), and went with Skinflick to work as a paralegal at David Locano's four-partner law firm, from which we were subsequently fired by a vote of the three other partners, apparently for spending too much money entertaining clients while not doing anything else. Fair enough.

At the time David Locano was still maintaining to both of us that he didn't want Skinflick to join the mafia. Which was probably even true, to the extent that any father can really want his child to surpass him or be different from him. But to warn us about what the life was like, and as a penalty for flunking out of the law firm, he sent us to work at a garbage truck dispatch facility in Brooklyn. And it's hard to see that as anything but a Very Bad Move.

For one thing, it wasn't much of a penalty. It was dreary and boring, but it was easy. It gave you a lot of time off. And it was impossible to get fired from, since all we were getting paid for was being connected to David Locano.

Also, some of the lowlifes, particularly the nostalgic ones, were interesting. Grown men named Sally Knockers or Joey Camaro,* who cowered in front of the blow-dried scumbags who came by *doo, free ties a week* to pick up half the take. Some of the scumbags were interesting too.

---

* Supposedly from the expression "bitchin Camaro." He did kind of complain a lot.

Kurt Limme comes to mind. Limme was about ten years older than we were. He was undeniably handsome, and well dressed for real, not goombah. He seemed like an uncle you might have in Manhattan who was making a killing as a stock-broker and fucking a lot of women. In reality he was under indictment for a series of extortion schemes involving the installation of cell phone relay towers, but even that seemed to be relatively forward thinking.

Skinflick fixated on him as a guy who was as cool, cynical, and relaxed—if not quite as smart—as Skinflick was. And who had *made* it. Limme, meanwhile, being the breakout member of a traditionally low level mob family, appreciated being worshipped by David Locano's son.

Limme started taking Skinflick with him on his endless errands in the city, which seemed to me to be mostly shopping trips. I knew I should have been discouraging Skinflick from hanging out with him so much, since among other things Skinflick did a lot of cocaine when he was with Limme, but I had started working jobs for David Locano regularly, and was glad Skinflick had someone to entertain him in my absence.

Regarding the actual jobs, I'm not going to say too much. I can't.

I *will* say that *if* it so happened that I killed a dozen or so people—people I wouldn't be able to talk about now, because the DA didn't know about them so they weren't part of my immunity agreement—then these would have been the years during which I did it. Not that I'm saying I did. I'm saying *if*.

Furthermore, *if* I killed these people—*if,* motherfucking *if*—I would have made sure that every one of them was some truly evil fuck. A guy who, if you knew he was out there, would make you want to keep your family in a bank vault. David Locano would have known better than to offer me anything else.

And—last point—I would have done every single one of those jobs right. No shell casings, no latents, no alibi gaps. No bodies, even, for most of them. So don't even try.

But anyway.

Skinflick and I were still working in trash-haul, at least on paper, when he found out Denise was getting married.

Elisabeth Kübler-Ross at one point said that our comprehension of death passes through five distinct stages—denial, anger, bargaining, depression, and acceptance.* When Skinflick got the news about Denise, he went straight to sullen and irritable, then started losing weight and spending a lot of time alone.

As it was, between the girls, the drugs, Kurt Limme, and the fact that we both had other places to stay (I still had my grandparents' house, he had his parents'), I wasn't seeing all that much of him anyway, even though we kept our two-bedroom condo in Demarest. But in the week before Denise's wedding, Skinflick failed to show up to work even once, and I didn't run into him anywhere else, either. And on the night before the wedding, Kurt Limme called me.

"Pietro, have you seen Skinflick?" he said.

---

* I say "at one point" because this progression is what we think about when we think about Kübler-Ross. But what we avoid thinking about when we think about Kübler-Ross is how she later changed her mind and decided we'll all be reincarnated. I wish I was shitting you.

"No. He didn't come to work this week."

"I saw him about three days ago."

It so happened that I had had lunch with David Locano a day earlier, because he was worried about Limme's influence on Skinflick, so I knew Locano hadn't seen Skinflick for a while either. "He's probably staying with some girl," I said.

"Not with Denise getting married," Limme said.

"Good point."

"I'm worried about him, Pietro."

"Why?" I asked. "How much coke did he have on him?"

Limme said, "I don't do cocaine or know anybody who does."

"Chill out," I said. "I just want to know if he's in trouble."

There was a pause. "Yeah, he might be," Limme said.

"All right. If I hear anything, I'll call you."

"Thanks, Pietro."

"Yeah."

Twenty minutes later the phone rang. I figured it was Limme again, but it was Skinflick.

Slurred. "Where are you?" he said.

"I'm at home. You called me."

"Yeah, I was trying all the numbers. Dress up. I'm coming over in a limo. I've got a girl for you."

I looked at the clock. It was only nine, but whatever this was sounded bad.

"I don't know," I said. "Hello?"

He'd hung up.

The inside of the limo was like a nightclub lit by penlights, and it took me a moment after I got in to adjust to the darkness. On the squishy leather couch at the back were Skinflick—glistening and pale except beneath his eyes—and Denise. Next to me, facing them, was a young blonde with good posture and strangely muscular bare shoulders and a broad neck. I later found out she'd swum competitively in college, which had ended for her three months earlier.

Skinflick was in a tuxedo with the shirt open. Denise was in a black sheath. The blonde's dress was weirder: green satin. "Jesus," I said, leaning over to kiss Denise as the car started up. "I didn't realize it was prom night."

"You look good enough, honey," Denise said. "This is Lisa."

"Hi Lisa."

Lisa kissed my cheek and breathed hot alcohol on me, saying she'd heard a lot about me.

"You too," I lied.

"Lisa's the maid of honor," Skinflick said.

"No shit," I said.

Skinflick keyed the intercom. "Georgie—you know where we're going?"

"Yes sir, Mr. Locano."

"Where are we going?" I asked, as we started moving.

"It's a surprise," Skinflick said.

I looked at Lisa, who had "weak link" written all over her as far as information pumping went, but she just shrugged at me as she leaned toward where Denise was holding out a coke spoon for her. It was a weird moment.

The limo turned north at the first big intersection, so the Midtown Tunnel was out. Denise scooped some coke for me as Skinflick licked a joint closed.

"Let me have a drink first," I said.

By the time we got to Coney I was completely drunk and stoned, and everyone else was worse. Skinflick was talking about coke spoons. Who made them, and whether they came as part of a whole tiny cutlery set. The driver, Georgie — he was a guy I knew, with a ponytail and a full chauffeur's outfit — parked in the same lot I'd parked in when I killed the Russians in 1993. After he let us out he got back in the car to wait.

I told Skinflick I didn't want to go to Little Odessa.

"We're not going to Little Odessa," he said. He took Denise's arm and led her out across the boardwalk, toward the ocean.

The Coney Island boardwalk has to be one of the widest in the world. When you're as fucked up as we were it seems endless. And that's when you're on *top* of it. Once we made it down the stairs to the beach, and the women got their high-heeled shoes off, Skinflick took a small Maglite out of his pants pocket and announced that we were going back the way we came, but *underneath* the boardwalk.

Like in the fucking Motown song.

"No fucking way," Denise said. "I'll cut my foot. I'm getting married tomorrow."

"Don't worry about it," Skinflick said. "If he doesn't take you I will."

"I'll step on a crack needle."

"It'll be worth it."

"To you, maybe."

"Just step where I'm stepping."

Skinflick headed in without looking back, and Denise followed him. It was that or lose the benefit of the flashlight he was holding. Lisa went next, with me in the back.

It was creep-out city down there. Somehow the Motown song doesn't mention the semivisible homeless people, or how they fast-shamble away from you like they're scared of something only they know is down there.

Still, even in the darkness and the moving shadows, and even with all the columns, Skinflick got us to the other side pretty quickly. It was like he knew his way around. At the time I thought it was just that he was so depressed about Denise getting married that he didn't give a fuck what happened to him or any of the rest of us, but when we reached the end—a chain-link fence that had long strips of plastic woven through it vertically—he already knew where the loose corner was. While Denise and Lisa complained about how cold the sand was, Skinflick pushed the corner in and held it open. Denise went first, and suddenly we were all back under the glare of the New York night sky.

We were on asphalt, at the rear of some kind of complex that looked like a cross between a power plant and a high school. A jagged line of cylindrical cement buildings, two or three stories tall, connected to each other at ground level by aboveground tunnels. No windows, just pipes coming out through the walls. There was a hum, and a strange smell of rot.

Also, strangely, there was an amphitheater off in the distance. You could see its aluminum bleachers from below.

"What is this, a sewage plant?" I asked. I couldn't even tell where we were in relation to the parking lot.

"Not even close," Skinflick said. He walked straight for the largest building. Denise and Lisa were still pulling their shoes on, and they cursed as they hopped after him.

By the time we all caught up, Skinflick was at an entranceway that stuck out of the building. And he had a *key*.

When he opened the door there was a blast of warm air like an exhalation. It smelled like ocean. Like ocean concentrated.

In the beam of Skinflick's flashlight, we could see a hallway that followed the curve of the exterior wall. The place looked like the inside of a submarine: metal pipes freshly painted blue and wet cement, with a lot of dials and a couple of tanks of some sort. "Shut the door behind you," Skinflick said as he started through it. The sea smell was far more intense than it had been on the beach.

I said, "Skinflick, are we in the Aquarium?"

"Sort of," Skinflick said. He waited for me to close the door.

"What do you mean, sort of?"

"It's kind of a back door," he said.

The hall ended, and a flight of yellow metal stairs took its place, continuing up along the inside of the wall until the darkness and the curvature of the building made it vanish.

"It smells *disgusting* in here," Lisa said.

"I think it smells like pussy," Denise said. She was into it now, joining Skinflick in his whacked-out mood. She took his hand and started pulling him up the stairs.

It didn't smell like pussy. It smelled like the front of a cave that had a giant sleeping in it.

"I don't think this is a good idea," Lisa said.

Denise looked down at her and put a finger to her lips. "Shh. Pietro will take care of you." To me she turned her fingers into a "V" and flicked her tongue out through them. Then she and Skinflick clanked up out of sight, though we could still see their flashlight moving up the curve of the wall.

"Fuck," Lisa said.

"We can stay here if you want," I said to her.

"Yeah, right." She looked back along the hall, which was now consumed by darkness. She pushed her sweat-lank hair off her face. "Will you go first?" she said.

"Sure." I started up the stairs.

It soon became completely dark, and as I slowed she came up close behind me and held on around my waist. She had very solid arms. Just as it started to turn me on, though, my foot clawed air, and I realized we were at the top.

"*Denise!*" Lisa hissed.

"Through here," Denise said. Her voice was throaty, and echoey. Lisa and I followed it through a low arched hallway, trying not to bang our heads, and suddenly we could see again, even though Skinflick had his flashlight off. Because the room into which we emerged had skylights in the ceiling.

"Room" might be the wrong word, but whatever it was, it was huge and hexagonal, and the grated metal catwalk we were on ran all the way around it like a balcony, leaving an open space in the center that was maybe thirty feet across.

Five feet below the catwalk, not just in the center but also below the grate we were standing on, there was water. Water glinting from the skylights but otherwise pure black.

We were above a giant water tank.

The whole fucking building was a water tank.

Skinflick and Denise were leaning over the railing, he behind her with his arms around her. "What do you think?" he said.

"What is this place?" I asked him. It sounded like a church.

"The shark tank."

"The one with the chest from the *Andrea Doria* in it?"

"Yeah, but that's been gone for years."

I was amazed. I'd seen the shark tank from below, through the glass, a dozen times, though not since I was a child. But from that side the Aquarium had seemed like one large indoor space. And now I realized that that was an illusion, allowed by the tunnel-like hallways that ran between the freestanding tanks.

The largest of the tanks was the one we were now above. I remembered it as a vortex of giant, nightmare animals circling past the glass with dead eyes, not needing to visibly propel themselves. In the center of the tank, on the sand, had been the treasure chest from the *Andrea Doria*.

"What happened to the chest from the *Andrea Doria*?" I said.

"Some dipshit opened it live on national TV. Before you got cable."

"No shit. What was in it?"

"What do you think was in it? They let it sit on the bottom of a shark tank the whole time we were kids. It was filled with mud."

Lisa cleared her throat. "Are there sharks in there now?" she said.

"Lisa, it's a shark tank," Denise said.

Skinflick turned his Maglite back on and pointed it down at the surface. It mostly just reflected back up.

"Can we turn on the lights?" I said. There were heavy arc lamps clipped to support beams running just under the sky-lights.

Skinflick flicked the flashlight beam over them, then clicked it off. "I don't think so. They're on a timer."

Lisa looked down at her feet. "Is this thing sturdy?" she said.

Skinflick jumped up and pounded his feet down on the grate, making it ring out and vibrate.

"Feels sturdy," he said.

"Thank you, Adam," Lisa said. "Now I'm going to vomit."

"It gets better," Skinflick said. He led the way around the ledge, past an open, freestanding metal closet that had bunched up wetsuits and a couple of scuba tanks in it. To a segment of grating that didn't have a railing, just a yellow nylon rope. He unhooked one end of the rope.

"Adam, what are you doing?" Denise said.

I stepped back. It was instinctive—you couldn't look at that section of ledge without thinking of falling in.

"I'm lowering the ramp," Skinflick said.

The ramp was folded back up onto the grate. Skinflick lifted it and let it drop out over the water.

The booming clang as the ramp bounced into place—not horizontally but pointed down toward the water, at a forty-five-degree angle—lasted forever, and the vibrating deck felt like it was going to hurl us into the water.

"Look, there's wetsuits," Skinflick said. "Anyone want to go for a swim?"

No one said anything.

"No?" he said. "Well I'm going to put my foot in." Then he actually started to step out onto the ramp.

"Adam, don't!" Denise shouted.

"You've got to be kidding," Lisa said.

I said, "Skinflick. Get the fuck away from that thing." I was gearing up to grab him, but even getting near the section without a railing was frightening.

Skinflick lowered himself to his ass and started crab-walking down toward the end of the ramp. "Somebody take my hand," he said. "It's too scary."

"No way," I said.

"I'll do it," Denise said. She went and lay down by the top of the ramp, and reached one hand down to Skinflick. Then she had to look away. He took hold of it and started to work his foot over the edge.

"Skinflick, don't do it," I said.

He grunted. There was a good ten inches of space between the end of the ramp and the surface of the water, so reaching it with his foot while retaining hold of Denise's hand required him to fully stretch out.

He kicked the toe of one shoe in the water, then pulled his foot back onto the ramp. "See?" he said. "No big deal."

Almost instantly there was an explosion in the water where

his foot had been, then another one. In seconds the whole surface was roiling with enormous, slimy bodies. They looked like giant snakes sliding over each other in a bucket.

"Oh shit! Oh shit! Oh shit!" Skinflick said, scrambling back up the ramp and all the way to the wall, taking Denise with him into his arms.

Now, as the water bucked and dropped in waves, you could see sharks all over the place. One rolled and broke the surface with a fin, wet and shiny in the light from the ceiling panes.

Eventually the water settled, and they were hidden again.

Skinflick started to laugh. "Holy motherfucking shit," he said. "That is the scariest thing that has ever happened to me."

Denise thumped him in the chest, and he grabbed her again and kissed her.

My own heart was pounding, and I realized Lisa and I had our arms around each other too.

Skinflick let his hands slide down Denise's back. "Okay," he said to me and Lisa. "Which side do you guys want?"

"Like, what, like we're supposed to have *sex* now?" Lisa said.

"It's a bachelorette party. So, yes."

"Jesus fucking Christ."

"It's not supposed to be romantic," Skinflick said. "It's supposed to be primal. Which it is. Right, Denise?"

"Fuck yeah," she said.

"So which side do you want?" he said.

Lisa said, "Denise—"

Denise looked at her, and shouted, "Choose a fucking side!"

So she did. The one with the wetsuits, and the cabinet.

Which you could sit in and hold each other, and eventually

even fuck in, without having to look down through the grate and see the water. Even if you could still smell it.

How young, or crazy, or callow do you have to be to have sex in a place that feels like you're suspended over Satan's eye?

I can't defend it. All I can do is point out that twenty-four hours later I met Magdalena, and my life became a completely different thing.

11

At the nursing station outside Assman and Mosby's room, a kid in a "volunteer" smock approaches me. He's a City College student from the neighborhood who believes he'll someday go to med school and become a neurosurgeon. He wants to be the grandfather who works his whole life to establish the family fortune. And maybe he will be.

I know all this because I once asked him why he wears an Afro pruned into the shape of a brain.

"Hey, Dr. Brown—"

"No time," I tell him.

"No sweat, just wanted to tell you I took that patient down to PT."

PT is physical therapy. I stop. "What patient?"

The kid checks his clipboard. "Mosby."

"Who told you to take Mosby to PT?"

"You did. It was in the orders."

"Orders? Fuck. How'd you get him there?"

"Wheelchair."

Fuck!

I turn to the nursing station. "Did somebody bring Mosby his chart, then take it back and put it in the orders rack?" All four people working there avoid my eyes, like they always do when something goes wrong. It's like something from a nature documentary.

"Did you actually take him into PT?" I say to the kid.

"No. They told me to leave him in the waiting room while they found his appointment."

"All right. You want to come on a trip?"

"Yes!" he says.

I turn to my med students, who are just now coming out of Mosby and Assman's room. "Okay, guys," I say. "Anyone asks where Mosby is, tell them he's in Radiology. If they say they already checked Radiology, tell them you meant PT. In the meantime, steal me some antibiotics for when the lab reports back on that shit I just got stuck with. I want a third-generation cephalosporin, a macrolide, and a fluoroquinolone. I also want some antivirals*—everything you can get a hold of. Figure out some

* Antivirals are not antibiotics because viruses, unlike bacteria, are not "biotic"—they're not alive. They're just pieces of genetic code that your body interprets as orders to make more, identical pieces of genetic code, then spread

138

combination that won't kill me. If you can't, just use what I wrote for Assman, and double it. Got it?"

"Yes, sir," one of them says.

"Good. Don't be freaked out."

I turn to the kid with the brain Afro and say, "Come with me."

In the elevator I ask the kid his name again. "Mershawn," he says. I don't ask him to spell it.

I've made him put on his overcoat. I'm wearing a lab coat that has "Lottie Luise, MD," stitched on the front of it. I don't know who Lottie Luise is, but she leaves her coat in convenient places. Or used to.

"Mershawn, don't get your tongue pierced," I mention as we get to ground level.

"Fuck *that* shit," Mershawn says.

In front of the hospital it's snowing and sleeting and everything's a mess. Visibility, as they say, is low.

I don't know what I was expecting—well, wheelchair tracks in the slush, now that I think of it—but the sidewalk's salted down and thirty people a minute are passing by. Plus there's a big metal awning that runs for fifty yards along the front. The sidewalk is wet with black water.

---

them around. Some viruses, like HIV, your body will even insert directly into your DNA for smoother copying, making them part of your identity.

"Which way did he go?" I say. Thinking: *If he even came out this entrance, since there's at least one on every face of the building.*

"This way," Mershawn says.

"Why?"

"It's downhill."

"Huh," I say. "I'm glad I brought you already."

Around the corner, the side street drops off toward the river even more steeply than the avenue we're on now. Mershawn nods, so we head down it.

A couple of blocks along, there's a twenty-five-foot patch of slush capable of holding prints. We know this because there are what look a fuck of a lot like wheelchair tracks running down it. The tracks angle toward a graffiti-covered metal door in a building with the windows boarded over, but die out before they actually reach there.

I go and bang on the door. Mershawn looks up at the building dubiously. "What is this place?" he says.

"The Pole Vault," I tell him.

"What's that?"

"Are you serious?"

He just looks at me.

"It's a gay bar," I say.

The door gets opened by a fifty-year-old black man with graying hair and a barrel chest. He's wearing a flannel work shirt and bifocals. "Help you?" he says, angling his head back to look at us.

"We're looking for an elderly black man in a wheelchair," I say.

For a moment the man just stands there, whistling a tune I don't recognize. Then he says, "Why?"

Mershawn says, "Because neither of us got one for Christmas, and they're all sold out at Elderly-Black-Men-in-Wheelchairs-R-Us."

I say, "He's a patient at the hospital, and he escaped."

"Mental patient?"

"No. He's got gangrene in his feet. Though he is demented."

The man thinks for a moment. Again with the whistling.

"I don't know why, but something about you idiots strikes me as well intentioned," he finally says. "He went down toward the park."

"Why'd he come here?" I ask.

"He asked for a blanket."

"Did you give him one?"

"I gave him a jacket a customer left. Put it over him." He looks around, and interrupts a new bout of whistling with a shiver. "That all?"

"Yeah," I say. "But we owe you one. You should come in and let us check out your emphysema."

The man squints down his nose at the "Lottie Luise, MD" monogramming on the front of my white coat. "Thank you Dr. Luise," he says.

"I'm Peter Brown. This is Mershawn. We'll get you in and out for free."

The man gives a wheezy laugh that tails off in a choke. "Figure I got where I am today by *not* going to the hospital," he says.

"Fair enough," I have to say.

On the way down Mershawn asks me how I knew the guy had emphysema, and I list the physical signs he was showing. Then I say, "Teaching point, Mershawn. Who whistles?"

"Assholes?"

"Okay. Who else?"

Mershawn thinks about it. "People who are thinking about something, then subliminally start thinking of a song about that thing. Like when you're doing a cranial nerve exam and you start whistling 'Keep Ya Head Up.' "

"Good," I say. "But a lot of people also whistle because they're subconsciously trying to increase the air pressure in their lungs, so they can force more oxygen through the tissues."

"No shit."

"Shit. You know the dwarfs in *Snow White* who work in a mine?"

"Yeah, okay."

"If you had silicosis, you'd whistle your ass off too."

"Damn."

"That's right."

For the rest of the block I feel like Prof. Marmoset.

Duke Mosby, when we find him, is on a flagstoned pavilion overlooking the Hudson from the heights of Riverside Park. It's a hell of a view, but the river's charging heavily for it, spitting back a wet and flurrying wind. The kind you can feel through the vents in your plastic clogs. Snowflakes are skittering up from the ground at the same time they're wheeling in from the sky. They're lodged in Mosby's hair and eyelashes.

"What's going on, Mr. Mosby?" I shout to him above the wind.

He turns, and smiles. "Not much, Doctor. You?"

"You know Mershawn?"

"Sure do," he says without looking at him. "Doctor, tell me this. Why is it so important to look at a river now and again?"

"I don't know," I say. "I think I may have missed that lecture in medical school."

"I think it's because we all have to see *something* God made once in a while. Like maybe if they put some plants around the POW camp, people wouldn't break out so often."

"If I have to see something God made," Mershawn says, "I'd rather look at some pussy."

"You see any pussy around here?" Mosby asks him.

"No sir."

"Then I guess we're stuck with the river." Mosby notices Mershawn's haircut, and says, "What the hell is that on your head?"

It occurs to me I might be losing my mind.

"Can we go back to the hospital now?" I say.

In the lobby I try Prof. Marmoset again, mostly as a reflex. I set my teeth for Firefly, but he picks up the phone himself.

"Yeah, hi, Carl —" he says.

"Professor Marmoset?"

"Yes?" He's confused. "Who is this?"

"It's Ishmael," I say. "Hold on one second." I turn to Mer-shawn. "Can I leave this on you?" I ask him.

"I can handle it, Doc," he says.

"I believe you," I say, looking in his eyes, which sometimes works. "Take him to PT, wait twenty minutes, ask why they haven't called him for his appointment. When they tell you he doesn't have one take him back up to the floor and say PT made a scheduling error. You got that?"

"I got it."

"I believe you," I say again. Then I turn away and uncover the phone. "Professor Marmoset?"

"Ishmael! I can't talk long, I'm expecting a call. What's up?"

What *is* up? I'm so happy to actually be talking to him that I can't precisely remember where I'd planned to begin.

"Ishmael?"

"I've got a patient with signet cell cancer," I say.

"That's bad. Okay."

"Yeah. A guy named Friendly's doing the laparotomy. I looked him up—"

"John Friendly?"

"Yes."

"And this is a patient of *yours*?"

"Yes."

"Get someone else to do it," he says.

"Why?" I ask.

"Because presumably you want him to live."

"But Friendly's the highest rated GI surgeon in New York."

"Maybe in a magazine," Prof. Marmoset says. "He inflates his statistics. He does things like bring his own blood supplies into the OR so he doesn't have to report transfusions. If we're talking about reality, he's a menace."

"Jesus," I say. "He didn't want the patient to have a DNR order."

"Exactly. When your patient's a vegetable, Friendly won't have to report him as a fatality."

"Fuck! How do I get him off the case?"

"Let's think about it," Prof. Marmoset says. "Okay. You call a GI guy named Leland Marker at Cornell. He's probably skiing, but his office will be able to track him down. Tell his scheduler Bill Clinton needs a laparotomy and is hiding out at Manhattan Catholic to avoid the press. Tell him Clinton's using a fake name, and give him the name of your patient. Marker'll be pissed as hell when he figures it out, but by then it'll be too late, and he'll have to operate."

"I don't think I have time for that," I say. "Friendly's operating in a couple of hours."

"Well, you could drop some GHB in his coffee, but from what I've heard he probably wouldn't notice."

I lean against the wall. There's a ringing in one of my ears, and I'm starting to get vertigo.

"Professor Marmoset," I say. "I need this patient to live."

"Sounds like someone needs some distancing techniques."

"No. I mean I *need* this patient to live."

There's a pause. Prof. Marmoset says, "Ishmael, is everything all right?"

"No," I say. "I've got to see this patient through."

"Why?"

"It's a long story. But I have to."

"Should I be worried about you?"

"No. It wouldn't do any good."

There's another pause while he decides what to do with this.

"All right," he says. "But only because I have a couple other calls coming in. I want you to call me when you can tell me about it. Leave a message. In the meantime, I think you should scrub in."

"*Scrub in?* I haven't done surgery since med school. And I sucked at it even then."

"Right, I remember that," he says. "But you can't be any worse than John Friendly. Good luck."

Then he hangs up.

12

I met Magdalena the night of Denise's wedding, August 13th, 1999. She was in the string sextet, playing viola. Ordinarily she played in a quartet, but her booking agent handled a couple of different quartets, so when people wanted a sextet, which was usually for a wedding, the agent made one up. Denise's wedding had a sextet and, for after dinner, a DJ.

It was a big wedding. It was at a country club on Long Island that the groom's family belonged to, since Denise had decided to do it back East, where most of her extended family was. Skinflick and I were seated about a mile away from her.

Somehow everybody seemed to understand that it was my job to babysit Skinflick, and that I was supposed to keep him either too sober or too drunk to do anything embarrassing. It was a pretty sordid job, and it got old fast. I was almost as hung over as he was, and I was tired of hearing him complain. Half of me thought if he was serious he really *should* make a scene, and steal Denise away. Ignore the constraints of tradition and family and be true for once to his *Golden Bough* bullshit.

But rituals turn us all into fucking idiots. Like those birds that sleep with their heads facing backwards because their ancestors slept with their heads under their wings. Plutarch says carrying new wives across thresholds is stupid because we don't remember that it refers to the rape of the Sabine women—and that's fucking *Plutarch,* two thousand years ago. We still draw the Reaper with a scythe. We should draw him driving a John Deere for Archer Daniels Midland.

So maybe it's understandable that Skinflick felt unable to step in front of a parade that went thousands of years back. It still made me kind of sick, though, and the humidity didn't help. At one point I took the long way back from the bar to have some time away from him.

That's when I saw Magdalena.

I'm not sure this is any of your business, but if you really want me to talk about her, here it is.

Physically: She had black hair. She had a widow's peak. She had slanted eyes. She was small. Bone-thin except for her lower body, which was muscled from running. Before I met her I'd always liked big blondes. She kicked all their asses instantly.

The white shirt she wore to play viola was too big for her, so it was rolled at the sleeves and open at the neck. You could see her collarbones. When she played she kept her hair back with a velvet band, but locks of it always escaped to arc forward from her widow's peak. When I first saw her they looked like antennae.

That night she was pale, but whenever she spent time in the sun she would turn brown, like she was from Egypt, or Mars. The waist of her bikini bottoms would stretch from one sharp hip bone to the other and float a centimeter off her stomach, so you could slide a hand down there. She had full lips. I'd kill everyone I ever killed all over again for those lips.

None of this says anything about her. It doesn't even tell you how she looked.

She was Romanian. Born there, moved to the U.S. at fourteen, late enough to keep a bit of an accent. She was feverishly Catholic. She went to church every Sunday and got sweat on her upper lip when she prayed.

It may strike you as odd that someone—the only one—I loved like that was so religious. I loved even that about her, though. It was hard to argue in her presence that the world didn't have *some* kind of magic going on, and she was completely undogmatic. To her, the fact that she was Catholic and I was not had to be as much God's intention as everything else. God wanted us to be together, and would never make her love someone He didn't love also.

Prior to meeting Magdalena when I thought of Catholicism

I thought of dusty icons, corrupt popes, and *The Exorcist*. But where I imagined creepy wooden statues of St. Margaret, she imagined St. Margaret herself, in the fields of Scotland, with the butterflies. What Magdalena was to me, the Virgin Mary was to her. It never made me jealous. It just made me grateful to be around her.

Speaking of the Sabine women, by the way, my favorite thing to do was carry Magdalena around. In the days when I had the condo in Demarest and Skinflick was never around, I used to do it for hours. Carry her naked in both arms, *Creature from the Black Lagoon*–style, or else seated on my bent right arm, facing forward with one of her own arms looped back around my neck. Sometimes I would put my arms out straight against the wall, and she would sit facing me with her thighs over my forearms, so I could lick her from her pussy to the sides of her neck, and get at her hip bones, and her ribcage.

I'm still not making this anywhere close to clear.

We knew the second we saw each other. How depressing is that? How far from anything that will ever happen again, to me or anyone else?

I saw her and I couldn't stop staring at her, and she kept staring back. I worried I just happened to be standing in the spot her eyes gravitated toward when she played, so I moved, and she followed me. During the times she wasn't playing, when she put her viola down, her mouth would open just a tiny bit.

Then Skinflick came up behind me and said, "Hey, that faggot's going off alone."

"Who?" I said, still looking at Magdalena.

"Denise's 'husband.' "

Faggot was a charming mannerism Skinflick had picked up hanging out with Kurt Limme. He'd started out using it ironically, like he was mocking goombah bigots, but it had stuck to him. At least he didn't use it to refer to gay people.

"Okay," I said.

"Let's go follow him."

"No thanks."

"Whatever, asshole," he said. "I'll go do it myself."

A few moments later I said "Fuck," and pulled myself away to go after him.

I saw Skinflick heading around the back of the catering tent. I followed.

Denise's new husband was standing there in the darkness, smoking a joint, alone. He was a blond guy with a ponytail and rimless glasses who worked as a computer animator or something in Los Angeles. I think his name was Steven, though who really cares.

"He's a motherfucking *pothead?*" Skinflick said.

The guy looked about twenty-six, which was four years older than we were, and six years older than Denise. He said, "You Adam?"

"Fuckin right," Skinflick said.

"You're the mob cousin?"

"The *what?*" Skinflick said.

"Must have the wrong guy. What *do* you do for a living?"

"Are you giving me fucking *lip?*" Skinflick shouted.

The guy flicked the remains of his joint away and put his hands in his pockets. I was impressed. He might have been able to kick Skinflick's ass if Skinflick was alone, but Skinflick was not alone.

"I'll have Pietro kick your head so far up your ass you'll be able to see out your own mouth!" Skinflick said.

"No he won't," I said, laying a hand on Skinflick's shoulder. To the guy, I said, "He's a bit drunk."

"I can see that," the guy said.

Skinflick slapped my hand off. "Fuck both of you."

I took Skinflick by the arm, too hard to slap off. "You're welcome," I said to him. "Say congratulations."

"Eat shit," Skinflick said. To the guy, he said, "You better treat her right."

The guy was wise enough to not answer as I dragged Skinflick back to the wedding.

I took him to our table and made him eat two Xanax while I watched. When they kicked in I left him there and went back to watch the sextet.

At nine o'clock they stopped playing so the DJ could take over and people could dance. They all stood up and started packing their instruments and music stands.

I went to the edge of the stage. Magdalena blushed and avoided my eyes as she packed. "Hello?" I said.

She froze. The others stared.

"Can I talk to you?" I said.

"We're not allowed to talk to the guests," one of the other ones said. The woman who had been playing cello. She had an underbite.

"Then can I call you?" I said to Magdalena.

Magdalena shook her head. "I'm sorry." It was the first time I heard her accent.

"Can I give you *my* number? Will you call *me?*"

She looked at me.

She said "Yes."

Later, I was standing around stunned, and Kurt Limme came up to me.

"Noticed you hitting on the help," he said.

"I didn't know you were invited to this," I said.

"I came here to support Skinflick. This is tough on him."

"Yeah, I know. I've been with him all night."

Limme shrugged. "I was busy. I was fucking his aunt in one of the Port-a-Potties."

"Shirl?" I said.

He looked uncomfortable. "Yeah."

"Yuck for her," I said. "I hope she was drunk."

But I didn't really care.

Love was in the air.

I spent the next three days in Demarest, killing my heavy bag and waiting for her to call. When David Locano called instead and asked me to meet him at the old Russian Baths on

10th Street in Manhattan, I jumped at it just to have something to do.

Locano was using the Baths regularly at that time, on the theory that the FBI couldn't build a microphone capable of surviving a steam room. This seemed overly optimistic—it was before 9/11, when we all learned how incompetent Louis Freeh's FBI really was—but we went with it.

For my part I kind of liked the steam room. It was dirty but it gave meetings a kind of ancient Rome feeling.

"Adam's getting his own apartment in Manhattan," Locano said when I got there. He looked depressed. He was hunched forward in his towel skirt.

"Yeah," I said. I sat down next to him.

"Were you going to tell me?"

"I figured you knew."

"Have you seen it?"

"Yeah, I went with him to look at it."

That made him wince. "Why didn't he tell me?"

"I don't know. You should ask him."

"Yeah, right. I can barely talk to him. Even when I get to see him."

"He's going through a phase."

Which was true. Skinflick was spending all his time with Kurt Limme. But I wasn't too upset about it. I had my own shit going on, and in a weird way the fact that Skinflick would rebel against me as well as his father was flattering. It showed that Skinflick saw me as an influence on him, just as he'd been an influence on me.

His father felt otherwise, though. "It's that fuck Kurt Limme," he said. "He wants to put Adam in the business."

"Skinflick won't go through with it," I said.

He nodded slowly. Neither one of us believed me.

"I really don't want it to happen," Locano said.

"Neither do I."

He lowered his voice. "You know it means he'd have to kill somebody."

I let that sit for a minute. "What about getting him an exemption?" I said.

"Don't jerk my chain," Locano said. "You know there aren't any exemptions."

I did know that, I guess.

It still freaked me out to hear him admit it.

"So what can we do?" I said.

"We can't let him do it."

"Right, but how?"

Locano looked away from me, and whispered. I couldn't hear him.

I said, "Excuse me?"

"I want you to kill Limme."

"*What?*"

"I'll pay you fifty grand."

"No way. You should know better than to ask me that."

"A hundred grand. Name it."

"I don't do that shit."

"It's not just for Adam. Limme is bad news."

"He's *bad news?* Who gives a shit?"

"He's a cold-blooded killer."

"How's that?"

"He shot a Russian grocery clerk in the face."

"To get made?"

"What difference does that make?"

"It makes a shitload of difference. You're telling me Limme shot someone what, five years ago? That sucks. He deserves to die for it, and I hope he at least goes to jail for it. But it doesn't give me the right to kill him. It doesn't give you the right, either. If you feel that strongly, call the cops."

"You know I can't do that," he said.

"Well I can't murder someone for being a bad role model for Skinflick. Who'd *you* kill to get made?"

His voice turned hard. "That's none of your fucking business."

"Whatever," I said.

"What the fuck's gotten into you?" he said. Then, a moment later, "I hear you and Limme spent some time together at Denise's wedding."

"We spent about thirty seconds insulting each other. I hate that dick."

"And Adam fucking worships him," Locano said. "It's gonna get him killed, or sent to jail."

"Yeah," I said. "Well maybe you should have thought about that twenty years ago."

What can I say?

Your best friend's dad. Somewhere along the way you start to think of him as kind of like your own dad, or your idea of what your own dad should be. You come to believe that he likes you, and that you can trust him, and even talk shit to him.

You never think *This guy's a killer, and he's smart. You piss him off, he'll turn on you. Like that.*

You never think it in time, I mean.

When I got back to my apartment there was a message.

"Hello. This is Magdalena." Breathy, like she was keeping her voice down. Then a pause, then a hang-up. Nothing else. No number.

It flipped me out. I played it five or six times, then called Barbara Locano, then called Shirl, feeling weird about the Limme thing. Shirl gave me the name of the wedding planner in Manhattan who had hired the sextet.

The wedding planner told me from the cell phone in her car that she didn't give out contacts, "for their privacy." She said, "I mean, I'm sure you'll find a perfectly nice orchestra if you arrange your own wedding."

I made an appointment to meet her at her office the following day for an estimate, and when she got all flirty and demanding I didn't bother to find out how serious she was, just did everything to her she asked for. I barely even noticed.

Getting Magdalena's upcoming schedule was easier. Marta, her booking agent, seemed to think of giving it out as advertising, and worth the risk—at least to Marta. Apparently no one stalks the booking agent.

Most of the parties on the quartet's schedule were in private homes, which might or might not be big enough to crash without drawing attention, so I picked a wedding in Fort Tryon Park, in upper Manhattan, that didn't begin until nightfall. When I got there it turned out to be in a single large tent attached to the side of the stone-walled restaurant in the middle of the park. The event wasn't large, but it was laid back, and as soon as it was even slightly crowded I was able to mix in. I was wearing a suit, having assumed, correctly, that no one would hold a black-tie wedding in Fort Tryon Park.

Magdalena had on the same white shirt and black waiter pants. I stayed out of her sight until the group took a smoking break on a roadway up the hill, and I approached her. She was talking to the cello player near their van.

"Hello," I said.

"Hello," the cello player said. The challenge in her voice made her underbite worse.

"It's all right," Magdalena told her.

The cello player said something in a language I couldn't even identify, and Magdalena said something back in what I assumed was the same language.

"I'll be over there," the cello player said to both of us, and walked off.

Magdalena and I stared at each other.

"She's protective," I said eventually.

"Yes. She feels she has to be. I'm not sure why."

"I understand it."

She smiled. "Is that a pickup line?"

"No. Kind of. I want to know you."

She put her head to one side and closed one eye. "You know I'm Romanian?"

"No. I don't know anything about you."

"It's not likely it would work out, with a Romanian and an American."

"I don't feel that way at all."

"Neither do I," she said.

On the off chance that I had heard her correctly, I said, "When can I see you?"

She looked away. Sighed. "I live with my parents," she said.

For an awful moment I wondered if she was sixteen or something. It was certainly possible. Just as it was also possible she was thirty, since she gave off a feeling of ancientness like you'd imagine from a vampire, or an angel.

To be honest, if she *had* been sixteen it wouldn't have stopped me.

"How old are you?" I said.

"Twenty. How old are you?"

"Twenty-two."

"Well then." She smiled. "Perfect."

"Come away with me right now," I said.

She touched the back of my hand with her strong slender fingers. I brought my hand up to interlace them.

Later, when she would sleep with my balls in those fingers, which were barely able to contain them, I liked to think back to that night in the park. But at the time she said, "I can't."

"When can I see you, then?"

"I don't know. I'll call you."

"I *need* you to call me."

"I will. But we only have one phone."

"Call me from anywhere. Whenever. Do you still have my number?"

She recited it from memory, which I knew would have to satisfy me.

But another entire week went by without her calling. Insanity. I forwarded my phone to work, then drove like a maniac to get there so I wouldn't miss her. I took the cordless everywhere in the house. People who weren't her I just hung up on.

She called on a Sunday night, late. I was doing handstand push-ups against the wall and screaming. Out the window it was raining. I rolled forward and came to my feet with the phone in my hand.

"Hello?"

"It's Magdalena."

I fell still. I was completely slick with sweat. My pulse felt ready to blow apart my fingertips, and I couldn't remember whether it had been that way a minute ago or not.

"Thanks for calling," I croaked.

"I can't talk. I'm at a party. I'm in the bedroom. Everyone's purse is here. They'll think I'm stealing something."

"I need to see you."

"I know. I need to see you too. Can you come meet me?"

"Yes I can," I said.

The party was at a brownstone in Brooklyn Heights. She was waiting for me under the awning of the apartment building across the street, to stay out of the rain. She had her viola with her in a nylon case. As soon as I saw her I swerved the car into the fire-hydrant half-space in front of the building. She ran over and put her viola in the back seat and got in the front. I already had my seat belt off.

We kissed for a long time. It was difficult because I needed so badly to look at her, but I was also so hungry for her mouth.

Eventually she put her head on my chest. "I want you but I can't have sex with you," she said.

"That's okay."

"I'm a virgin. I've kissed a couple of boys, but that's all."

"I love you," I said. "I don't care."

She grabbed my face and looked into it to see if I was serious, then started kissing me again, a thousand times harder. I heard a zipper, and she took my hand and put it on her crotch, then pulled the cotton of her underwear aside.

Her pussy was blazing, and sopping. When she squeezed her thighs together it forced my fingers up into it.

Skinflick approved, by the way. Magdalena was completely honest and never questioned herself, and while Skinflick was no longer exactly like that, he still respected it in other people, and recognized how rare it was. Once when he and I were alone together he said "She's perfect for you. Like Denise was for me."

The three of us smoked pot together sometimes. Magdalena would announce that she wasn't feeling it at all, then go lazy-lidded, then start kissing my neck and whisper, "Take me to the bedroom." Skinflick, on the other side of me, would say, "Make Pietro do it. I'm watching cable."

But that was later, when Skinflick was living with me again.

What happened was this:

One night in October I came home to find him sitting in my living room with a gun in his hand. A chunky .38 revolver. I'd been out running, something I'd started to do with Magdalena, but right then she was either playing with the quartet or at night school, where she was studying accounting.

When I came through the door Skinflick didn't point the gun at me. But he didn't put it down, either.

"What's up?" I said.

"Did you kill him?" he said.

He looked fucking awful. He was pale, and a weird mixture of skinny and flabby.

"Who?" I said. Thinking: *Oh shit. David Locano is dead.*

"Kurt."

"Kurt *Limme?*"

"You don't know anyone else named Kurt."

"How the fuck would you know? I haven't talked to you in weeks."

"Did you?"

"No. I didn't kill him. I didn't even know he was dead. What happened?"

"Someone shot him in the face in the doorway of his apartment," Skinflick said. Limme's apartment was in Tribeca. "Like he buzzed the person in."

"What do the police say?"

"They say it wasn't a robbery."

"Maybe it was your Uncle Roger," I said. Shirl's husband.

"Is that supposed to be funny?"

"Yeah, I guess. Sorry." For a second I wondered if I *had* killed Kurt Limme, and somehow forgotten about it. "What does your dad say?"

"He says you didn't talk to him about it, so if you did it you did it alone."

"Nice," I said. I pulled a chair over from the table. "I'm going to sit down now. Don't shoot me."

Skinflick tossed the revolver onto the coffee table heavily as I sat. "Fuck you. I wasn't going to shoot you," he said. "I'm just worried they'll come after me."

"Who?"

"I don't know. That's the point."

"Huh," I said. "I'm sorry about Kurt."

"It's not gonna stop me."

"Not gonna stop you from what?"

He turned away. "From getting made," he said.

"I didn't realize that was on the agenda," I said.

"Yes you did."

"You're right: maybe I did. But it's a shitty idea, and maybe you shouldn't think about it right now."

"I don't need to think about it. I'm doing it."

"You're gonna murder someone to impress a bunch of scum-bags?"

"It's what Kurt would have wanted."

"Kurt's dead."

"Exactly. And I'm gonna say 'fuck you' to whoever killed him."

I said, "You think whoever killed Limme cares whether you get made?"

"I have no fucking idea!" Skinflick said. "I don't even know who did it!" He sulked for a moment. "Anyway, who are you to question me? You got revenge for your grandparents."

"That doesn't mean it was right."

"But it was, wasn't it?"

"Well, it sure as hell doesn't mean it's right for you."

"What's the difference?"

"Between me and you?"

"That's right."

"Jesus," I said. I sincerely did not want to get into that. "For one thing, I had someone to kill. I wasn't just killing to do it."

Skinflick's face flashed a hint of relief.

"Well, fuck, dude," he said. "I'm not gonna kill somebody *innocent*. I'm not an asshole. I'm gonna find some scumbag. Like the ones my dad finds for you. Some sick fuck who's begging for it."

"Yeah?"

"Yeah. I'll run the whole thing by you first if you want."

"Okay," I finally said.

That's all I said: *Okay*.

Now, you tell me.

Was that some kind of promise?

13

First I go up to Medicine to get my antibiotics and antivirals, which my med students have thoughtfully placed in a urine sample cup.

"Sir, you may want to check—"

"No time," I say. I use a random patient ID number to open up a fluids cabinet and take out a bottle of water with 5 percent dextrose.* I bite the cap off and slug down the pills.

---

* Most bottled water in hospitals has 5 percent dextrose. This is to prevent the phrase "Liter of plain fucking water: $35" from appearing on your bill.

And if my students are wrong, and I overdose?

It probably won't shorten my life by all that much anyway.

My watch keeps scaring the shit out of me on my way up to the visiting surgeons' office.

Outside the office door, Dr. Friendly's resident is leaning sullenly against the wall. He gives me a look, then stands and walks away.

The interval between my knocking on the door and Friendly finally saying "What?" makes me want to bang my forehead on the wood. I don't answer, just go in.

The visiting surgeons' office is meant to look like someone's real office. There's an oak desk you can sit behind to deliver bad news, and the wallpaper has a repeating pattern of diplomas on it that from a distance looks better than you would think.

Friendly's behind the desk. Stacey the drug rep is sitting on the edge of it, right near him, surprised to see me. Friendly, noticing me looking at her, leans and puts his hand on her thigh just below the hem of her short dress. Which I can see up.

"What is it?" Friendly says.

"I'd like to scrub in on your procedure on Mr. LoBrutto."

"No. Why?"

"He's my patient. I'd like to help if I can."

Friendly thinks about it. "Whatever. If it's not you, it's my resident, so it's no loss either way. I'll leave it to you to tell him you're taking his place."

"I'll go find him," I say.

"I'm starting at eleven, whether you're there or not."

"All right."

Stacey shoots some kind of facial expression at me, but I'm too grossed out to try to decode it.

I just leave.

In order to make it to Squillante's surgery I figure I'll have to do about four hours of work in the next two hours, then another four hours of work in the two hours afterwards. I realize right off that this will require draping my med students with a bit more responsibility than is usual or legal, and also keeping at least one Moxfane under my tongue at all times. To balance things out ethically, I don't give my med students any Moxfane.

We start. We see patients. Oh, fuck do we see patients. We see them and wake them up and shine lights in their eyes and ask them if they're still alive so fast that even the ones who speak English don't understand what the fuck we're doing or saying. Then we replace their IV bags and tap their arteries and shove medications through their veins. Then we slash through their paperwork. If they're in a tuberculosis tank, which you're not supposed to enter without suits and masks, we fuck the HAZMAT procedures and just get in and out as fast as we can.

Speaking of HAZMAT, we dodge the two hospital teams— Occupational Health and Safety and Infectious Disease Control—that are trying to run me down and ask me about my needlestick with the Assman sample. Right now the injection site barely hurts, and I don't have time for that shit.

As we move we get reminded, again and again, of what a

fascinating mix a hospital can be of people in a huge hurry and people too slow to get out of their way.

We even save a couple of lives, if you can call correcting a medications error saving a life. Usually it's just some nurse about to give someone milligrams per pound instead of milligrams per kilogram, but occasionally it's something more exotic, like a nurse about to give *Combivir* to someone who needs *Combivent*.

A couple of times we get asked to help people make difficult decisions, the outcome of which will affect whether they live or die. We do this quickly too. If there's a clear solution, it would have presented itself up front, and since it didn't, there's not much we can say to these people. That's what crackpots on the Internet are for.

"Go home," I tell my med students when we're finished. We've got, like, ninety seconds to spare.

"Sir, we'd like to watch the surgery," one says.

"Why?" I say.

But I can use the help.

We all race down to Prep.

The anesthesiologist is there, but Friendly isn't. The nurse asks why, and whether I'll do the paperwork and get the fucking patient down here already.

I "do" the paperwork with the speed and legibility of a seismograph. Then I send my students to look up some shit about abdominal surgery, and go myself to get Squillante.

"I screwed you, Bearclaw," he suddenly says as we're waiting for the elevator. He's still in his roller bed.

"No shit."

"I mean I screwed you a little more than I meant to."

I press the button again. "Yeah?"

"Yeah. I thought Skingraft was in Argentina."

"I don't understand."

"He's here in New York. Right now. I just found out."

"No. I mean, who the fuck is Skingraft?"

I figure it's probably one of Skinflick's two younger brothers, though as people to be afraid of they're both a bit lacking.

That or it's more bullshit with the nicknames.

"Sorry," Squillante says. "Skin*flick*. I forgot you guys were friends."

"What?"

The elevator arrives. It's packed. "Hold on a second," I tell Squillante.

"Everybody out," I say. "This patient has rabbit flu." When they're gone and we're on board with the doors closed, I use the same button Stacey did to stop the elevator.

"Now what the *fuck* are you talking about?"

"Skinflick," Squillante says. "They call him 'Skingraft' now because of his face."

"Skinflick's dead. I threw him out a window."

"You did throw him out a window."

"Yes. I did."

"It didn't kill him."

For a second I can't say anything. I know it isn't true, but my guts don't appear to be so sure.

"Bullshit," I say. "We were six stories up."

"I'm not saying he enjoyed it."

"You are fucking with me."

"I swear it on St. Theresa."

"Skinflick is *alive?*"

"Yeah."

"And he's *here?*"

"He's in New York. I thought he was in Argentina. He was living there, learning to knife-fight." Squillante's voice drops even further, embarrassed. "For when he found you."

"Well, that's fucking great," I finally say.

"Yeah. I'm sorry. I figured you'd have a little time if I died. But now you probably won't, is what I'm saying. If I do die, you'll probably just have a couple hours to get out of town."

"Thanks for the consideration."

To keep from hitting Squillante I palm-strike the "stop" button, and speed us toward surgery.

14

At the beginning of November Magdalena took me to meet her parents. They lived in Dyker Heights, in Brooklyn. A place I'd never been to before I started dropping her off there.

I'd already met her brother, a tall gangly blond high school kid who wore soccer uniforms all the time and was strangely shy, even though he spoke half a dozen languages and had been born five thousand exotic miles away. His name was Christopher, but his friends called him Rovo, because the family's last name was Niemerover.

Like I say, I'd already met him. The parents were news, though.

They were blond and tall like Rovo, but also husky. Next to the three of them Magdalena looked like she'd been raised by greyhounds.* The father worked for the subway system, as a shift manager for the IRT out of Grand Central, though in Romania he'd been a dentist. The mother worked in a bakery owned by a friend of theirs.

Dinner was spaghetti instead of Romanian food, out of "politeness" and a desire to point out how alien Magdalena and I were to each other. We ate in the dining room of the family's crazily narrow three-story half of a townhouse. Everything in the room—the rugs, the dark wood clocks, the furniture, the yellowed photos and their frames—ate light. Magdalena and I sat along one edge of the table opposite Rovo, with Magdalena's parents at the ends.

"When did you become interested in Romanians?" Magdalena's father said shortly after we started eating. He had a mustache and was wearing a tie and what looked like a detachable collar, but couldn't have been.

"When I met Magdalena," I said.

I was trying to play it harmless and respectful, but I had too

---

* Magdalena looked *Rom*, which medieval Europeans called "Gypsy" because they thought the *Roma* originated in Egypt. They originated in India. It's a pretty good joke that Romania, which is historically one of the most racist countries on earth—when it got its first political party primarily based on Jew-hating, in 1910, both its Liberal and Conservative parties were already officially "anti-Semitic"—is also one of the most racially mixed, because it lies in a mountain pass used by every army in history. Unless you think jokes should be funny.

little experience and wasn't doing very well. Plus Magdalena kept sliding over practically into my lap to prove to her parents how serious she and I were.

"Which was how, exactly?" her father said.

"At a wedding," I said.

"I didn't know the quartet was so sociable."

I didn't tell him it had been a sextet that night. I didn't want to correct him, and I didn't want to say "sextet" in front of him, either.

"It was a sextet," Magdalena said.

"I see."

Magdalena's mother smiled and looked pained. Rovo rolled his eyes. He was slumped so low in his chair that it looked like he was about to slide off.

"Do you speak any Romanian?" Magdalena's father said.

"No," I said.

"Do you even know who the president of Romania is?"

"Ceauşescu?" I was pretty sure I was right.

"I sincerely hope you're kidding," he said.

I couldn't help myself. I said, "I am. Comedy about Romania's a sideline of mine."

"So is sarcasm, evidently. You know, our Magdoll is not some American girl who will have sex with you in your car."

Rovo said, "Jesus, Dad. Gross."

I said, "I know that."

"You appear to have nothing in common with my daughter at all."

"Nobody has anything in common with her," I said. "I wish they did."

"That's right," her mother said, approvingly. Magdalena's father glared at her.

Magdalena herself just got to her feet and went and kissed her father's forehead. "Papa, you're being ridiculous," she said to him. "I'm going home with Pietro now. I'll be back tomorrow or the next day."

It stunned all three of them.

It stunned me too, but not so much that I didn't let her grab me and get me the hell out of there.

Around that time, David Locano asked me to meet him at the Russian Baths again. I still had athlete's foot from the last time, but I went.

"Thanks for telling Skinflick I killed Kurt Limme," I said as soon as I sat down next to him.

"I didn't. I just said it wasn't me."

"Was it?"

"No. Word is it was some dipshit he was blocking on a relay tower deal."

I wondered why I'd bothered to ask. If Locano *had* killed Limme, or hired someone else to do it, why would he tell me? And what did I care anyway? Just because I had refused to murder Limme didn't mean I had to mourn him.

"So what's up?" I said.

"I've got a job for you."

"Yeah?"

I had decided in advance that if he offered me a job I would say no. And that I would continue saying no until he understood that I was leaving the business behind.

Magdalena had changed the way I thought about it. Not that she knew I killed people. She didn't. She knew I worked with scumbags, though, and she was afraid to know the details, which was bad enough.

"You won't be able to turn it down," Locano said. "You'll be doing the world a lot of good."

"Well—"

"I mean, these guys are foul."

"Right. But—"

"And it'd be the perfect job for you to do with Adam."

I stared at him. "Are you kidding?" I said.

"He wants to join. He's got to pay the price."

"I thought the idea was to keep Adam *out* of the mafia," I said.

At the word "mafia," Locano looked around. "Don't be a Chatty Cathy," he said. "Even in here."

"Mafia mafia mafia," I said.

"Enough! Jesus."

"I'm not interested," I said. "Not even in doing it alone. I'm done."

"You're quitting?"

"Yes."

It was a huge relief to say it. I had thought it would be much harder. But I was still unsure how Locano would react.

He stared into space for a moment. Then he sighed. "It'll hurt to lose you, Pietro."

"Thanks," I said.

"You're not going to ditch me and Adam entirely, are you?"

"Socially, you mean? No."

"Good."

For a while we just sat. Then he said, "Tell you what. Just let me pitch this to you."

"I'm really not interested."

"I hear you. But I've got to do my best. Will you let me just tell you about it?"

"Why?"

"Because I think you'll feel differently once you've heard about it. I'm not saying you have to change your mind. I'm just saying I think you will."

"I doubt it."

"That's fine. Just let me tell you. This one's like the Virzi Brothers all over again, but a hundred times worse."

Right then I knew I really didn't want to hear about it.

"Okay," I said. "As long as you don't mind if I say no."

"You know how prostitutes get turned out?" Locano asked me.

"I've read *Daddy Cool*."

"*Daddy Cool* is sixties bullshit. Nowadays they get them en masse from the Ukraine. Hold a modeling audition then ship them to Mexico, where they beat them and rape them conveyor-belt style. A lot of the time there's heroin involved too, so the girls won't run away. We're talking fourteen-year-old girls here."

"And you're involved in this business?" I said.

"No fucking way," he said. "That's the point. Nobody I work with can stand that shit, but there's not a lot we can do about it when it's out of the country."

That seemed like bullshit already, but I just said, "Okay."

"But now there's a guy doing it stateside. In *New Jersey*. You know where Mercer County is?"

"Yes."

"I'll get you a map anyway."

The door to the steam room opened, and a pulse of cold air entered. Then a guy holding a towel around his waist.

"Excuse us for a minute," Locano said to him.

"What you mean?" the man said. He had a Russian accent.

"I mean, please leave for ten minutes. We'll be done then."

"Is public steam room," the man said. But he left.

"Where was I?" Locano said.

"I don't know," I said.

"Mercer County. There's three guys out there: a father and two sons. They call it the Farm. They still fly the girls into Mexico and smuggle them up in NAFTA trucks, but they do the beating and raping right here. That way more of the girls survive the trip. But with what these guys end up doing to them, not as many more as you would think."

"Is this about production quotas, David?" I said.

He looked at me. "No," he said. "Not even slightly. This is about it being part of my job to look shit in the face before anybody else has to. As soon as I found out about this, I decided to stop it. And as soon as I told the people I work with about it, they said 'Go ahead.' " He paused. "It pays a hundred and twenty thousand dollars."

"I don't care about that."

"I know. I'm just trying to show you how seriously everyone is taking this. It's a hundred and twenty thousand dollars, and that's for you. Adam I'll cover myself."

I'd almost managed to forget that detail. "Why would you send Adam into a situation like that?" I said.

"Because I've got the Farm rigged," Locano said.

What he meant by "rigged" was this:

A couple of months earlier, the owner of the Farm, Karcher the Elder, first name Les, had called some plumbing contractors out to extend the water pipes from the kitchen out to a shack he and his sons had built alongside the house. The plumbers thought the shack might be for a meth lab, so they looked around for anything they could steal, paying particular attention to smells. This led them to another outbuilding, farther off in the back yard, which turned out to have what seemed to be a naked, decomposing teenage girl in it, though the flies on the body were too thick for them to really tell.

On the way back to their truck, completely freaked out, one of the plumbers looked in through Karcher's office window and saw what he believed was a rack, like from a medieval torture chamber.

The crew was so bothered by the whole thing that they almost called the cops. Then their training kicked in, and they passed the information up the mob line instead, where it eventually reached Locano. If you believed Locano's story—which I must very much have wanted to do—this was the first time anyone realized what the Karchers were doing, even though the Farm had been supplying prime product for almost two years.

Not that it mattered. The mob now wanted Karcher dead, either because someone who really had been ignorant now wasn't, and objected, or else because someone had decided that any operation that could be discovered by a vanful of consistently stoned plumbers was probably riskier than it was worth.

Whatever the case, Locano had quickly decided that this was the job for me to walk Skinflick through. He'd had the plumbing guys go back to the house to finish the pipes, but had them use cardboard instead of drywall to edge off the hole between the house and the new shack.

According to the plumbers, they had covered the cardboard with wax paper before painting it to keep it from warping, and the patch was so low to the ground, and so impossible to see from inside the house, that the Karchers had basically no chance of discovering it. Once Skinflick and I got into the shack, it would be a simple matter to tunnel through the wall and go shoot Les Karcher and his sons in their sleep.

Locano even had a plan to get us to the shack. For five grand and a leg up in the organization, the kid who delivered the Karchers' huge grocery order every week was willing to take us in the back of his pickup truck. Both this kid and the plumbers reported that there weren't any dogs on the premises.

How I came to sign on to this plan—the first I'd ever followed that came from someone else, or even involved someone else, or that anyone else even knew about, and which had so many variables about which I myself knew so little—remains something of a mystery to me. When I recall that time now, it seems like my mind was fogged. Though maybe it's my memory that's off.

I wanted Magdalena and I wanted out. And I knew both would require a sacrifice. I also hated myself pretty significantly, and understood that freedom, let alone Magdalena, were things I could in no sense claim to deserve.

Or maybe it was that I still trusted David Locano—if not in his intentions toward me, then in his intelligence and protectiveness toward Skinflick. I had to believe that no one with Locano's amount of experience would lead the two of us into a situation that was fucked.

Let alone one as fucked as the Farm turned out to be.

I told Magdalena everything.

I had to. Watching her love me without really knowing me was like watching her love someone else, and the jealousy was killing me. I fantasized all the time about having a different life, and past. About actually being just some garbage scumbag, even.

But that wasn't reality. So I told her. Even though the thought that she might leave me was fucking awful.

She didn't leave me. She cried for hours and kept making me tell her over and over again about the people I had killed. How evil they were, and how likely they were to kill again. Like she was searching for permission to keep loving me.

Part of what I told her was that I was going to kill the man and his two sons who ran the Farm, then never kill anyone again unless they threatened *her*. Shutting down the Farm would be a favor to Locano that would smooth my way out of the business. And it would be justified by the lives it would save.

"Can't you just call the police?" she said.

"No," I said, with more certainty than I felt.

"Then you have to do it right away," Magdalena said.

I thought she meant she needed me to get it over with so she could stop sharing me with the Devil, and start working on trying to forgive me.

"To keep any more girls from dying," she said.

That may be the most shameful part of it. Not that I felt I couldn't betray David Locano's "trust" by calling the police. But that it hadn't yet occurred to me that each passing day was a day in hell for the girls I was supposedly about to rescue.

It shows something, though: if you're going to be soulless, you should at least consider outsourcing your conscience to someone else.

"It has to be a Thursday," I said. "That's the Karchers' grocery day."

Magdalena just looked at me. Thursday was four days off. Not nearly enough time to get ready.

Another rule broken. Another step taken into fog. Another among many.

"I'll move it to this Thursday," I said.

15

A couple of nurses and the anesthesiologist and I use Squillante's bedsheet to lift him from his wheelable bed to the fixed table in the center of the operating room. It's not that he weighs anything, but that the operating table is so narrow you need to get him perfectly squared up on it or he'll fall off. As it is, his arms flop down until I lock a couple of armrests into place under them.

"I'm sorry," he says as I screw them to the rails.

"Shut the fuck up," I say through my mask. Squillante's

the only one in the room not wearing scrubs, a mask, and a shower cap.

The anesthesiologist gives Squillante an opening salvo through one of his IVs. A mix of painkiller, paralytic, and amnestic. The amnestic is in case the paralytic works but the painkiller doesn't, and Squillante spends the whole operation conscious but unable to move. At least he won't remember to sue.

"I'm going to count backwards from five," the anesthesiologist says. "When I get to one you'll be asleep."

"What am I, a fuckin infant?" Squillante says.

Two seconds later he's out cold and the anesthesiologist has a steel laryngoscope that's curved like a crane's beak down his throat. Shortly afterwards there's a respirator tube down there too, and Squillante is, as the anesthesiologists say, "sucking the plastic dick." The anesthesiologist checks airflow, squirts some K-Y-looking shit onto Squillante's eyeballs, and tapes the lids shut. Then he bags Squillante's head so that just the respirator tube sticks out. It instantly makes Squillante look like a medical school cadaver, where you bag the head for the first few months of anatomy class so it won't dry out before you get to it.

I push Squillante's empty bed out into the hall, where it will shortly be stolen and given to another patient, probably without the sheets being changed. But what am I going to do, use a bicycle lock? Then I go back in and velcro his arms and legs to the table, like in a monster movie. "Is this table electric?" I ask. Somebody laughs. I find a crank and arch Squillante's back by hand.

A nurse finishes cutting Squillante's gown off with scissors, revealing the fact that his scrotum drapes halfway down his thighs, like an apron. The nurse reaches for an electric razor. Another nurse is wrapping Squillante's limbs in what looks like an inflatable mattress. If anyone remembers to turn it on later, it will fill with hot air and keep him from getting frostbite.

"Sir," one of the medical students says, behind me.

"You want to scrub in?" I ask.

"Yes sir!"

"Go," I say. To my other med student I say, "Go look up the LD_{50} of defenestration."

Then I ask the circulating nurse to get Dr. Friendly on the phone.

Friendly answers after five rings, out of breath. Instead of "Hello," or any other acceptable thing, he says, "I'm not the father. Kidding. It's Friendly. Who's this?"

"It's Dr. Brown," I say. "Your patient's almost prepped."

"I thought you said he was prepped," Friendly says, when he finally shows up. Stacey comes in behind him, sheepish in her own mask and cap. Friendly has his hands up, soaking wet, with the backs facing forward.

Squillante *is* prepped. He's just not draped.

Draping is when you cover everything but the precise area you're operating on. Most surgeons want to be there when it happens, so that the patient doesn't turn out to be, say, face down by mistake.

Then again, most surgeons don't wear knee-high rubber boots to a gastrectomy, like Friendly is wearing. It can't be a good sign.

Washing your hands, by the way, which Friendly has just done and which I did forty-five minutes ago, is the best part of surgery. You do it in the hallway, smacking the front of the steel sink with your hip to turn the faucet on. Despite the frigidity of the air, perfectly hot water comes out. You peel open a presoaked sponge pack that you get from the dispenser (presoaked in either iodine or an eight-syllable synthetic sterilizer made by Martin-Whiting Aldomed—your choice, though iodine smells better) then wash the *shit* out of your hands, including under your nails. You always wash upwards, from the fingertips to the elbows, making sure no water runs back down toward your fingertips. You're supposed to do it for five minutes. You do it for three, which feels like a vacation, then bang the water off. The sponge you just drop in the sink. Cause you are done doing *anything* menial for the next few hours.

Right now, the five of us in the room who are "scrubbed in"—Dr. Friendly, the scrub nurse, the instruments nurse, my med student, and I—literally can't scratch our own asses. In fact, we can't pass our hands above our neck or below our waists, or touch anything that isn't blue.*

Dr. Friendly dries his hands on a blue towel, then does the little dance where you plunge your arms into the paper gown the scrub nurse holds out, then into the gloves, and then you tear the cardboard card off the front of your gown (touching only the blue half) and hand it to the circulating nurse, who holds it while

---

* This brings up an obvious paradox, which is that everything blue in an OR is supposed to have been sterilized, but our scrub suits, which are blue, have all been in at least one fast-food restaurant since the last time they were washed. What can I say? It's an imperfect science.

you spin around once, so that the belt of your gown tears loose and you can tie it. Friendly does his best to look bored during this, but I don't buy it. It probably never gets old.

"I'll take chain," he announces. The instruments nurse opens a pair of chain-mail gloves and drops them onto the scrub nurse's large blue table, where Friendly picks them up himself and puts them on over his rubber ones.

He clanks his fingertips together. "Now another pair of Dermagels." He winks at me. "HIV risk. The patient was wearing a pinkie ring. And in my book, gay gets you the chain mail."

The scrub nurse, a small Filipino man, rolls his eyes.

"Oh, what?" Friendly says. "You're offended? I can't say the word 'gay'? Worry about that on your own time. Let's work." To the circulating nurse he says, "Music, please, Constance."

The circulating nurse goes over to the boom box on one of the carts, and shortly afterwards that U2 song comes on about how Martin Luther King was shot in the early morning of April fourth. Martin Luther King was shot in the evening, even if you're on Dublin time, but the U2 greatest-hits album is something you learn to live with in medicine. Every white surgeon over forty plays it. You learn to be grateful it's not Coldplay.

The scrub nurse and I unfold a blue paper sheet over Squillante and tear out the section above his abdomen. Then we drop a square of iodine-perfused polymer onto the revealed skin. It fuses to Squillante's wrinkles.

Friendly, meanwhile, wanders around with a stapler, stapling the paper sheet to Squillante's skin. Stapling is pretty shocking the first time you see it. But the damage it does is minor compared to the damage from the surgery, and the old-schoolers swear by it. So people who want to act like the old-schoolers swear by it too.

As Friendly's finishing up, my other med student comes into the room and whispers "The LD_{50} of defenestration is five stories, sir."

To review, "LD" is "lethal dose," and the LD_{50} is the lethal dose for 50 percent of people. Defenestration is being thrown out a window. So the student is telling me that if you throw a hundred people out a fifth-floor window, half of them will live.

"Jesus fuck," I say. I threw Skinflick out a *sixth*-story window. What does *that* make the odds?

And why can't I catch a break? "What's the usual cause of death?" I say.

"Aortic rupture," the med student says.

"Okay." The aorta, our largest artery, is essentially a long thin balloon, like the ones pedophiles twist into the shapes of animals.* Since it's filled with blood, it makes sense that it would burst on impact. "What's next?" I say.

"Head injury, then bleed-out from organ laceration," the med student says.

"Good work," I say.

My mouth fills up with bile as I think about it. Although my mouth has been filling with bile regularly since I ate my last four Moxfanes half an hour ago. At least I'm alert.

"Labs from the needle stick aren't back yet, sir," the med student says.

---

* Apparently they're hoping the squeaking noise will drive away the parents.

"Don't worry about it," I say. True, my forearm is throbbing, but Assman's sample has probably long since been thrown out. If it ever got sent in the first place. Too many people's workday would be lengthened by five minutes if it survived.

"Let's do this," Friendly says. He kicks a metal step stool into place on Squillante's right and gets on it. The scrubbed-in med student kicks a stool into place farther down. I go to Squillante's left side. The instruments nurse is already on a stool by the head, with his trays in place on their various booms.

"Okay, everybody," Friendly says. "The patient is PMS. I know we'd all like to treat him specially because of that, like he's a cop and we work at a drive-through. But we don't work at a drive-through. So let's be professionals."

"What do you mean by 'PMS?' " my med student asks.

"Post–Malpractice Suit," Friendly says. "Settled a claim nine years ago."*

I'm thankful my student asked, since I didn't know what Friendly was talking about either. But I'm distracted. The Mox-fane has just given me the weirdest feeling. Like I just lost consciousness, but only for a thousandth of a second.

"Signor?" Friendly says.

---

* People think (and their attorneys often encourage them to think) that a malpractice suit is a no-risk proposition because 90 percent get settled prior to trial. But you can't just *threaten* a malpractice suit. In most states the statute of limitations on personal injury is so tight (two and a half years in New York) that no insurance company will take you seriously until you actually file a claim and agree to deposition. And at that point you're marked for life — either as a litigious, possibly fraudulent complainer, or (of even more interest to employers, who are the primary consumers of this kind of data) as actually having ongoing health problems.

I shake the sensation off.

"Pen," I say.

An instant later there's a pen with the cap off in my hand. I'm not sure if the scrub nurse just uncapped it and handed it to the instruments nurse incredibly quickly, or whether I blacked out again for a moment. Either way, it's creepy.

I stare down at Squillante's abdomen. I'm assuming the incision is going to be vertical, since the only times I've seen transverse incisions on an abdomen have been in C-sections. I just have no idea how long the incision's supposed to be, or where it's supposed to start.

So I wave the pen slowly through the air above Squillante's midline, like I'm trying to make up my mind, until Friendly finally says, "Right there is fine. Go, already." Then I draw a line from that spot, which is just below the ribs, to Squillante's pubic bone. I curve around the navel, since that's basically impossible to repair if you slice it.

I hand the pen back to the instruments nurse and say "Knife."

16

On the day Skinflick and I hit the Farm, I had the grocery kid pick me up at a gas station about ten miles north of there at two thirty in the afternoon. I got there at six in the morning to look for cops. When the kid arrived and stood by the payphone to wait for the call I'd told him was coming, I came up behind him and dropped my left elbow over his chest. Took hold of his chin. He went stiff.

"You're fine," I said. "Just relax. But don't turn around, and don't look at me. This is going exactly as it was supposed to."

"Yes sir," the kid said.

"I'm letting go of you now. Let's walk to the truck."

When we got to it, I was still just behind him. I said, "Keep the window down and set the odometer. Let me know when it's at almost six miles." Then I swung up into the bed and sat with my back to the glass and my feet against the boxes of groceries. I was wearing a "U MASS" baseball hat, a sweatshirt with the hood up, and a full-length cashmere overcoat. The idea was to look like a frat asshole and be impossible to identify.

When we turned onto a dirt road and the kid called out that we were almost at the six-mile mark, I told him to slow the truck down, and Skinflick came out of the trees ahead of us. Skinflick was dressed like I was, but he didn't look like a frat asshole. He looked like a Jawa. He had covered up our stolen car pretty well, though, off in the brush by the side of the road.

I gave him a hand up into the truck, and we tucked into the left side of the bed, because we knew the security camera was going to be on the left. The road got progressively rougher. Skinflick's body next to mine felt like a cashmere-covered duffel bag.

We reached the gate. You could hear the hum of the electrified fence. After a while a man's voice said, *"Yeah, who's that?"* through a loudspeaker. The voice had that nasal George Bush fake-cracker accent that resentful white men all over America now use.

The driver said, "It's Mike. From Cost-Barn."

"Lean out so's I can see you."

I guess Mike leaned out. An electric motor started, and the gate rolled noisily aside. When we drove through, I could see that the fence had rails of barbed wire, slanted *inward*.

The truck banged and fishtailed uphill for a while, then stopped. The kid came around and opened the fantail, doing his best not to look at us as he lifted out a box that had a bunch of large cans of food and bottles of detergent in it. He looked nervous, but not so nervous I was worried he would fuck up.

The second he was out of sight I slid out the back of the truck to the ground, and Skinflick came down after me.

The face of the house was done in brown overlapping planks, like it was shingled. Four windows in front, one on either side of the doorway, and another two up top. To our left you could just see the green fiberglass shack at the side of the house that Locano's plumbers had run the pipes into. The back of the truck was angled toward it to give us another couple feet of cover.

When the driver pushed the doorbell, I ran for the front of the house, putting my back against the wall beneath the corner window. Skinflick landed hard beside me just as the door opened up. I put a finger to my lips in annoyance, and he gave me an apologetic thumbs-up. When the kid disappeared inside, we dashed around the corner.

This was the part we knew would be bad. The side of the house had the same two-up, two-down window setup as the front, though the rear ground-floor window was covered by the shack. The entrance to the shack, meanwhile, faced the back yard. To go around to it we'd have to make ourselves visible from at least two windows and the back yard.

So instead we ran in a crouch along the side of the house. The feeling of being watched was intense, but I'd warned Skinflick not to look up or back. I already knew by then that people can see almost anything and convince themselves they didn't, but that human faces tend to be undeniable. Half your visual cortex lights up when you see one. So we didn't raise our faces, and we reached the shack not knowing whether we'd been spotted or not. I held two sheets of the fiberglass back wall apart just long enough for us to slip through.

Inside the shed everything looked green, because the ceiling was the same translucent fiberglass as the walls. The doorway facing the back yard was just a cutout with a blue tarp hung over it from the outside. As promised, the wall shared with the house had a low spigot coming out of it. There was a steel bucket with a hose and a nozzle gun, and a drain in the muddy ground.

I went and looked out through the tarp door. The back yard was about three hundred yards deep before it hit the barbed-wire fence. There were some picnic tables and a cement barbecue pit. I could just see the edge of another fiberglass hut. I wondered if that was the one the dead girl had been found in.

I tried not to wonder whether the dead girl had really existed, or whether she had, just somewhere else. The job was blind. I'd known that coming in, and there was no point to opening my eyes now. The best I could hope for was that some evidence showed up before the killing began.

The fantail of the truck slammed, and as the engine started we could hear a man's voice speaking to the delivery kid in a tone that was casual enough for us to assume we hadn't been seen.

That meant the dangerous part was probably over. Now the boring part—the twelve hours of waiting before we went through the hole in the wall and started shooting people—was about to begin. I went and sat down by the spigot, on the tails of my new cashmere coat.*

Skinflick stayed standing, pacing the walls, and after a while I started to feel a bit embarrassed. Like I had some office job that sounded glamorous but really wasn't, and now my kid had come to visit and I had to show him how Daddy waits all day and night in the mud and then sneaks into people's houses to shoot them in the head.

Then I started thinking about how it was that my life had turned out like this.

How there'd been a time when I used to read books, and had a pet squirrel.

"Pietro," Skinflick whispered, jolting me. "I gotta take a piss."

This was not entirely unexpected on a twelve-hour layover. But we'd only been there for five minutes.

"You couldn't have pissed in the woods?" I said.

"I did piss in the woods."

"So go," I said.

Skinflick went over to the corner and unzipped. When the urine hit it, the fiberglass rattled like a steel drum. Skinflick stopped pissing.

He looked around. Let loose a few experimental drops into the mud just short of the wall. They made a splatting sound, and he stopped again. He started to look desperate.

"Get down low," I whispered.

Skinflick tried various crouches and kneelings, and ulti-

---

* Rule One from *The Hitman Handbook:* Never try to spare your clothes.

mately lay on his side in the mud, pissing toward the wall in a fanning motion.

It worried me. Skinflick was as immune to shame as anyone I knew, but even he had his limits. And the journey from shame to resentment is the shortest one there is.

But as Skinflick shook his dick, he just said, "Fuck. I hope the FBI can't DNA-test for urine."*

A moment later he said, "Holy shit. Look."

I went over and looked. They were almost invisible in the greenish gloom, but there were footprints all over the mud floor. *All* over—even where I'd been sitting.

Adolescent-girl-sized footprints. From many different feet.

It wasn't evidence, but at least it was creepy.

Then the front door opened, and a teenage boy's voice yelled, "Dad—I'm letting the dogs back out!"

Given the slowness with which some things reveal themselves, it's amazing how fast other things become clear. Like how, if someone has dogs but has to keep them inside when a plumber or the grocery guy is there, then those must be some pretty bad-assed dogs.

The feeling of surrealism, and passiveness, and fogged stupidity, lifted from me instantly. I had placed myself here. Now I had to survive.

I pulled my gun out of one pocket and my silencer out of the

---

* It turns out they usually can't, since healthy urine doesn't have cells in it. And if you *are* dropping so many cells that a lab as bad as the FBI's can strain them out of mud, prosecution is the least of your worries.

other, and heard loping sounds as I screwed them together. Two enormous, Doberman-shaped shadows appeared on the fiberglass wall.

I later found out they were something called "King Dobermans," which you get by crossing a Doberman with a Great Dane, then backcrossing it until all that's left of the Great Dane is the size. "Fuck," I said at the time.

Like all sane people, I love dogs. A dog is a hell of a lot harder to make vicious than a human. And it was clear we'd have to kill them.

The dogs started sniffing along the base of the wall that Skinflick had just pissed against. Then one of them started to push against the fiberglass, and the other stood back and started to growl.

The front door of the house slammed. That meant that either whoever slammed it was now outside, and should be taken out as fast as possible, or else was inside, and maybe wouldn't hear what was about to happen.

Either way, it was time to do something.

The dog that was standing back woofed. Prelude to a bark. I shot it twice in the head through the wall, flipping it backwards, then shot the nearer one twice in the chest. It went down squealing.

I quickly switched magazines, listening. The shots had been silenced, but all four of them had made a loud impact noise going through the fiberglass, and the walls of the shack were still rattling. The bullet holes had frayed edges, like cloth.

The front door of the house opened up again.

The same teenage-boy voice said, "Ebay? Xena?"

I started toward the tarp-covered doorway at the back of the shack.

"Ebay!" the voice screamed, much closer.

"I've got this one," Skinflick said.

"No!" I hissed.

But Skinflick was already running toward the wall of the shack, with his gun in his hand.

"No!" I shouted.

It was action movie bullshit. Skinflick jumped, and hit the back wall of the shack high with one shoulder, parting two sheets of fiberglass outward far enough for him to see, and shoot, through the V-shaped gap. Then the wall recoiled, flinging him back into the middle of the shack.

In a movie, though, he wouldn't have missed. Or forgotten to put his silencer on.

The gunshot sounded like a car crash. If you're in the trunk. It rang in my ears as I swung through the tarp-covered doorway and around to the front of the shack, almost slipping in dog blood, just in time to see the door to the house slam shut.

"Did I get him?" Skinflick said, as he came up behind me.

"I don't think so," I said. "He's back in the house."

"Oh, shit. What should we do?"

Like his fucking us like this was something I had planned for.

"Get moving," I said.

And not into the back yard, either. With the exception of their drywalling, these guys knew their house a lot better than we ever would.

I ran back into the shack. Kicked in the wall around the spigot and stomped the painted cardboard to the ground.

The opening it left was ridiculously small. Eighteen inches diagonally, maybe. And that was after I bent the spigot out of the way.

I could barely compress my shoulders enough to squeeze, head first, into the hole. And when I did, I blocked out all the light. I grabbed onto some pipes in the darkness and used them to pull myself into the mold smell.

My face knocked over a bunch of half-filled plastic bottles, and the smell turned to chlorine and dish soap. I almost laughed. Then I pushed open the cabinet door and squirmed out from beneath the kitchen sink.

The light was blinding. There was a wide stove on one side of me and a butcher's block on the other. I got to my feet quickly.

The butcher's block was no yuppie accessory: it was gore-stained and had a giant meat grinder screwed to one end. Also, there were two women standing on the other side of it, staring at me.

One was about fifty, the other maybe half that age. Both of them had that look you get after every bone in your face has been broken at least once and then allowed to set without medical attention. Though the older one's was worse.

They were armed, sort of. The older one held out a carving knife two-handed, and the younger one had a raised heavy iron grate from one of the stove burners. Both women looked terrified.

I kept my gun on the women and helped Skinflick to his feet

as he came through the crawlway. "Careful," I said to him. "We've got two bystanders. Don't shoot them."

When Skinflick saw them he swung his own gun up. "Bystanders?" he said. "One of them's got a knife!"

"Put your silencer on," I told him. To the women I said, "Where are all the girls?"

The younger one pointed to the floor. The older one scowled at her, then saw me noticing and stopped.

"In the basement?"

The younger one nodded.

"How many people in the house besides them?"

"Three," she said, hoarsely.

"Including you two?"

"Three besides us."

"Are you the police?" the older woman asked.

"Yes," I told her.

The younger one said, "Thank God," and started to cry.

"Time to go," I said to Skinflick. To the women I said, "Both of you stay here. If you move, we *will* kill you."

Not too police-like, but whatever. I backed into the carpeted hallway that led out of the kitchen, then turned and ran down it.

The hallway was claustrophobic, turning twice under shelves stuffed with crap like plaid sleeping bags and old board games. It smelled like cigarette smoke. Near the end there was a cork bulletin board with yellowing photographs of family vacations and, I think, people fucking, though I didn't stop to examine them.

The hallway opened into a cluttered foyer with the front door at one end. There were two additional doorways and a staircase leading up. The doorway on my right was just an arch, but the one on the left had an actual door, which was closed. Skinflick came up behind me.

I covered the open archway and the top of the stairs with my gun and backed toward the closed door. Pulled it open in a crouch.

Coat closet. Lots of rubber boots. I pushed it shut again.

Between the closet and the front door there was a painting of Jesus that seemed so incongruous I lifted it up. Controls for the intercom and the front gate.

I considered just running for it. Opening the gate from here and trying to make it to the woods on the other side of the fence.

But that was a lot of open ground to cover, and an obvious move. And whatever my odds were, Skinflick's were half that. I motioned for him to come out of the hallway and follow me, and crossed to the open archway.

This led into the room at the right front corner of the house. We had crouched under its front-facing window when we'd first gotten out of the truck. Out the side-facing window you could see the shack. The room itself had a large-screen TV, a couch, a weight bench, and some shelves with plaques and trophies on them—most, apparently, for skateboarding. Above the couch there was a framed poster of Arnold Schwarzenegger from his bodybuilding days.

As I glanced at it, my peripheral vision caught motion out the side window, and I ducked and pulled Skinflick down with me.

It was a tall thin guy coming around the side of the shack toward the front of the house with the kind of fast cross-step you only learn in the military or from gun-maniac videos. He had an aluminum riot gun in his hands that he kept focused on the shack.

"Clear out back!" he yelled, by which he seemed to mean behind the shack.

His voice was weird. Also he was weirdly skinny, and his cheeks and forehead had the kind of acne you could see from twenty feet away.

Jesus, I thought. There was no way he was over fourteen.

I looked up just in time to knock Skinflick's gun aside from where he was about to shoot through the glass above me.

"What the fuck?" he whispered.

I yanked him down below the sill. "Don't shoot without telling me, don't shoot glass that's right in front of my face, and if your target is talking to someone, wait till you can see that person. And don't kill any children. Understand?"

Skinflick avoided my eyes, and I pushed him onto his back in disgust. "Just stay the fuck down," I said.

A man's voice yelled, "Randy—get clear!" It sounded like the voice from the loudspeaker at the gate.

A machine-gun roar came right through the wall at us. Skinflick and I both covered our ears as much as we could without putting our guns down.

I rose just enough to look over the sill.

The shack was gone. Torn up islands of green fiberglass drifted toward the ground like leaves, and spun all the way into the front yard. It was like someone had just taken out the shack with a leaf blower.

I turned to the window at the front of the house. The kid with the shotgun was there, three feet away, in profile. If he had looked in he might have seen me. Instead he started walking back toward the spot where the shack had been.

Two other men came into sight from the back of the house and met him there.

One of the two was another teenager, but older—eighteen or nineteen. He had a Kalashnikov assault rifle.

The other man was a nasty-looking middle age, with a foam-front baseball hat and untinted aviator glasses. He was about five nine, with a lot of the kind of hard fat they don't teach you about in med school, but which you see all the time on guys who like bar fights. He was carrying something that looked like a chain saw, only with a Gatling gun where the blade should have been. Smoke and steam pulsed off the whole length of it. I had never seen anything like it.*

The two men and the kid kicked through the shredded fiber-glass, then the middle-aged one noticed the hole in the side of the house. "DON'T LOOK LIKE WE GOT EM," he shouted. It occurred to me that none of the three were wearing ear protection.

It was clear that they were about to move closer to the side of the house, at which point we would have to lean out the window to shoot them.

Skinflick, on his knees next to me, said, "We have to shoot."

He was right. I made a tactical decision. I said, "You take the fat one. I'll shoot the kids."

We opened fire, and the window collapsed in front of us.

---

* For the gun freaks: this turned out to be a .60 GE M134 "Predator" motor gun, firing a kind of depleted uranium bullet supposedly available only in China.

What I was thinking when I divided up the targets was that I would shoot both sons in the leg—ideally in the lower leg—and that Pops was so fat even Skinflick couldn't miss him.

The problem was that *I* kept missing. It's not that easy to shoot someone in the leg. It took practically my whole clip to shoot the older Karcher son in the shin and blow the younger one's foot off.

Meanwhile, Skinflick fired off *his* whole clip without hitting Karcher once. At which point Karcher turned the motor gun on us.

As I yanked Skinflick backwards, the roar lit up again. Entire chunks of the corner of the wall we'd been kneeling against just evaporated, like in one of those movies where a time traveler changes something in the future and things start to vanish in the present.

The air filled with plaster dust and shrapnel and it became impossible to see. Skinflick squirmed out of my hands and I lost sight of him. I crawled inward, away from the corner, then behind some fallen masonry. Only when I noticed I was coughing did I realize I could barely hear.

After an amount of time I couldn't judge, a gust of November wind pumped through the house, and the air cleared. The front and side walls of the room were mostly daylight. Big chunks of the ceiling were missing, showing a bedroom up above and some pipes spraying water down the remains of one wall. I could see all the way across the foyer. The Jesus painting, and the controls behind it, were wreckage.

Karcher himself was standing near what was left of the foot of the stairs. Skinflick was on his back at Karcher's feet.

Skinflick still had his gun, but the slide was blown back to show how empty it was.

"OH, YOU ARE IN SOME FUCKIN TROUBLE NOW, BOY," Karcher screamed at him. Apparently his hearing was coming back a lot slower than mine was.

"I AM GONNA KILL YOU SLOW, THEN FEED YOU TO YOURSELF."

Deliverance is *The Godfather* for crackers.

It occurred to me that Karcher didn't realize there were two of us.

I took my time standing up, and shot him cleanly through the head.

The rest you've read about. You've probably seen reenactments of it on true-crime television.

The older Karcher son, Corey, whom I shot in the shin, bled to death. The younger one, Randy, I tourniqueted. He might have lived, except that when I went to get the car, Skinflick shot him in the head. Welcome to the mafia, Adam "Skinflick" Locano.

When we loaded the three bodies into the trunk, the women came out on the front lawn and watched us, the older one howling on her knees, the younger one just staring. Later that night the bodies got divided into a half-dozen children's coffins by a tech in the Brooklyn ME's Office who owed the mob from betting on the *Oscars*, for fuck's sake, and the six coffins were buried at Potter's Field.

Before Skinflick and I left, I located as many of the Ukrainian girls as I could. There was one on the rack in Karcher's "office," who I couldn't get to wake up, and who I would have taken with us if I'd thought we could get her to a hospital any faster than the cops would.*

There was a still-alive girl chained up in the upstairs bedroom of one of the sons—by pure luck not the room above the TV room. And there were a couple of dead ones hanging from chains in another shack.

The entrance to the storm cellar, where the rest of them were, was around back. It was the worst thing I smelled until I went to med school.

Skinflick and I stopped at the same payphone I'd used to meet up with the delivery kid, and I called the cops to tell them where to go and what to expect when they got there. Locano we called by cell phone. After we'd dropped the Karchers' bodies off, we went home and took showers, and Skinflick got drunk and high and I went off to find Magdalena.

Skinflick and I had barely spoken to each other since the shooting began. We were both deeply shaken, but we also both knew that Skinflick's decision to cap a wounded fourteen-year-old was enough to destroy our friendship, and would have been even on a day when nothing else went wrong.

And two weeks later I was arrested for the murder of Les Karcher's two wives.

---

* It's true, by the way, that up close you could still read the "Home Depot" stencils on the planks of the rack. The ones that weren't too covered in blood and shit.

17

The instruments nurse gives me a tiny-headed scalpel. I pull it lightly down the center of the newly inked line on Squillante's abdomen, causing the ink, iodine wrap, and skin to spring apart about an inch. For a second, before the cut fills with blood, its fatty walls look like cottage cheese. Then I hand the scalpel back. It won't be used again this operation. Scalpels cut cleanly, but they can't stop bleeding.

Friendly says "Clamp."

I say "Bovie and suction."

A "Bovie" is an electrocautery, a device shaped like a pen

with a cord coming out the back and strip of metal extending from the tip. It looks like a tiny cattle prod, so it's unfortunate that "Bovie" is the name of its inventor, and not short for "bovine."

A Bovie not only cuts but also burns, so it closes blood vessels as you go. (It also leaves a trail of ugly carbonized flesh, which is why you don't use it to cut skin.) The idea is to suction the blood out of the incision, then quickly spot the cut ends of the arteries and use the Bovie to fry them shut. You have to do it fast, because suctioning only gives you a split second of visibility. Then it's all just blood again.

I hand the suction to my student, who won't look as stupid overusing it. Every time the student sucks the blood out, I wait until the tiny dots of blood appear, then pick one and try to electrocute it before it goes back to spurting.

At this rate the operation will take several days, and on top of that my periods of consciousness and unconsciousness are starting to alternate, lasting a thousandth of a second each, like the peaks and troughs of a radio signal. Sweat drips off my forehead into Squillante's incision.

Eventually Friendly gets bored and starts poking around with his "clamp," which looks like a pair of needle-nosed pliers. He grabs at arteries I can't see, so that all I have to do is touch the Bovie to the metal of his instrument and fry the arteries by conduction, on faith.

When the bleeding's stopped, Friendly jabs down into the gunky membrane at the bottom of the incision and spreads the jaws of his clamp, tearing the membrane apart. Then he picks out some more vessels for me to burn.

As he does so, Friendly looks at the instruments nurse, who's

a black man in his twenties. "So I can't say 'gay' in the OR,"
Friendly says. "Too many fragile people in here. I need to ask
permission first. I forget the whole thing's *collaborative* now."

The instruments nurse doesn't respond, so Friendly turns to
my med student. "You know what 'collaborative medicine'
means?" he says.

"No, sir," the student says.

"It means an extra ten hours of unpaid bullshit a week. Look
forward to it, kiddo."

"Yes, sir," the student says.

Friendly turns back to the instruments nurse. "Can I say
'black' in here? Or do I have to say something else?" He pauses.
"How about 'the artists formerly known as Negroes'? Can I say
that? Or do I need to ask permission to say that, too?"

Operating rooms, I should say, along with construction sites,
are the last safe havens for sexists, racists, or anyone else with a
Tourette's-like condition. The idea is that harassing people
teaches them to stay calm under pressure. The reality is that so-
ciologists could study ORs to learn what workplaces were like in
the 1950s.

"What do you say, Scott?" Dr. Friendly says to the instruments nurse.

The instruments nurse looks up at him coolly. "Are you talking to me, Dr. Friendly?"

"If I am, I have no idea why," Friendly says. He tosses his
bloody clamp right into the middle of the instruments tray.
"That's it. Let's open up." He digs his fingertips into the incision,
then leans over and tugs it wide like an enormous leather change
purse. You can see Squillante's beet-red abdominal muscles,

which have a bright white stripe down the middle where we'll make the next incision, because this stripe has almost no blood supply.

"Sister Mary Joseph negative," Friendly calls out to the circulating nurse, who's now at the computer. "There's also no Virchow's node, though you'll have to take my word for it."*

I Bovie along the white stripe.

"Will you be using Japanese or American lymph-node guidelines?" my med student asks.

"That depends," Friendly says. "Are we in Japan?"

"Sir, what's the difference?" my other student asks, from the floor.

"In Japan they spend all day hunting down nodes for preventative resection," Friendly says. "Because in Japan they have socialized healthcare." He pulls the twin bands of muscle apart. "Retractor," he says. "We're in the abdomen."

The instruments nurse starts assembling the retractor, which is a large hoop that can be locked into place to hold the incision open.

While we wait, Friendly looks back at the student who's not scrubbed in. "Don't worry, we'll get the socialized stuff over here soon enough," he says. "Stacey. You want to check my beeper?"

"Sure, Dr. Friendly," Stacey says. "Where is it?"

"In my pants."

Suddenly there are a lot of downturned eyes in the room. Stacey gamely walks over and pats Friendly's ass.

"Front pocket," he says.

---

* Cancer talk!

As I think I've mentioned elsewhere, scrub pants and shirts are reversible. So that while the back pants pocket is on the right, outside your pants, the front one's on the left, *inside* your pants.

Stacey reaches under Friendly's surgical gown and roots around his crotch. She wrinkles her nose at me while she's doing it, in a way that's actually fairly winning.

"There's nothing there," she finally says.

"We already knew *that*," the scrub nurse says.

Everyone laughs uproariously. Friendly turns red, then blotchy, above his mask. He grabs the retractor out of the instruments nurse's hands and wedges it roughly into Squillante's abdomen.

"You know what?" he says when it's in place. "Fuck all of you. Let's get to work."

We do. For a while, all you can hear is the beeping of Squillante's EKG. To me, each beep feels like an alarm clock after an eternity of restless sleep. My Assman-injected forearm is starting to twitch.

But we're making progress, at least. First we pile through Squillante's intestines, each loop of which is anchored to a thin sheet of tissue that supplies it with blood and so on. So that while they can slide all over each other, like sharks in a tank, you can't just unspool them like a rope. You have to leaf through them, like the pages of a Rolodex, or a phone book.

"Give me some reverse Trendelenburg," Friendly says.*

---

* "Reverse Trendelenburg" means the patient's feet are lower than his head. "Trendelenburg" means his feet are higher than his head. No surgeon on earth would be caught dead saying "head up" or "head down," though. In case you're wondering why your appendectomy took four hours.

The reverse Trendelenburgness helps us finish folding the intestines out of the way, and at last reveal Squillante's stomach.

As with the initial incision, the complexity here will not be in removing the stomach, since any Aztec priest could take out five of them and be on the links by noon. The difficulty will be in controlling the bleeding—finding and cutting off the dozens of arteries that enter the stomach like the spokes of a wheel—so that Squillante doesn't die. Friendly picks up a second Bovie and starts picking out arteries on his side as I work on mine.

"Funny stuff, you assholes," Friendly starts up again, suddenly. "How many years of training do I have? Eleven? Fifteen? More, if you count high school. For what? So I can spend all day with a bunch of uneducated morons, breathing in genital wart particles from the Bovie and watching my salary go to my ex-wife and half the HMO executives in America. I mean, you people breathe the particles in too. But still."

His movements are getting a little jerky. Or else maybe that's just my rapid sleep-wake cycle.

"Oh, but *that's* right," Friendly says. "*I* get to *save* people. People like this pinkie ring asshole, who's spent his whole life eating beef and smoking cigarettes, and sitting on his ass."

I say, "Suture," and start tying off one of the larger arteries. The stitch breaks in my hand. I ask for another one.

"The fucking beef industry and the fucking HMO industry," Friendly says. "Al-Cowda and the HMOsamas. They make my life hell while other people slack off. I bet tobacco's a lot of fun. All kinds of things I never did are probably fun. Like when I was in med school, and you all were out in the park, smoking weed and listening to Marvin Gaye while you fucked each other."

This time I tie my stitch more gently, and it holds. I'm surprised at how quickly the knot tying comes back to me, particularly with my forearm starting to make my fingers stiffen up. But anything someone teaches you to do first to the foot of a dead pig, then to the foot of a dead human, and finally to the foot of a live human, probably sticks in your memory permanently.

"Suture," Friendly says. The instruments nurse gives a stitch to Friendly, but it gets tangled in Friendly's fingers, and Friendly angrily shakes it off into Squillante's open abdomen.

"You know what I should have done?" Friendly says. "I should have been a snake handler. It's the same job but the pay is higher. Instead I save the lives of people who hope they'll die on my table so I can get the shit sued out of me. Because that's all anybody wants: a chance to take a queen out with a pawn."

"Dr. Friendly?" the scrub nurse says.

"What?" Friendly says.

"Who's the queen in this scenario?"

There's another round of mask-hidden laughter.

"Fuck you!" Friendly says, grabbing up the knotted length of stitch and throwing it at the scrub nurse's face. It's too light to make it that far, though, and it arcs toward the ground.

For a second none of us realize that Friendly's other hand has plunged his Bovie into Squillante's spleen.

Not just into it, either. *Along* it, slicing as it went. As we watch, the incision beads with blood, then starts to gush.

"Oh, fuck," Friendly says, yanking the Bovie free.

The spleen is essentially a bag of blood about the size of your fist, to the left of your stomach. In seals, whales, and racehorses it's large and holds an extra supply of oxygenated blood. In humans it mostly strains out old or damaged red blood cells, and also has places where antibodies can go to clone themselves when they get activated by an infection. You can live perfectly well without a spleen, and people who survive car crashes or have sickle-cell anemia frequently do. But you don't want to rupture it suddenly. Because almost as many arteries lead to the spleen as lead to the stomach, so losing blood from there can kill you fast.

Friendly rips the Bovie out of its power source and throws it to the ground, shouting "Give me some clamps!"

The scrub nurse calmly says "Bovie down," and tosses a handful of clamps onto the tray. Friendly grabs a couple and starts trying to pull the edges of the spleen wound together.

The clamps tear right out, taking most of the surface of the spleen tissue off with them.

Squillante's blood starts to pulse out in sheets.

"What's happening?" the anesthesiologist yells from the other side of the curtain. "BP just dropped ten points!"

"Fuck off!" Friendly says, as we both go into action.

I grab a couple of clamps myself and start hunting out arteries. Just the biggest ones, since they're all I can see through the fountaining blood.

Friendly doesn't hassle me when I clamp the left gastroepiploic artery, which runs toward the spleen along the bottom of the stomach. I'm not sure he even notices. But when I go for the splenic artery itself, which comes off the aorta like a spigot, he swats my hand away, causing me to almost kill Squillante out-right.

"What the fuck are you doing!?" he yells.

"Hemostasis," I tell him.

"Fucking up my arteries, more like!"

I stare at him.

Then I realize that he actually thinks it's possible to save Squillante's spleen, rather than tying it off and removing it.

Because if he saves it he won't have to report slicing it open as a complication.

The alarm goes off on Squillante's blood pressure monitor. "Get him under control!" the anesthesiologist yells.

Leading with my shoulder in case Friendly gets rambunctious again, I try once more for the splenic artery, and this time I get it closed off about an inch downstream of the aorta. The blood loss out the spleen slows to a wide, shallow leak, and the blood pressure alarm shuts off.

"Suture and needle," Friendly says through his teeth.

Friendly starts to sew the wreckage of Squillante's spleen into an ugly little lump. Halfway through, the needle breaks off.

"Stacey!" Friendly screams. "Tell those fuckers to learn to make sutures, or I'm going to Glaxo!"

"Yes, doctor," Stacey says from somewhere that sounds far away.

The next stitch holds better, or Friendly doesn't yank on it as hard or something. "Can I have one of my arteries back now?" he asks me.

"It's not going to hold," I say.

"GIVE ME THE FUCKING SPLENIC."

I separate the handles of the clamp that's holding the splenic artery closed. The spleen slowly reinflates.

Then it splits in half along either side of the sewn-up incision, and sprays blood everywhere. As Friendly hurls the clamp in his hand against the wall, I reclose the splenic artery.

"Clamp on the floor," the instruments nurse says casually.

"I'm taking the spleen out," I say.

"Fuck you. I'll do it," Friendly says.

"I want to transfuse," the anesthesiologist says.

"Fine!" Friendly yells at him. "Hook him up, Constance."

Constance opens up a Coleman ice chest that says "Friendly" on it in permanent marker, and pulls out two bags of blood.

"Is that shit cross-checked?" the anesthesiologist asks.

"Do your job," Friendly tells him.

Together, Friendly and I remove Squillante's spleen. It takes about an hour and a half. Friendly then orders one of my med students to run it down to Pathology, so that he can later claim he took it out on purpose, looking for cancer. Which I have to admit is a nice recovery.

After that, the actual removal of the stomach is slow but mindless. We've already whacked half the arteries in Squillante's abdomen. There's nothing left to bleed. He's lucky he still has blood going to his liver and colon.

Reconnecting the esophagus to the intestine is more irritating, like sewing two pieces of cooked fish together. But even that gets done eventually.

"Go ahead and close," Friendly finally says to me. "I'll go do the op report."

Closing will take at least another hour, and I'm as tired as I've ever been in my life. Plus the fingers of my right hand are cramping almost to the point of uselessness.

But I'd rather close Squillante up alone than with Friendly. There are so many layers in the human body that even a good surgeon will skip sewing some of them up if the operation's running late. As long as the layers closest to the surface are done, the patient won't know the difference. They'll just be more likely to rupture later on.

And I, for one, want Squillante trussed as tightly as possible. Snug and waterproof as a latex dress.

When I finally stumble out of the operating room, Friendly's standing in the hall, drinking a Diet Coke and stroking the ass of a frightened-looking nurse.

"Remember to will the thrill, kid," he says to me.

I'm not even sure if I'm awake. I've gotten through the last half hour by promising myself I'll lie down the second I can. So maybe I already have and am now dreaming.

"You're out of your fucking mind," I say.

"Then I'm lucky this isn't a democracy," he says. "It's an asskisstocracy. And I'm the king."

This last part he says to the nurse. I don't care.

I'm already staggering past him down the hall.

I wake up. There's an alarm going off like a truck backing up. Also a bunch of voices.

I'm in a hospital bed. I have no idea why or where. Every wall except the one behind me is a curtain.

Then my beeper and the alarm on my watch go off at the same time, and I remember: I lay down for a twenty-minute nap. In the recovery room. In the bed next to Squillante's.

I jump up and swat aside the curtain between his bed and mine.

There are people all around him. Nurses and doctors, but also, near the foot of the bed, a pack of civilians. Aggressive family members, I figure, come to see how it has all turned out. The noise level is incredible.

Because Squillante is coding.

As I watch, his EKG stops jagging all over the place and flatlines, setting off yet another alarm. The medical people shout and throw hypodermics to each other, which they jab into various parts of his body.

"Shock him! Shock him!" one of the civilians yells.

No one shocks him. There's no point. You shock people whose heart rhythm is wrong, not absent. That's why they call it "defibrillating" instead of "fibrillating."

As it is, Squillante stays dead. Eventually the ICU assholes start giving up, and pushing the civilians away to have something to do.

I try to figure out which civilian is Jimmy, the guy whose job it is to get Squillante's message about me to David Locano in the Beaumont Federal Correctional Complex in Texas. My money's on the guy in the three-piece suit who's already pulling out a cell phone as he leaves the recovery room. But there are other contenders as well. Too many to do anything about.

So I go to the head of the bed and tear off the printout from Squillante's EKG machine. It's perfectly normal up to a point about eight minutes ago, where it starts spiking all over the place.

The spikes aren't even close to normal. They form a bunch of "M"s and "U"s, like they're trying to spell "MURDER." I pick up the red "biohazard" bin and take it back around the curtain to where I was napping. Dump it out on the bed.

Even with all the used syringes and bloody gauze squares, it doesn't take long to find the two empty vials that say "Martin-Whiting Aldomed" on them.

And which used to be filled with potassium.

18

Both of Les Karcher's wives had been named Mary, though the younger one had been affectionately known within the family as "Tits." The cops and paramedics found Older Mary in front of the house, where Skinflick and I had left her. Her skull had been crushed in, presumably by the iron stove grate that was found near her body, with (according to the Feds) no recoverable prints but a fair amount of Older Mary's brain tissue on it. Tits, like the three male Karchers, was simply gone.* Unlike them, she hadn't left any blood.

* Look, I'm sorry to call her "Tits," but everybody did. Even the prosecution, including one time in *court*, though it mysteriously failed to appear in the transcript.

That the Feds would charge me with the murders of the Marys and not those of the Karcher Boys, as the father and sons came to be called, made a certain amount of sense. The Marys were a hell of a lot more sympathetic, and the Feds had one of their corpses. And if the case didn't fly, they could always charge me with the Boys' murders later.*

On the other hand, trying me for the murders of the Marys was in other ways a bad move, because I hadn't actually done them. Any evidence the prosecution presented would be either fabricated or misinterpreted, and it would be impossible for them to disprove the "alternative explanation": that Tits, after God knows what mistreatment over the years, had brained Older Mary and run off with the 200,000 dollars that one of the Ukrainian girls had overheard was in the house.

Let me state for the record, by the way:

Tits, if this *is* in fact what happened, then I bear you no ill will. Even if you were off somewhere the whole time, reading

---

* The idea that you can't be tried twice for the same crime in the U.S. turns out to be horseshit. You can be tried twice on the same *charge*—once in Federal and once in State court—and you can be *charged* any number of times for the same crime. For example, my own Federal trial was on charges (two counts each) of: First-degree murder; Manslaughter in the first degree; Murder committed by the use of a firearm during a crime of violence or a drug trafficking crime; Murder during a kidnapping; Murder for hire; Murder involved in a racketeering offense; Murder involving torture; Murder related to a continuing criminal enterprise or drug trafficking offense, or drug-related murder of a Federal, State, or local law enforcement officer; Murder related to sexual exploitation of children; and Murder with the intent of preventing testimony by a witness, victim, or informant. The large number of charges was designed to make sure the jury convicted me of *something,* and also to hike my potential sentence to four figures. But even then the Feds retained the option of trying me again on other charges, and of throwing me over to the State.

about my trial in the *New York Post* every day and laughing about how you could step in to save me at any time but weren't going to—which I doubt—your actions are completely understandable.

Though I can't swear I'd feel this way if things had turned out differently.

My "defense team" was assembled by the firm of Moraday Childe. It included, notably, both Ed "The Tri-State Johnnie Cochran" Louvak and Donovan "The Only Member Of Your Legal Team Who Will Ever Return Your Calls, Even Though Everyone Else Will Bill You $450 An Hour, Rounded Up, To Listen To Your Messages" Robinson.

Donovan, who is now a Special Assistant in the Office of the Mayor of the City of San Francisco—*Hi, Donovan!*—is about five years older than I am, so at the time was around twenty-eight. He was sharp but looked stupid—*Sorry, Donovan! I know what it's like!*—which is exactly what you want in a defense lawyer. He did his best to help me, I think because he believed I was innocent. At least of those specific charges.

For example, Donovan was the first to pick up on how weird it was that I was being charged with murder involving torture, given that there was no evidence supporting the charge, and there *was* direct witness testimony from several of the Ukrainian girls that Older Mary had, if not directly participated in, then at least provided ancillary services to a couple of pretty horrific sessions. So it wasn't a topic you'd think the prosecution would want to raise.

Donovan came to see me one day in jail—funny, I don't remember Ed Louvak ever doing that—and said, "They've got something on you. What is it?"

"What do you mean?" I said to him.

"They have some piece of evidence they haven't told us about."

"Isn't that illegal?"

"Technically, yes. The rule is they have to show us anything they've got 'in a timely fashion.' But if it's something good, the judge will allow it anyway. We can try for a mistrial on that basis, but we probably won't get it. So if you have any idea what they might have, you might want to think about telling me about it."

"I have no idea," I said. Which was the truth.

David Locano was paying for all this, by the way, though not directly. He didn't want a formal link to me, and probably also wanted to be able to cut me off if he thought I was turning dangerous to him or Skinflick.

But at the moment there wasn't any reason for that to happen. We all knew the Feds would hold off on prosecuting Locano for solicitation of murder until they had proven that I had, in fact, murdered someone. And Skinflick wasn't even a suspect.

Locano had kept Skinflick scrupulously clean. He had forbidden him to take credit for the hits unless it became clear that there wasn't any heat. And he himself had never once mentioned Skinflick in connection to the Karchers outside of the steam room of the Russian Baths on 10th Street.

Unfortunately, he had been a bit looser when it came to me. The Feds had about eight hours of recorded phone calls in which he referred to me as "The Polack." As in *"Don't worry about the*

Brothers K. The Polack's visiting them next week." But at least that gave Locano a strong incentive to try to keep me from being convicted.

The Feds told us about the tapes early, to encourage me to turn on Locano. They also told us they had some already-incarcerated mob guy who was willing to testify that, in general, I was a hitter who was known to do work for Locano.

But the Feds were keeping the Mystery Evidence, if Donovan was right and they had some, a secret till the last moment.

And in the meantime I rotted in jail.

Wendy Kaminer, that genius, says that if a Republican is a Democrat who's been mugged, then a Democrat is a Republican who's been arrested. You might think a mafia hitman is not exactly the guy to be representing that argument, and in fact *fuck* me, but let me point a couple of things out.

One is that, if you are accused—*accused*, mind you—of a capital crime, you will not be offered bail. I was in the Federal Metropolitan Correctional Center for the Northeast Region (FMCCNR), across from City Hall in downtown Manhattan, for eight months *before my trial even started.*

Another is that, unless you're a scary-looking famous hitman like I was, what will happen to you in jail will be a fuck of a lot worse than what happened to me. I was never forced to sleep next to the lidless aluminum toilet, for instance, which had a perfect surface-tension dome of urine, shit, and vomit at all times, just waiting to slop over any time anyone used it. I was never forced to do what they call "taking out the laundry," or any of the other thousand fantastically imaginative degradations incarcerated people come up with to demonstrate their power over each other and to fight off boredom. Even the guards kissed my ass.

And remember: this wasn't prison. It was *jail.* The place they send people who are presumed *innocent.* In New York City, getting sent to Rikers Island (where I would have gone if my charges hadn't been Federal) just means you've got charges pending.

And you might think you'll never end up there, because you're white, so the justice system works *for* you, and you never smoke pot or cheat on your taxes or leave any other opening for anyone who wants to hurt you—but that doesn't mean you won't. Mistakes get made, at which point you will fall into the hands of what is essentially the DMV, but with much less stringent hiring requirements.

And—even in New York City, and no matter who you are— your odds of getting arrested are about 150 times your odds of getting mugged.

Plus, newsflash: jail sucks.

Like they promise, it's *loud.* Dog kennels are supposedly loud because any noise over ninety-five decibels is painful to dogs, so once one dog starts barking from the pain, all the rest start too, and the decibel count just keeps rising. In jail it's the same thing. There's always someone too crazy to stop screaming, and there are always the fucking radios, but those things are only part of it.

People in jail talk constantly. Sometimes they do it to hustle each other. In jail, even the people so stupid you're surprised they know how to breathe are constantly on the make. Because odds are good they'll find someone even stupider than they are: someone more stressed-out, or more fucked-up on drugs, or whose mother drank more alcohol when she was pregnant with them or whatever.

But people in jail also talk just to talk. Information, in a place that chaotic, comes to seem vital no matter what the quality.

The real value of conversation in jail, though, seems to be that it *keeps* people from thinking. There's no other way to explain it. People in jail will have a conversation with someone four cells away rather than shut their fucking faces for two minutes. Like there's not enough noise from the guy knifing and/or raping someone near you, or sharpening his homemade syringe on the wall. People you threaten with *death* will keep talking to you.

What they're all hoping for is that in the mindlessness of the place you'll tell them something you shouldn't, which they can then go sell to the warden. People in jail talk all the time about how much they hate *snitches,* and how people shouldn't *snitch,* and how you'll have to excuse them for a minute while they go off to knife someone for *snitching.* "Snitch" is one of their favorite words.* But *all* those fuckheads, no matter how many times they tell you they'd rather die than be a *snitch,* spend most of their day trying to dig up something to snitch about. To lessen their sentence, or kiss ass, or just to fight the boredom.

---

* And sounds even more Dr. Seuss–like when paired with "bitch," which is another of their favorite words.

Another favorite topic in jail is where everyone is headed.

As a mob guy and a killer, it was clear I'd be sent to one of the two facilities that make up Level 5, the highest level of security in the Federal system. The question was which one—Leavenworth or Marion.

What's interesting about Leavenworth and Marion is that although they're the only two Level 5 prisons, and although they're also the two worst prisons in the U.S., they're complete opposites. At Leavenworth the cell doors are open for sixteen hours a day, during which the prisoners are free to "mingle." Apparently the mingling gets particularly baroque from June through September, because that's when the warden leaves the lights off in the upper tiers. He has to: it gets so hot in Leavenworth that if he turns the lights on, the prisoners will destroy them to cut down on the heat production.

At Marion, meanwhile, the esthetic is completely different. You're in "Ad Seg," or "Administrative Segregation," which means a tiny white cell, alone, with a fluorescent diffusion light over you that never shuts off and is the only thing you have to look at. You spend twenty-three hours a day there, with the other hour spent showering, going out to a solitary twelve-foot pacing run, or putting on and taking off your leg irons, which you have to do any time you do anything. In your cell you start to feel like you're floating in fluorescent white nothingness, and that nothing else really exists.

If Leavenworth is fire, Marion is ice. It's the Hobbesian hell vs. the Benthamite one. The dipshits I was in jail with all said

Leavenworth was preferable, because at Marion you inevitably go insane. They also said that in free-range Leavenworth I, particularly, would do well, since as a mob guy I would get *respect*. At least as long as I was young enough to defend myself.

"Respect," by the way, is the third word people in jail say all the time. As in *"You tryin to start a war, dog? It ain't respect to call that punk bitch Carlos! You got to call her Rosalita, dog. No, I mean it ain't respect to the violators who are men in the block!"* Which a guard actually said to me once.

I figured all told I would prefer Marion. But I didn't worry about it too much, because the choice of whether you spend the rest of your life at Marion or at Leavenworth is not one you get to make. Bizarrely, it's not one *anyone* gets to make. It gets decided randomly, on the basis of available beds.*

And anyway, I was planning to avoid both places. By snitching or whatever else it took.

I was willing to tell the Feds everything I knew, about the mob in general and David Locano in particular. True, I had once loved Skinflick like a brother. His parents had been closer to me than my own parents. Also true, I loved Magdalena so badly that I would have sold the Locanos and anything else I had access to in an instant, for one hour alone with her, anywhere.

I just didn't know how long to wait. If it turned out that I would somehow walk, it would be crazy to tangle with the mob

---

* A Brooklyn wiseguy once told me you could choose Leavenworth by having a bed there "cleared," i.e., by having someone killed. Sounds like bullshit to me.

unnecessarily. But if I waited too long, and got convicted, it would be a lot harder to plea-bargain.

Locano's guys were smart enough not to threaten Magdalena—or me, for that matter—directly, because they knew that if they did I'd start thinking about how to hurt them, and never stop. But they didn't have to say much. I was in a cage, and they were out there, where she was. The ones who came to visit mentioned her all the time: *"The case is bullshi'. It's shi'. You'll be back out wit your girl again. Wha's her name? Magdalena? Nice name. Gray girl. You'll be wit her in no time. We'll sen her somin."*

Magdalena herself came to visit me four times a week.

Visitation rights are looser in jail than they are in prison— because *Hey, you're innocent!*—and apparently they're looser in Fed than they are in State. You're not allowed to touch, but you can sit at opposite ends of a long metal table that has no divider, as long as the prisoner keeps his hands in sight on the tabletop. The visitor can keep her hands wherever, and do things to herself with them while you talk, and after a few weeks you don't even think about the guards being there when this happens. And if you and she are fast you can stand at the same time, and you can kiss her or she can get her fingers into your mouth before you're pulled apart and she's thrown out and you get searched by a dentist. Because the warning that she won't be allowed back turns out to be bullshit. And the guards, those sorry derelicts, are all willing to lie for you.

I loved Magdalena more and more with each visit and with each of her strange, formal letters. *"In the quartet they keep telling me I am playing out of time. I am, because I am thinking about you. But it makes me play better, not worse, as I am so much more alive then, so*

I do not feel I am letting them down. I play best when I play from my heart, and you are my heart, I love you."

If that feels to you like one of those fucked-up prison romances where the obese woman writes to the celebrity wife-murderer, I don't care. It saved my life, and my sanity. Her visits blotted out the squalidness of that shithole for days after she left.

Magdalena talked to Donovan more than I did. After he suggested to both of us separately that we might want to get married in case she was subpoenaed,* Magdalena told me that of course she would. That she would do anything.

I told her I didn't want to, because I wanted to marry her for real. She said, "Don't be stupid. We've been married for real since October Third."

I'll leave that one for you to figure out. It would be like trying to describe what the surface of the sun looks like.

Not that anyone seriously thought Magdalena would be subpoenaed. She would break a jury's heart like *that*.

She brought me books, which were hard to read because of the noise. Then she brought me earplugs.

And, without telling me, she began the process of applying to become a Federal prison guard, so she'd have a chance in hell of being near me if things went badly.

Early in the summer of 2000, I was taken out of my cell and brought to an office in the FMCCNR I'd never been to before.

---

* She could still have been compelled to testify about crimes committed prior to the marriage, but juries still think it's illegal, so prosecutors don't like to do it.

That itself was not unusual, since every couple of weeks or so there was an "initial appearance" or "pretrial hearing" or whatever, to verify things like that I was who I claimed to be or who the Feds claimed I was, and that a crime had been committed at all. But this time the guard left me in the office alone and went and stood outside. Which felt extremely strange, even though I had wrist-waist and ankle cuffs on.

I immediately searched for a phone to call Magdalena. There wasn't one. The wooden desk, like the wooden bookshelves, was empty. The wooden chair was the old slat-back kind. Out the window there was a ledge, and if I'd wanted to escape that would have been a good time for it. For a minute or two I considered it, and I was still looking out the window when the door opened behind me and Sam Freed came in.

He was in his late sixties then, immediately likable in a wrinkled gray suit. When I started around the desk he held a hand up and said, "Sit." So I took the desk chair and he pulled over one of the ones along the walls.

"I'm Sam Freed," he said. I'd never heard of him.

"Pietro Brnwa." There was something about him that made you feel, even in your orange jumpsuit and leg irons, like a human being.

"I'm with the Justice Department," he said. "Though I'm mostly retired now."

That's what he said. He didn't say, for instance, "I invented WITSEC," though that would have been true. He didn't say, "I broke the mob's back, and the people I gave immunity to have the lowest recidivism rates ever seen."

Of course, he also didn't say that he was one of the most

loathed people in law enforcement. Because sure, he'd struck the mafia a deathblow, but only at the cost of setting a bunch of scumbags up with new lives, which most cops and even Feds found unforgivable.

He was Jewish, of course. Who else would fight that hard for justice in a way guaranteed to make him a pariah? His father had worked the Fulton Street Fish Market, paying 40 percent off the top to Albert Anastasia.

Like I say, though, at the time I had never heard of him. "Huh," I said.

He said, "I heard about you from Baboo Marmoset."*

"I don't know who that is," I said.

"Indian kid. Doctor. Long hair. He did your physical a couple of months ago."

"Oh, right." I remembered him now, though only someone of Freed's generation would say he had long hair. Marmoset had talked on the phone and done my paperwork at the same time he'd examined me. Then he'd said, "You're fine." I was pretty sure that was the extent of our interaction.

"I'm surprised he remembered me," I told Freed. "He seemed a bit distracted."

Freed laughed. "He always does. God knows what he'd be capable of if you could get his attention. I'll tell you a story."

Freed put his feet up on the desk. "My wife and I like to go out to dinner theater," he said. "These things at a Chinese restaurant where some actors stage a crime and you have to solve it.

---

* "Baboo," which is a common nickname for the youngest male of an Indian household, obviously isn't Prof. Marmoset's real first name. His real first name is Arjun.

It's ridiculous, but it feeds us and it feeds the actors, so there you have it.

"Sometimes Baboo comes along. He never seems to pay attention at all. He's usually got some date, in fact. Spends the whole night with his face in her boobs or else checking his voice mail. At the end of the evening, though, when it's time to guess who committed the crime, he's always right."

"No kidding," I said.

"None," Freed said. "Anyway, he's the best judge of character I know. And I've known a few."

He didn't say, "Like Jack and Bobby Kennedy," though he could have.

He said, "Baboo called you 'an interesting and possibly redeemable individual.' By which I assume he meant not only that you deserved a second chance, but that you probably had enough information to trade to earn one."

I shook my head. I already felt like Freed was someone I didn't want to disappoint, and I didn't want to lie to him, either. "I barely talked to that guy. And I'm not willing to testify," I said.

"Okay. It can wait. But not for long. Speed the plow. The opportunity won't keep forever."

"I'm not interested in entering protection unless I have to. I'm not ready for it."

"I don't know about that," Freed said. "Protection's not what you think. It's not about becoming someone else. It's about becoming who you were meant to be in the first place."

"That's a little deep for me," I said.

"I don't believe that for a second," he said. "Think about what your grandfather would have wanted."

"My *grandfather*?"

"I'm sorry to get personal. But I think I know what he thought of you, and what he'd think about you being here, and I think you know too."

"Do you do this to all potential witnesses?" I said.

"Absolutely not," he said. "But Baboo Marmoset thinks you can take it."

"He doesn't even know me!"

Freed shrugged. "The man has a gift. He probably knows you better than you know yourself."

"That wouldn't take much," I said.

"No it wouldn't, toughguy," Freed said. He swung his legs off the desk and stood up. "But I think you know what this mob stuff is worth. It gives you a couple of headwaiters kissing your ass because you pay them and they're afraid of you, and it takes everything else away. Including that lovely young lady of yours."

Somehow when *he* said it, it didn't bother me. But intellectually I knew better.

"You're conning me," I said.

"Takes one to know one," he said. He opened the door but turned around before he went out. "You know, if I *was* conning you, I'd say this: Why did the the mob want the Karchers dead?"

"I don't know anything about that," I said.

He ignored me. "You saw how isolated the Karchers were. Who could they identify? You think they knew people higher up in the chain?"

I just looked at him.

"They didn't. They knew people *below* them. That's why the

mob wanted them gone. So the business itself could keep going, under a different subcontractor.

"I'll be in touch later. But if I was conning you I'd ask you to think about that, and what your grandfather would have said about it."

Freed was right about the Karchers, of course. It had occurred to me a million times before.

But that night I slept without my earplugs so I wouldn't have to think about it.

The trial itself you already know about, you child of Fox News, you. But you have no idea how injuringly boring it was, even to me. The Feds had been running "Operation Russian Doll" for months before I stepped in and fucked things up for them, so there were thousands of financial documents that anyone capable of getting a job in the private sector would have known better than to read to the jury. And which had almost nothing to do with the Italian mafia. Or, as the FBI calls it, "the LCN."

"LCN" stands for *la cosa nostra*—"the our thing," or "the thing of ours." I have never once heard anyone in the mafia actually say *"la cosa nostra,"* let alone "LCN." Let alone *"the* LCN." Why would they? It'd be like a bunch of French criminals calling themselves the LJNSQ, for "the *le je ne sais quoi.*"*

---

* Supposedly, FBI agents are still required to say "the LCN" because when J. Edgar Hoover had to explain to the McClellan Committee why he denied for so long that the mafia existed—despite, for example, Hoover's own tapes

Anyway, for a while the trial was just a slog. Then, about ten days into opening arguments—right after they played the recording of my 911 call from the gas station, which a speech expert said was my voice "to about eighty-five percent certainty"—the prosecution produced the Mystery Evidence, and the whole thing took off.

The Mystery Evidence, of course, was a skinned, severed hand, which the prosecution said they would prove had once belonged to Tits.

The Hand was disgusting. You had to admit that it looked too delicate to be anything other than female, but also just a little too large to be that of an adolescent Ukrainian girl. And it was easy enough to take the Feds' word for it that the Hand had been found *outside* the compound, right near where the car had been parked that they said they were going to prove I had driven away. And that the knife marks all over the Hand made it clear that it had been skinned, and not, say, picked over by some weasels or whatever.* It was a thing of deep horror. Particularly when the Feds projected it, huge, onto a screen at the front of the courtroom.

Naturally, Ed Louvak objected, but Donovan had been right: although it ran contrary to *Brady v. Maryland* for the prosecution

_____

of Sam Giancana calling in orders to the floor of the U.S. Senate—he tried to pass the whole thing off as a semantic misunderstanding. Like everyone else had just been using the wrong name.

* By the way, the medical term for something getting skinned, intentionally or otherwise, is "degloving," but any part of your body with skin can be "degloved." In the ER, for instance, dicks that have been stuck into vacuum cleaners are perennial favorites.

to have kept the Hand secret from the defense, the judge allowed it into evidence anyway, since it was so grotesque and so likely to generate press coverage. And also, I suppose, because it was the only thing likely to get a conviction.

You have to understand that, relatively speaking, July 2000 was a terrific time to be tried for murder. Five years earlier the O. J. Simpson trial had managed to slander the concept of circumstantial evidence, which up to that point had been the basis for almost every criminal conviction in history. Circumstantial evidence includes everything except physical evidence and direct eyewitness testimony. If you buy a speargun, tell everyone in the bar you're about to go shoot someone with it, then come back in an hour with the gun but not the spear and say you did it, that's all just circumstantial evidence. The O.J. trial managed to make even *physical* evidence look suspect, because any gap in the "chain of custody" made it conceivable the cops had fucked with it.

And eyewitness testimony, by that time, had been under fire for years as being unreliable. Which it is. Though in my case there wasn't going to be much anyway—just Mike the Grocery Boy, on what he might or might not have seen in his rearview mirror.

The Feds, meanwhile, had barely any physical evidence other than the Hand. There was mud all over the Farm, but none of the footprints in it were large enough to be mine.*

---

* This was because I had cut the soles off a pair of shoes three sizes too small and glued them to the bottom of some shoes that actually fit me, so that according to the size/depth chart the Feds use to extrapolate body measurements from footprints I was five foot four and three hundred pounds. I don't flatter myself that this fooled the detectives, but try explaining it to a jury.

So the Hand had been scrupulously protected, and supposedly kept under direct observation at all times from the moment it was found. Which seems silly. I mean, whose job is *that?* Do you have to sit in a refrigerator to do it? But it got the point across.

The Feds didn't even have to DNA-test it—which they couldn't have, because they had no reliable sample from Tits to compare it to. The O.J. trial had made DNA testing seem like a conspiracy by a bunch of assholes with jobs to fool jurors they thought were stupid. The *defense* was welcome to DNA-test the Hand—and come across as smart-ass elitist dickheads, for a result the jury would just ignore anyway—but the prosecution wasn't about to.

It all confused the shit out of me.

I mean, there it was. The Hand. I couldn't remember whether Tits had had long nails or not. But it was *somebody's* hand. If the Karcher Boys hadn't cut it off, then somebody else had, which meant I had to think about whether someone was setting me up.

But who, and why?

The prosecution referred to the Hand constantly, no matter what boring shit they were shoveling in the foreground. Like the surveillance tapes, which had so much static that the prosecution had to project subtitles up at the front, causing half the courtroom—and two thirds of the jury—to fall asleep. Until the prosecution said "Bear in mind they're talking about the kind of vicious criminal who would do *this* to a woman's hand," and put the image of the Hand back on the screen, and everybody woke back up.

Things got more interesting when the prosecution started showing photos of the Farm, including the storm cellar, and then again when they finally called Mike the Grocery Boy to the stand about driving us into the compound in his truck. Mike was impressively sullen, and he got a laugh by saying, "From what I saw, it could have been Bigfoot back there." The prosecution also began to lead up to calling the imprisoned mob turncoat, which might have been interesting.

But, as you know, the trial ended before that was necessary.

One night Sam Freed came to my *cell*. At *midnight*. He wouldn't talk to me until a guard had taken us to the office where Freed and I had first met, and left us alone there.

"Look, kid," he said then. "Something's about to happen. I'm not going to tell you what it is, because I want you to focus on what I'm saying. And when you find out, you're not going to be able to focus on anything."

"Oh, don't give me that shit—" I said.

"I'm giving it and you're taking it. So listen. I made you an offer that would have been the best thing that ever happened to you. You could have been a goddamned *doctor*, like your grandfather. You could have been anything or anyone you wanted to be. Want to join the country club? I could have made you a WASP. You hear me?"

"I never wanted to be a WASP."

"You hear me?"

"Yes."

"I will do everything I can to get that offer back for you after everyone calms down," he said. "But for a while things will be squirrelly, and out of control. Just remember people will come to their senses eventually. You testifying against David Locano will always be worth something to the DOJ. Are you hearing me?"

"I'm not sure," I said. "I have no idea what you're talking about."

"You will tomorrow morning, believe me. So spend tonight thinking about what I'm telling you—about taking a deal if I can get you one. With your permission, I'll call your girlfriend and give her my number. Can I do that?"

"Well . . . yes, but . . ."

"You'll understand it all tomorrow morning," he said. "And when that happens—for Christ's sake, use your head."

At eight the next morning, the judge dismissed all State and Federal charges against me on grounds that the Hand should have been discovered under *Brady v. Maryland* after all. Six hours later they let me out of a holding cell. Donovan came and got me and took me out to lunch and told me what the hell had happened.

My defense team had had the Hand DNA-tested. They figured the public wasn't as stupid about that kind of thing as they had been during O.J., and what could it hurt. When the results had come back they'd had the Hand examined by a radiologist. Then a PhD in anatomy, and then a zoologist.

The Hand was not a hand. It was a paw. From a bear. A *male* bear. And just like that, it was over.

That afternoon, the prosecution tried to seal the record. There wasn't any point. The headlines started immediately:

"ESCAPE CLAWS." "BEARLY LEGAL." "WITLESS FOR THE PAWSECUTION."

Those fuckers never had a chance.

Which wasn't fair. Everyone went on and on about what a colossal fuckup it was, and how stupid someone would have to be to mistake a bear paw for a human hand. But I was in that courtroom, and so were a lot of other people. And not one of us doubted it for a second. In photos, at least, it was impossible to tell.

Even after I got to med school I was amazed by the similarities—particularly if you take off the claws, which people do when they skin bears. Bears are the only nonprimates that can walk on their hind feet. They look so much like people when you skin them that the Inuit, Tlingit, and Ojibwa all thought bears could *become* people by taking their skins off. And the Inuit, Tlingit, and Ojibwa dissected a lot more bears than some drunk at the FBI ever did. Let alone the *New York Post*.

Anyway.

That, kids, is how the Bearclaw got his name.

19

I'm standing by the curtained-off bed next to Squillante's in the recovery room, rolling the two empty potassium vials around in one hand. I should be rounding on my patients, then getting the fuck out of the hospital. Or else forgetting about my patients, and going straight to the getting-the-fuck-out part.

What I should not be doing is standing here trying to figure out who killed Squillante. I mean, who cares, and what difference does it make? Is there some hitman still in the hospital who's about to get a call saying *"Wait up. While you're there, would you mind whacking the Bearclaw, too?"* Unlikely. I probably have about ninety minutes.

But no one's ever whacked a patient of mine before, and I can't get past it. It pisses me off in a whole new way.

I give myself one hundred seconds to think.

The obvious suspect is someone from Squillante's family. Someone who was hoping Squillante would die in surgery so there could be a big malpractice suit, but was willing to take matters into his or her own hands when Squillante pulled through. So an insurance beneficiary.*

But it's also someone who knew to use two whole vials of potassium. Any less than that might have allowed Squillante to live, or even helped him. Any more would have been pointless, and would have caused streaks in his aorta that would scream out on autopsy.

But if the person wanted to hide the fact that it was murder, why inject Squillante so quickly that his EKG spiked? The insurance company would love that. The money's never coming out of probate.

Maybe the person *did* care, but didn't have the time or training to do it right.

Again, though, who gives a shit? Enough time wasted. I'll go see those of my patients who might die if I don't, and leave the rest to Akfal.

Then get the fuck out.

---

* You see this all the time—not people actually killing their relatives, but people sorely disappointed when their relatives survive. It usually takes the form of someone asking you to take their mother off life support even though her surgery went great and Mom's up and walking around and about to check out.

I know: *Sterling. And fuck the Pakistani, eh?* But he might as well get used to it, since I doubt I'm coming back.

In the hallway outside the recovery room, though, I run into Stacey. She's still in her scrubs, and she's crying.

"What happened?" I ask her.

"Mr. Squillante *died*," she says.

"Oh," I say. Wondering how it's possible to hang out with Dr. Friendly and still be surprised by the death of one of his patients. Then I remember Stacey's new on the job. I put an arm around her.

"Hang in there, kid," I say.

"I don't know if I can deal with this job," she says.

Something occurs to me. I say, "Yeah." Then I count to five as she sniffles. Then I say, "Stacey, do you have any potassium chloride samples?"

She nods her head slowly, confused. "Yes . . . I don't usually, but I've got two of them in my bag. Why?"

"Why do you have them now, if you don't usually have them?"

"I don't do the ordering. They just FedEx me the stuff and I bring it into the hospital."

"They FedEx it to your office?"

"I don't have an office. They FedEx it to me at my apartment."

I'm amazed. "You work out of your *home?*"

She nods again. "So do my roommates."

"Do all drug reps work out of their homes?"

"I think so. We're only supposed to go in twice a year, for the Christmas and Labor Day parties." She starts sobbing again.

Jesus, I think. *Every day's a lesson.*

"You wouldn't have any more Moxfane, would you?" I ask her.

"No," she says through the tears, shaking her head. "I'm all out."

"Go home and get some sleep, kid," I tell her.

I'm doing respirator settings on a patient I haven't mentioned and won't mention again, dripping time like blood, when I get a page from Akfal. I call him back.

"Assman's got jaundice," he says.

Great. It means his liver is malfunctioning so badly that it's stopped correctly processing dead blood cells. My own arm has started to feel a bit better. But he, at least, is fucked.

I should skip it. Not so much because it can wait, which it sounds like maybe it can't, but because I can't think of what to do for him even if I take the time. I know if I called WITSEC and said "I really should run for my life, but I've got a patient who's gone from ass pain to liver failure in less than eight hours due to an unknown, spreading pathogen," and they knew what they were talking about, they'd say "Run for your life. You might as well save *someone*."

Or maybe they wouldn't. WITSEC is not the most sympathetic organization in the world. Their universal word for witness is "scumbag"—which is fine for actual criminals like myself, but gets a bit grating when they're talking about a young widow with a baby who's just testified against three gangsters who came into her store and shot her husband in front of her.

And most relocated witnesses are lucky to get a job at a Staples in Iowa. So you can imagine how the Feds feel about *me,* who as far as they're concerned got placed in a gold-plated, tax-dollar Porsche en route to a golf course, with a license plate reading, "FUKUFBI."

What actually happened is that I got placed into the two-year premed program at Bryn Mawr, which I paid for myself. But even that was only because I had Sam Freed backing me. Sam's retired now. If I get relocated again, it'll be to paint fire hydrants in Nebraska. It will never be to work as a doctor.

Of course, I could run *without* being relocated. Participation in WITSEC is strictly voluntary. In fact, if you do something they don't like they kick you out, and half the time "accidentally" rat you out in the process. But to keep my name, and therefore my MD, I'd have to find some shithole so far away the mob couldn't find me to *mail* me a bomb. And even those places have surprisingly strict licensing requirements. Like wanting to know who you are.

The fact is, once I leave this hospital I leave medicine, almost certainly forever.

The concept is dizzying. I race up to Assman's room.

As I'm passing the nursing station, the Jamaican charge nurse calls out: "Doctair."

"Yes, ma'am," I say. The Irish crone is asleep on her computer keyboard, drooling into the AS/ZX region.

"There's a woman keeps calling to talk to you. Leaving a number," the Jamaican one says.

"How long's she been calling?"

"Several hours."

So it's possibly legitimate. "Can I have the number?" I say.

She slips it across the counter to me, written on a prescription pad.

"Thanks," I say. "Don't let your friend electrocute herself."

She scowls and holds up the unplugged cable from the computer keyboard. "This is a *hospital*," she says.

I make the call. A woman says, "Hello?" There are traffic noises in the background.

"This is Dr. Peter Brown," I say.

"You're Paul Villanova's doctor?"

"Yes, ma'am."

"He was bitten by a flying rodent."

"What do you mean?"

I hear the clunk you can only get these days by hanging up a payphone.

I enter Assman's room.

"How you feeling?" I ask him.

"Up yours," he says. I touch his forehead. He's still burning up. I feel a bit guilty about the fact that my forearm barely hurts anymore, and that I have movement back in my fingers.

"You ever been bitten by a bat?" I ask. Not that a bat is a

rodent—it's a chiropteran. But sometimes you need to put yourself in the shoes of the common man to practice medicine correctly.

Plus, no one gets bitten by a flying squirrel.

"No," Assman says.

I wait for him to equivocate, but he doesn't. He just keeps his eyes closed and sweats.

"Never?"

At least it gets his eyes open. "What are you, a retard?" he says.

"Are you sure?"

"Yeah, I think I would probably remember that."

"Why? You can't even remember the last four presidents."

He rattles them off.

"Or what day of the week it is."

"It's Thursday," he says.

So at least his mind's still working. Mine, meanwhile, is blurring.

"Are you married?" I say.

"No. I wear this ring to keep supermodels from rubbing up against me in the subway."

"Where's your wife?"

"How the fuck should I know?"

"Is she in the hospital?"

"You mean as a patient?"

"Any time you want to stop being a smartass," I say to him.

He closes his eyes and smiles through the pain. "She's around here somewhere," he says.

I pull the curtain and check on Mr. Mosby. He's managed to

undo his wrist restraints but has left the ankle ones on out of courtesy. He's asleep. I check the pulses in his ankles and leave.

I scribble "R/O bat bite per wife" in Assman's chart,* then finish the note with two horizontal lines and a diagonal one. I don't even sign it.

Because right now I'm in a strange state of purity. One way or the other, "Dr. Peter Brown" will not exist long enough to be sued, or even to check lab results. There is nothing to do but actual medicine, and even then only what is strictly, imminently necessary.

Or what I feel like doing. I check the speed on a couple of chemotherapy drips, then spend all of thirty seconds fixing the dressing on the girl missing half her head.

Osteosarcoma Girl, in the next bed over, is ashen, staring at the ceiling. The bag on her knee is filled with blood and blood clots.

Her other knee's propped up. I pull her gown down to cover her pussy, which still has a blue tampon string hanging out of it, and which anyone walking into the room can see.

"Who gives a shit?" she says. "No one's going to ever want me again."

"Bullshit," I say. "Thousands of people will want you."

"Yeah. Losers who think they can trade up by fucking a gimp."

---

* "R/O" means "rule out," as in "You deal with it."

Huh. Seems pretty astute to me. "Where'd you get a mouth like that?" I ask her.

"I'm sorry," she says, sarcastically. "None of the *boys* are gonna want to take me *dancing*."

"Sure they will," I say. "Down at the hop."

"You fucker!" she says.

I wipe the tears off her cheeks. "I have to go."

"Kiss me, you asshole," she says. I do.

I'm still doing it when there's a throat clearing noise behind me. It's two surgery techs come to wheel her away so she can get her leg cut off.

"Oh shit I'm scared," she says when they lift her to the stretcher bed. She's holding my hand, which is sweating.

"You'll be okay," I say.

"They'll probably cut off the wrong leg."

"That's true. But the second time they operate it'll be harder to fuck up."

"Fuck you."

They wheel her away.

When I get beeped to the ER by a doctor I know who works there, I think: *No problem.*

It's on my way out.

Just outside the ER I pass the fuckhead who tried to mug me this morning. He still hasn't been examined yet, since long wait times are how they discourage people without insurance from coming to the ER. His face is covered with blood, and he's holding his broken arm. When he sees me he jumps off his stretcher and gets ready to run, but I just wink at him as I jog by.

Under less extreme circumstances, I love emergency rooms. People who work there are as slow and calm as houseplants. They have to be, or they fuck up and burn out. And in the Manhattan Catholic ER you can always find the doctor who paged you, because it's all been one open space since an incident you really don't want to know about.*

The doctor is hosing out a low-back knife wound on a patient who's writhing and screaming but being held in place by a couple of nurses.

"What's up?" I ask her.

"The ER's a fucking nightmare," she says, sedately.

"Sorry, I'm in a hurry. What can I do for you?"

"I've got a biker status post–motorcycle accident with heavily contused testicles."

"Okay."

"And he's mute."

"He's *mute*?"

"That's right."

"Can he hear?"

"Yes."

So he's probably not mute.

I look at my watch, like it's going to say, "Ten minutes to hitmen."

"Show me," I say.

---

* All right, fine. A nurse there turned out to be keeping his patients tied up and sedated for days at a time while he "experimented" on them.

She puts down the sprayer and takes me over.

The biker's not some jackass with a weekend Harley. He's an actual biker-gang biker, like from *Gimme Shelter*. He's got green tattoos and is wearing sunglasses in the Emergency Room. There's a bunch of ice packs on his groin, with his purple and black water-balloon scrotum showing through them.

"Can you hear me?" I ask him.

He nods.

I squeeze his nose shut. He looks surprised, but not as surprised as when he realizes he's not strong enough to claw my hand off his face.

Eventually he opens his mouth to breathe, and I take the bag of heroin out.

I toss it to the doctor. "Okay?" I say to her.

"Thanks, Peter," she says.

"Any time," I say, wishing it were true.

I walk out through the ambulance entrance.

20

After I got out of jail, I didn't give a shit about anything but Magdalena.

We moved into an apartment in Fort Greene, close enough but not too close to her parents, and spent all our time together. If she went out to play a gig I drove her and lurked nearby.

Twice a week we went to see her family. Her parents were polite, but got teary-eyed every time. Rovo, Magdalena's brother, seemed in awe of me, a fact that shamed but also flattered me.

My other family, the Locanos, I avoided to the extent that

I could. I owed them and they owed me, and beyond that every-thing was broken. I don't know how many friends you can stand to hear talking about you on tape like that, calling you "The Polack" and appearing to give no shit whatsoever about what kind of trouble they're getting you into. I don't know how many friends could stand knowing you've heard those tapes, either. We started disentangling from each other, but slowly to be safe.

Skinflick, meanwhile, just seemed bewildered. What we'd gone through together at the Farm was now useless to him. What was he going to do, come out *now* and say he'd whacked the Karcher Boys? *Helped* whack the Karcher Boys, even? Shot an injured fourteen-year-old in the head while I was off getting the car?

It had all been for nothing, and now it wasn't so much shame as envy I felt from him. Even after I got out of jail, we barely spoke.

The worst thing was that I couldn't avoid the wider mafia. Within the "LCN community," and among its many hangers-on, I had achieved the worst kind of celebrity: the kind where people you don't know recognize you instantly as a cold-blooded killer, and love you for it. Those lowlifes had paid for my defense, and they were touchy, vain, insecure, and dangerous. I could turn down some of their invitations, but not all of them. There was a limit to how hard I could snub them.

At least the mob guys didn't want me to go back to killing people. They understood that the myth that I was now bullet-proof because the government would be too embarrassed to ever charge me with anything again was worth a lot more to them untested.* But *fuck* those assholes wanted me around. It was during that time that I met Eddy "Consol" Squillante. Among many, many others.

"Assholes" really doesn't do them justice, by the way. Those fuckheads were hideous. Proudly ignorant, personally repellent, absolutely convinced that their willingness to hire someone to beat money out of someone who worked for a living constituted some kind of genius and an adherence to a proud tradition. Though whenever I asked one of them about that tradition—the one thing I was interested in hearing about from those slime-hags—they'd usually clam right up. I never knew whether this was because of the oath they'd taken or because they just didn't know anything. Though I never stopped asking, because, at the least, getting those fuckers to shut up was its own kind of victory.

Skinflick invited me to a couple of parties at the apartment he'd moved into on the Upper East Side. If I went I'd show up when I thought it would be the most crowded, seek him out to shake his hand, and leave. He'd say something like, "I miss you, dude," and I'd say, "Me too," and in a way it would be true. I'd miss *something,* and whatever it was, it was definitely gone.

In fact, if I'd only had more faith in that—in how dead things had become—I might have been able to save all of us.

It was April 9, 2001. I was home, but Skinflick called me on my cell phone. It was night. I was waiting for Magdalena to get back

---

* Time between John Gotti being nicknamed "The Teflon Don" and getting sent to prison for life: eighteen months.

from playing an anniversary party. I had recently bought her a car.

Skinflick called me and said, "Dude, fuck, I am in *huge* huge trouble. I am *fucked.* I need your help. Can I come pick you up?"

"I don't know," I said. "Is it going to get me arrested?"

"No," he said. "It's nothing like that. It's not illegal. It's a lot fucking worse than that."

And because I hadn't finalized my break with him, I told him, "Fine. Pick me up."

The whole way out to Coney, Skinflick chewed his nails and took hits of cocaine out of an Altoids tin by licking his fingertip, dunking it, sniffing off the powder, then rubbing the rest around his gums like he was brushing his teeth.

"I can't tell you. I need to show you," he kept saying.

"Bullshit," I said. "Tell me."

"Please, dude. Please. Just be cool. You'll understand."

I doubted that. I felt like Skinflick and I were having the conversation I'd had with Sam Freed the night before the Feds dropped the charges. Only I knew that this time the surprise was not going to be anything good.

"Want some coke?" he said.

"No," I said.

By then I'd stopped doing drugs. I'd done a fair amount in jail, to fight the boredom, but compared to a six-mile run with Magdalena, let alone fucking her chilled sweaty body afterwards, that shit just didn't hold up. The amount Skinflick had on him, though, and the amount he snorted as he drove, were impressive and frightening.

He drove us to Coney, and parked in the same place we had almost two years earlier. Then we took the same underworld walk beneath the pier, though this time he had a larger Maglite.

We went through the fence gap and straight to the shark tank building. It looked smaller than I'd remembered it. The door was already unlocked.

I figured by then that Skinflick had lied to me about the illegal part, and that he'd killed someone and needed my help hiding the body. He pulled the door closed with a bang, and led the way up the curving metal stairs.

He turned his flashlight off as we ducked into the tank room itself, and for a moment all I could see was the gray glow of the skylights and, down below, their reflection in the black water.

Then I heard the noise — a high-pitched *"Mmmmmmmm!"*

The most accurate way to reproduce it would be to put gaffer's tape over your mouth then try to scream through it. Since gaffer's tape was what was over Magdalena's mouth.

I recognized the sound of her instantly. The adrenaline jacked my pupil size. Suddenly I could see.

There were half a dozen mob assholes, more or less, around the balcony. It's hard to count in those situations. I recognized a couple of them. All of them were armed.

The rope across the missing section of banister had been removed, and the ramp was unfolded out over the water. Magdalena and her brother Rovo, who was hulking behind her, were standing near the top of the ramp. Their arms, legs, and mouths were taped—sloppily, like the webs spiders weave when you test toxic drugs on them. There was an asshole with a gun just behind them.

An impulse hit me. *Kill.* All around the room, knees, eyes, and throats lit up like targets in a shooting gallery.

But I didn't target Skinflick. I could have—I could have lashed out backwards with my heel, and buried it so far past his sternum that I'd crush his heart. But somehow I didn't yet believe he could be part of this. He'd known about it, yes. But maybe he'd been forced to bring me here. Or *something.* So I spared him when I started killing.

The creep to my left wasn't so lucky. He had a Glock pointed at me. I moved in from the outside of it, visualizing the front of his shoulder blade through his chest and then feeling my shoulder crush toward it through his collarbone and lung. I clawed his throat out backhand as I took his gun. With my throat hand I grabbed Skinflick's flashlight and used it to blind two more of those fucks. Then I shot them through the chest.

But Skinflick, for once, was *fast.* Because this time all he had to do was flinch backwards through the doorway, and flinching was what he was expert at. From the safety of the arch he yelled *"Shoot!"*

I shot two more before they could start. Then the creep behind Magdalena and Rovo shoved them off the edge of the ramp, and they started dropping toward the water. I shot that creep through the forehead, and vaulted the railing.

I couldn't fall fast enough. I could see that Magdalena and Rovo, in addition to being taped up, were taped *together.* Just a couple of strands, but enough to hold. I was moving toward the water so slowly I wanted to scream. I shot another thug as his stomach came into view below the banister, just for something to do.

Someone else started shooting at me. I saw a muzzle-flash blossom slowly from the balcony, though by then I couldn't hear.

Then I finally hit the water, and things began to happen.

Water's always shocking, but I was shocked already, and the water felt as thin as air as I moved through it toward where I thought the Magdalena-Rovo bundle was. My knee hit something slimy that at first gave way like a leather bag filled with water, then sprang into life and lashed back at me.

A lucky grab got me Magdalena's hair. Something slapped me on the neck. I got hold of some gaffer's tape and thrashed for the surface. Breathed air that turned out to be water, then spasmed and finally got my head out. I kept kicking things with my legs. At one point I kicked something that felt like a giant slimy rock, so hard I almost sprained my ankle.

I didn't have time to think about it, though. I couldn't find Rovo's head. Finally I got smart and rotated him separately from Magdalena, and they both gasped in horribly through their nostrils.

I sank again, pushing them upwards. Something nosed into my stomach, hard. I needed support. I wondered if there was a shallow end, and if so how to find it.

When I came up for air again, someone on the balcony was

shooting. It didn't seem to matter all that much. I'd long since dropped the gun and the flashlight. What I needed was some way to keep us above water.

Something slammed me in the back and took us all toward one of the walls. I kicked us into the space where two of the hexagonal tank's walls came together, and tried to use the friction of the glass to lodge Magdalena and Rovo in place with their heads above water. I kicked and thrashed to keep the sharks away. The second it seemed to be working I reached up and tore the tape off Magdalena and Rovo's mouths.

Magdalena started choking at once. Rovo I had to thump on the chest. Every time I stopped kicking as hard as I could, something sideswiped my legs. Rovo and Magdalena starting wheezing, then hyperventilating. "Breathe!" I shouted.

The waves began to subside, though the butting from below kept up. I wasn't sure why the sharks hadn't attacked yet, but from the way they became more aggressive when my attention lapsed, it seemed clear they were testing me out.

And maybe the bullets had helped. I could hear someone moaning on the walkway above us.

After a long while Skinflick called out from somewhere else. "Pietro?"

I debated whether to respond. I was pretty sure he couldn't see us. I couldn't see him, in any case, just dim, grated light through the walkway directly overhead, and a small part of one skylight if I looked back over my shoulder. So Skinflick might not know whether we were still alive, and he might be trying to locate us by sound. I was thrashing quite a bit, but that could have been sharks.

I did know this, though:

I'd been stupid not to kill him up above. He, and no one else, had done this.

But he was also our only way out. As repugnant and hopeless as I knew it would be, I had no choice but to try to talk him out of it.

"Skinflick!" I said. My voice felt harsh and weak.

"How you feeling?" he said. His voice echoed around. At least it seemed impossible to pinpoint anything that way.

"What the hell are you doing?" I said.

"Killing you."

"Why?"

"My dad found out it was you that killed Kurt Limme."

"That's bullshit! Your dad killed Kurt Limme. Or paid some Russian to do it."

"I don't believe that."

"Why would I do it? What did I give a fuck? Get us out of here!"

"It's a bit too late for that," he said.

"For what? You know I'm telling you the truth!"

"Don't think you'd know truth if it bit you on the ass, pal. Which I believe it is about to do."

"Skinflick!" I shouted.

He was silent for several moments. Then he said, "You know why my dad hired the Virzis to kill your grandparents?"

"*What?*" I said.

"You heard me. You know why?"

"No! And I don't care!"

I didn't, actually. I didn't know whether it was true, I didn't know what it meant if it was, and I didn't want to hear Skinflick go on about it.

"It was a favor to some Russian Jews," he said. "Your grandparents weren't actually the Brnwas. They were Poles. They worked at Auschwitz as teenagers."

His voice intermittently cut out as the water got above my ears. I was pushing against both glass walls at once, trying to keep Magdalena and Rovo lodged into the corner. But they kept slipping down the front of my body.

"The real Brnwas died there," Skinflick went on. "And your grandparents took their identities to get out of the country after the war. But they met a Russian guy in Israel who recognized them, and who had known the real Brnwas. A friend of his called my dad."

I couldn't help taking part of this in. It had the feeling of something that would require figuring out, and possibly feeling bad about.

If, say, I was alive in a week.

Right now I needed Skinflick to shut up and help us.

"So what?" I screamed.

"So you don't know shit."

"Fine!" I said. "I forgive you! I forgive your dad! I forgive my fucking grandparents! Get us out of here!"

Skinflick didn't answer. Then he said, "I don't know, dude. You killed all my guys."

"That's a good thing," I said. "No one knows about this. Come on!" When he didn't say anything, I added, "You want me to help you kill someone else, I will!"

"Yeah. Like last time?" he said. "I think I'll take what's on the table, thanks. And that's you. Literally."

"The Farm wasn't my fault. You know that!"

I started to panic. My legs and arms were burning. Living things were sliming along my ankles. And I was having no luck whatsoever pulling the tape off Magdalena's and her brother's bodies. I could only stare into their terrified eyes, and feel their hot breath on my face.

"Whatever, pal," Skinflick said. "Or maybe I should say 'chum.' As in 'feeding time.' "

The guy dying over us dropped his gun into the water. It hit about three feet away, but there was nothing I could do about it. Skinflick fired a couple of shots into the water randomly when he heard the sound.

"Now I've got to get these fucking bodies out of here," he said, when the echo died down. "You know, I thought about bringing some meat in case the fish weren't biting. I guess that's not going to be necessary."

I figured that meant he was planning to throw one of the bodies into the water, and wondered if that might help us: a chunk of food the sharks could compare to us, and use to decide we *weren't* food.

Then I felt something on my face, and tasted copper. I looked up, and a big drop hit my eye. It stung. It was warm.

"At least let Magdalena and her brother out of here!" I yelled at Skinflick. "They didn't do anything to you!"

"Casualties of war, chum. Sorry."

Two seconds later the sharks began to strike.

The sharks had a choice of me or Rovo, because as soon as I real-ized what was happening I covered most of Magdalena's body with my own.

Rovo was throwing a lot fewer elbows than I was. The surface of the water bucked and splintered as they attacked him.

People sometimes say that all sharks do is swim and kill, but that gives them too much credit. They use the same muscles, along their sides, for both. They clamp their jaws shut on some-thing, then just whip side to side until a mouthful of it tears free. Then, if they feel they have the luxury, they back off until their target bleeds to death.

The sharks at Coney did not have that luxury, and they knew it. There were too many of them. That tank was an obscenely concentrated slice of organic hell, packed with animals that in the wild would swim hundreds of miles a day, and stay the fuck away from each other. Here, if they bit and backed off, there wouldn't be anything left. So the ones that struck Rovo pulled him off the wall toward the center of the tank, and dragged Mag-dalena and me with him.

It felt like we were being flushed down a drain. Underwater, with my legs around Magdalena, I found the tape around her arms and ripped it with my teeth. It tore out my lower left canine tooth and the one just behind it, but it got her free.

At the surface, though, she flailed away from me toward Rovo, who was being turned and yanked from every direction, and was still screaming blood in the light from above. I grabbed the tape around Magdalena's legs and pulled her back into the darkness just as Skinflick started firing again.

I think that's what actually killed Rovo. I fucking well hope so.

I got Magdalena back to one of the corners and pressed a hand over her mouth. I think she could see over my shoulder. She didn't have to. The water was *alive,* and you could feel the tearing and the snapping of the sharks fighting over her brother's body.

I don't know how long we stayed like that. I was holding us both against the walls, kicking to keep us afloat and also freaking out every time I felt or imagined I felt something brush against my feet or legs. Which was constantly.

What felt like a couple of hours went by. Over time the skirmishes got less violent and less frequent, until they ceased to break the surface of the water. God knows what pieces of Rovo were still worth fighting over. Things turned relatively quiet.

Then there was a voice up above. "Mr. Locano—Jesus fuck."

Somebody else spoke: "Holy shit!"

"Yeah," Skinflick said. "Just clean it up, would you?"

Someone started to drag bodies. It took a long time. The toes of the mob assholes' shoes made xylophone noises on the metal grating of the balcony.

Eventually they finished. Skinflick shone a flashlight around, but I kept us mostly underwater.

"Pietro?" he said.

I didn't answer.

"Nice knowing you, pal," he said.

He went and retracted the ramp before he left.

When I look back on it, half the time I ever spent with Magdalena seems to be that night.

We moved with infinite slowness around the perimeter. I kept her as high as I could against the glass, and she reached up into the darkness, searching for some low-lying strut or faucet or anything else we could use to pull ourselves out. I also searched with my feet for the rock I'd hit earlier. Neither one of us had any luck. The grating, five whole feet off the water, might as well have been a mile away.

In the corners you could sort of push outward against both panes of glass, even though the angle was wide, and hold yourself up. If you pushed too hard, you pushed yourself backwards off the wall. If you didn't push hard enough, you sank. My arms and neck were in agony.

And of course there were other, more trivial problems. The salt that made us buoyant enough to keep our heads above the surface was harsh in our eyes and mouths. The water itself was about eighty degrees, which feels warm at first but is easily cold enough to kill you if you're in it long enough.

When it came to saving Magdalena, though, I felt indestructible, and immune to fatigue. I came up with a technique. I put Magdalena's legs over my shoulders with her facing me so that I could keep as much of her as possible out of the water. I did it for hours, I think. Eventually we took her clothes off, since she was warmer without them. And eventually after that she let me lick her, although she never stopped crying, even while she came.

Judge me if you want. Judge her and I'll break your fucking head. You'll learn about the primordial when it enters your living room. The sharpness and the richness of Magdalena's pussy, the nerves down my spine that were receptive to no other stimuli, made the ocean seem weak. They meant life.*

Throughout the night we heard a snorting noise, maybe once every fifteen minutes. As the skylight brightened, slowly then ridiculously quickly, I started to see a small, round head appear at the surface, black eyes gleaming, to blow water out reptilian nostrils.

When I could read my watch, it was just past six AM. We were shivering and nauseated. Just as it became bright enough to see the sharks through the water, they turned a lot more aggressive. Apparently they like dawn and dusk. They came darting in like the shadows of a bouncing ball.

But they'd missed their chance. All it got them was a lot of shoe heel in the face. The tank brightened further. We could see that the snorting animal was a large sea turtle, and was probably also the thing I had thought was a rock. Then we could see that there were two of them. Then that the tank was packed with animals.

There were at least a dozen human-length sharks (twenty minutes later I was able to put the count at fourteen for sure), of two different types, neither of which I could identify. Both were brown and looked like they were made of suede, and had a sur-

---

* People think the ocean's about life, and freedom. But beaches are the most impassable barriers in nature. People worship them like they worship outer space, or death, or anything and anyone else that says no to them and means it.

prising and revolting number of fins along their sides. One type had spots.*

A slow, fluid stingray that looked like half its tail had been bitten off moved along the sand and cement bottom of the tank. Higher up there was a school of parrot fish, more than a foot long each, herding and striking at the remains of Rovo's body, driving them around the edges of the tank as they fed like he was dancing.

There wasn't much left of him: the torn-up head, the spine, the bones of his arms. His hands were shredded, the tendons splayed like pompons. Occasionally a shark would rake the body anyway for the fibrous remains of its meat, and send it head over heels until the fish got hold of it again. At one point I dunked and caught it as it went by, thinking that if I could keep the fish off it Magdalena might stop hyperventilating so much. But it made the sharks too aggressive, and the feel of it made me retch. The only place you could really hold on to it was at the sharp, slimy base of the spine, next to the holes through which both kidneys had been taken. So I just let it drift again and told Magdalena not to look at it. We both kept looking at it, though.

Around 7:30 the sharks steered away from us as if they'd heard some signal, and the feeder guy appeared.

He was in his twenties with a shaved head and sideburns, in yellow rubber pants. He stood and stared at Magdalena's spiked-

* They were tiger sharks or nurse sharks or something. Who gives a shit? Any shark that large will attack a human if it thinks it can get away with it. And all shallow-water sharks are brown on top and white underneath, so that fish above them will think they're sand, and fish below will think they're sky.

out nipples. She was completely naked. At least it kept the fucker from noticing Rovo.

"Get us out of here," I rasped.

He came and folded down the ramp, and I launched off the wall with Magdalena in my arms, ready to tear the eyes out of any shark that fucked with us now. Pulling myself up after I'd pushed her out made my head spin so hard my vision went to static for a moment.

"I'm calling the cops," he said.

"How?" I said. "You don't have a cell phone."

"Yeah I do," he said, taking it out.

Shithead. I smashed it on the railing, and dropped the pieces into the water after I knocked him unconscious.

The twenty-four hours that began at that moment were the worst and most important of my life. During them—though this is the least of it—I traveled close to two thousand miles, only to end up back in New York, one full day after Magdalena and I crawled out of the water.

Specifically, I ended up in Manhattan, where Skinflick's doorman recognized me and let me into the building. The two goons in Skinflick's apartment I killed with his glass coffee table.

Skinflick himself, still awake and coke-fried, I picked up by the hips, like I used to pick up Magdalena. Then I hurled him, twisting and screaming, face-first through his living room window.

Immediately afterwards I wished I had him back so I could do it all over again.

And from the street, where the crowds were already forming, I called Sam Freed, and for the second time that day told him where to pick me up.

21

I reach the street as a civilian. Free. I have given it all up. I will treat no more patients. And whatever a uniform and a prefix before my name have done for me, they will now stop doing. I have left the priesthood, molesting no altar boys along the way.

I should feel awful. I know that. It has taken me seven years to become a doctor. Essentially I have nothing else. No job. No safe place to live, even.

But somehow the freezing wind spitting ice up off the sidewalk tastes like night spring air full of fireflies and drunken female barbecue guests.

Because I don't feel bad at all.

I am in New York City. I can go rent a hotel room and call WITSEC from there. Then I can go to a *museum,* or a movie. I can ride the Staten Island Ferry. I probably shouldn't, since every male on Staten is either a mob guy or a cop, but I can. I can go buy a fucking *book* and read it in a *café.*

And fuck, how I have *hated* being a doctor.

Since med school I have hated it. The endless suffering and deaths of patients whose lives I was supposed to fix but couldn't, either because no one could or because I just wasn't good enough. The filth and the corruption. The corrosive hours.

And I have particularly hated this New York Death Star of a hospital, this fluorescent Moria known as ManCat.

I have remained a doctor as long as I could. I owe a debt, I know, and I appreciate that being a doctor has forced me to pay it, bringing me my good deed for the day, every day, so that I have not had to go looking for it.

But I can only pay what I can pay. Getting killed on top of giving up seven years won't help anyone. In fact it will just eat up resources. There is nothing more for me to do in this profession.

Which is hardly the end of the world. Maybe after I'm resettled I can work in a soup kitchen. Malpractice insurance for *that* can't be too high.

Dr. Friendly's term—"Post–Malpractice Suit"—comes to mind and makes me laugh.

Then it makes me think of something else, and I stop like someone's spiked my foot to the ground. I almost fall over.

I think it through to find the way it's wrong.

I keep thinking.

But it's pointless.

I know how to save Osteosarcoma Girl's leg.

Standing in the wind and muck, I try Surgery on my cell phone. No answer.

Orthopedics. Busy.

Akfal. Dvořák's *New World Symphony* comes on, which means he's taken a patient into MRI.

Meanwhile, at the end of the block ahead of me, two limousines pull up, and six men get out without speaking to each other.

All six have coats that go past their waists, to cover their weapons. There's a dark-haired guy and a Hispanic-looking one, but the other four look midwestern. Jeans and sneakers. Faces lined by too much time in the sun on their ranches in Wyoming and Idaho that they think no one knows about.

I've visited some of those ranches. On business, if you know what I mean.

The hitters split both ways at the corner, to block off all exits. I look behind me. Another two cars.

I've got about half a second to decide whether to cross the street and be gone or head back into the hospital.

I'm an idiot. I choose the hospital.

I race back up the escalators to the operating floors. If the guys outside are the first ones here, this will buy me some time, since they'll probably sweep from the ground up.

If.

I cut through the recovery room, where the ICU guys are still looking around the cubicle where Squillante died, trying to figure out where the printout from his EKG went. Eventually they'll get IT to print a new one. Like in a month.

In the Surgery locker room there's a flat-screen TV on the wall that shows the operating schedule. It says Osteosarcoma Girl had her leg removed three hours ago. Which is impossible, because I just saw her. At least there's a room number, one floor up.

When I get there, though, some schmuck in scrubs and a face mask is mopping the floor, and there's no one else there. Which *probably* means the schedule has the wrong room on it, but isn't a guarantee.

"When's the next procedure?" I ask the guy with the mop.

He just shrugs. Then, when I turn to leave, he drops the mop and loops a wire over my head.

Cute. The guy's probably been waiting here since he overheard me talking to Osteosarcoma Girl outside her room. Playing the long odds to keep Locano's reward money for himself. And he's a wire psycho.

A wire is simple to make, simple to get rid of, and simple to hide, even in scrubs. But only a psycho uses a wire. Who else wants to get that close to someone? I barely have time to get my hand up in front of my throat before he yanks it tight.

I realize then that it isn't going to kill me. At least not fast. With my hand palm-out in front of my voice box, and the tube of my stethoscope caught beneath the wire on both sides, the psycho can't generate enough force to cut off the arteries, even with the wire crossed behind my neck. He can cut off the veins, which are closer to the surface than the arteries, but that will just stop blood from *leaving* my head. I can already feel the heat and pressure building up. But I won't be unconscious for a while.

Then the guy does a back-and-forth sawing motion, quick enough that I can't take advantage of it, and the wire cuts deeply into my palm and the sides of my neck. The psycho's braided something into it—glass, or metal or something. The head of my stethoscope clanks as it bounces off the floor.

Apparently this *is* going to kill me fast.

I stomp on his foot. He's wearing steel-toed shoes. Of course he is—he's a wire psycho. He's expecting this. The toe cap caves a little, causing him to grunt as his toes get pinched, but it doesn't change his plans much. You can run a car over steel-toed shoes.

So I shove us both backwards, hard. He's expecting this too, and easily braces us against the operating table with his legs.

But this is *my* house. I drive my heel into the pedal that unlocks the table's brakes, and this time when we go flying it takes him by surprise.

I land on top of him on the floor. There's a satisfying grunt as his air goes. But his grip on the wire holds.

So with my free hand I reach back and grab a bunch of hair—which, stupidly, he has—on the left side of his head. Then I sit up, yanking him up and over my shoulder, and twisting him at the same time.

This only works if the wire psycho's right handed, or at least has his right wrist crossed over his left one. But I'm running out of options.

It works: the wire's no longer around my neck as he goes over.

The psycho hits the floor pretty hard and missing some hair, face up with his head toward me. Where it's not too much trouble for me to rapid-strike his face with alternating elbows and knife-hands—back and forth, back and forth—until he's unconscious and bleeding out the back of his head.

I get dizzily to my feet.

Wrong day to mop, fucko.

In the supply corridor between surgery rooms, I use a staple gun to close up my palm. The pain is maddening, but it'll keep my hand functional. My neck I wrap in a bandage. There's not much more I can do about it without being able to see it, and the most mirrorlike object I can find is an instruments tray.

While I'm changing into a new pair of scrubs, I notice the kit shelf, which has steel shoeboxes with the instruments for various surgeries. They're labeled things like "CHEST, OPEN" and "KIDNEY TRANSPLANT."

I pull out the one that says "LARGE BONE TRANSECTION." Select a knife that looks like a machete with a grip cut out of it and use it to slice open the side of my new pants. Then I attach it to my outer thigh with surgical tape.

When I go out to the sink to try to wash the blood off, there's a nurse there scratching his armpit with the needlelike camera of a laparoscope that will later be inserted into someone's abdomen by doctors wearing moon suits to prevent contamination.

He takes one look at me and scuttles off.

I go from room to room on the Surgery floors until I find Osteo-sarcoma Girl. It's the fastest way to do it. When I get there, she's unconscious, with the anesthesiologist holding the mask on her.

She's laid out naked on the table. The residents are squabbling over who gets to shave her pussy, which isn't necessary in the first place.

The scrub nurse's eyes go wide when he sees me. "You're not wearing a mask! Or a hat!" he shouts.

"It doesn't matter," I say. "Where's the doctor?"

"Get out of my operating room!"

"Tell me who's doing the surgery."

"Don't make me call security!"

I pat the front of his paper gown, contaminating it, and he shrieks. If the operation does happen, I've just extended it by half an hour. "Tell me where the fucking doctor is," I say.

"I'm right here," the doctor says, behind me. I turn. Above the mask he's patrician. "What the hell are you doing in my operating room?"

"This woman doesn't have osteosarcoma," I tell him.

His voice stays calm. "No? What does she have?"

"Endometriosis. It only bleeds when she's menstruating."

"The tumor is on her femur. Her distal femur." He looks at my neck bandage, which I imagine must be seeping again. It hurts like fuck. "Are you a physician?"

"Yes. It's migrated uterine tissue. It can happen. There have been cases."

"Name one."

"I can't. I heard about it from a professor."

In fact I heard about it from Prof. Marmoset, once when we were on a plane together. He was talking about the stupid shit you have to learn in medical school that you never see again in your life.

"That is the stupidest thing I've ever heard."

"I can pull a case up on Medline," I say. "She has uterine tissue in the anterior compartment of her quadriceps, attached to the periosteum. You can take it out. If you take her leg off instead, Pathology will realize that I'm right and fuck you. They'll fuck everybody in this room. I will make *sure* of that."

I stare around at each set of eyes I can find.

"Hmm," the doctor says.

I wonder if I'll have to touch the front of his gown too.

"All right, calm down," he finally says, tearing his gown off by himself. "I'll go do a lit search on Medline."

"Thank you."

"And with whom do I have the pleasure of speaking? Just so I can have you fired when you're wrong."

Good luck, dickhead.

"Bearclaw Brnwa," I tell him as I leave.

The escalator landing, though, is staked out: a hitter at each end, and two riding up to the next floor.

Fuck, I think. *How many of these guys are there?*

I have a Rambo moment in which I consider yanking a Purell alcohol hand gel dispenser off the wall and using it as napalm, but then decide that burning down a hospital filled with patients kind of crosses the line. Instead I double back to the fire stairs, which are echoing with the careful footsteps of people looking for me, and sprint up the three flights to Medicine as quietly as possible.

Heading back toward the center of my lair.

Which has its bonuses. Like my having hidden that fuckhead mugger's handgun up here.

I just have to find it.

I have no recollection whatsoever of where I put the gun. When I try to think back I feel only a haze of drugged-out exhaustion.

I decide to use a Prof. Marmoset trick.

According to Prof. Marmoset, you should never bother trying to remember where you put something. You should just imagine needing to put it somewhere *now*, then go to the place you pick. Because why would you pick a different location now than you did earlier? Your personality is more stable than *that*. It's not like we wake up each day as different people. It's just that we don't trust ourselves.

So I give it a shot. I use the Force. I imagine myself at 5:30 in the morning, with a handgun to hide and practically nothing on my mind.

It leads me to the nurses' lounge behind the Medicine station. To the antique textbooks on the high-up shelf that runs around it, which haven't been used since the advent of the Internet. To a large book in German on the central nervous system.

Behind it is the handgun.

Score another one for Marmoset.

Out in front at the nursing station I can see that there are two hitters at each end of the hall, searching rooms. Coming toward me.

If I want a straight-up shootout I can cross to the parallel hallway on the other side of the station, and fire at these guys from there. Which in addition to killing an unknown number of bystanders will bring every armed person in the hospital running. I think about this for a moment, then discard the idea. I've met those security guards.

I duck into a patient room behind me. I know it's empty because just before Squillante's surgery I discharged one of the patients who was in it, and the other one was the woman I found dead in her bed this morning. Nothing in this hospital happens fast enough for someone to have even pretended to change the sheets between then and now.

I search the cabinets. The largest gown I can find is a medium. I kick my clogs and clothes off into the bathroom, pull the tiny, warmthless thing on, and hop into the bed the woman died in.

A couple minutes later two hitters come into the room.

I'm lying back. They look at me. I look at them. The crappy gun I'm pointing at them from beneath the sheet feels ready to dissolve in my hand. Most of its weight is in its bullets.

I try not to look in their eyes. Even so, I realize what I must look like to them now that they've searched all the other rooms. Way too healthy, even with my stupid neck bandage on. A complete impostor.

They reach into their jackets simultaneously. I aim the fuckhead's gun at the nearer of the two and pull the trigger.

The hammer clicks but nothing happens. I pull the trigger again. Another click. Within two seconds I've tried all six cylinders, and the trigger is starting to bend. It's not the bullets, it's the firing pin or something.

Fucking cheapie bullshit gun. I throw it at them and reach for the knife taped to my thigh.

Apparently they Taser me.

I wake up.

I'm in a checkered linoleum hallway, face down. The two guys holding my arms know what they're doing: at least one of them has a foot on my back, so I can't roll forward to escape. The knife is gone. Most of what I can see are shoes. Most of what I hear is laughter.

"Just fucking do it," someone says. "This is making me sick."

"It's a precision job," another guy says, and there's more laughter.

I look around wildly. On the wall to my left there's a brushed aluminum door. A walk-in freezer. I'm still in the hospital.

Over my shoulder I can just see a guy crouching behind me with an enormous plastic syringe that's full of some brown fluid.

"We heard you got stuck with something nasty earlier, but it didn't kill you," he says. "So we thought we'd stick you with something even nastier."

"Please don't say it," I manage to say.

But he does: "If you weren't full of shit before, you will be now."

Hilarity. Meanwhile I'm still in the fucking hospital gown, which is untied at the back and lying open. The guy jams the syringe into my left buttock and injects the whole burning mess. At least he flicks the air bubbles out first.

"You'll be good and ready by the time Skingraft gets here," he says.

Apparently they Taser me again.

22

Magdalena and I left the Aquarium in the shark-feeder guy's green Subaru hatchback. I had to lean on the steering wheel with my chest to drive. I couldn't extend my arms.

Magdalena was in one of the yellow raincoats from the metal cabinet. She had her legs under her on the passenger's seat. She was keening so hard, her entire face red and wet with tears, that when she first spoke I didn't realize she had, or understand what she was saying.

Which was, over and over, "Stop."

"We can't," I said. My gums were hot and fat where I'd lost a tooth and ground down the socket.

"We have to tell my parents."

I thought about this. Her parents needed to leave. Once Skinflick found out we were still alive, he would go after them. They had to be warned.

But they also had to stay calm. If they called the cops before the Feds had protection in place, Skinflick would just find out sooner.

"You can't tell them about Rovo," I said.

"What do you mean?" Magdalena said. Both our voices were hoarse. Parody voices.

"You have to tell them to leave. To get out of New York. Get off the East Coast. Go to Europe. But if you tell them Rovo's dead they'll freak out, or they'll stay, or both."

"They deserve to know," Magdalena said.

"Baby, you can't," I said.

"Don't call me baby," she said. "Never call me baby. There's a payphone. Pull over."

I pulled over. If she hated me, which she was right to, there was certainly nothing else worth worrying about.

I think she did lie to her parents about Rovo, though. Because she was crying while she talked to them, but silently, with her chest jolting in and out.

Whatever she said, she said it in Romanian.

For which I am eternally grateful.

It was night by the time we crossed into Illinois. There was a restaurant pretty high above the highway in a long strip of widely spaced motels. It was Somebody's Pies or something. It was a chain.

Magdalena came in with me to order, shivering the whole time. It was stupid to be seen together, but I couldn't let her out of my sight. I felt rootless to the point of nonexistence.

What Skinflick had said about my grandparents, I knew, had been right. It explained too much: all those years of avoiding other Jews, their silence about their families before the war, the wrong tattoos on their forearms. I didn't know what to make of it, or of their attempt to live their lives as other people, but I knew I had only one connection to humanity now, and that was Magdalena.

The restaurant we stopped at I don't remember much about. I'm sure it was orange and brown, like all highway restaurants. We ate in the car. Then Magdalena fell asleep in the hatchback with the seats folded down, and I snuck out and called Sam Freed, and told him we were ready to come in.

"This may take a little while," he said. "I don't know who I can trust with this." He thought for a few moments. "I don't want to call anybody I don't have to, but we may not have a choice. I'll get a few people and fly out there myself. It shouldn't take more than six hours."

I woke up in the back of the Subaru, with Magdalena curled away from me.

It was still night, but the shadow of someone's head had

jumped onto the fogged-over back window, because whoever it was was backlit by the streetlight behind the restaurant parking lot.

The head was not wearing a police hat. I heard no radios, and saw no flashlight. The owner of the head was doing his best to move as quietly as possible as he worked his way around the car. When the shadow was outside the right rear door, I kicked the door open and into the guy's stomach, then launched myself out after him.

The guy stayed on his feet for about five sideways steps, then went down, and I was on him. His nylon coat hissed on the asphalt as I dragged him behind the dumpster, out of the light.

I didn't recognize him. He was early twenties. Thin, glasses, white guy. I slammed him face-first into the side of the dumpster.

"You with the Feds?" I said. He was too nerdy to be a hitman.

"No, man! I thought that was my car!"

"Bullshit." I slammed him again.

He started crying. "I just thought you guys were effing," he says.

"What?"

"I wanted to watch!"

He was sobbing. I searched his pockets, but there was nothing there but a velcro wallet. His driver's license was from Indiana.

And his fly was open.

"Jesus," I said.

I leaned out to tell Magdalena it was all right. She was sitting up in the back of the Subaru.

Then, suddenly, she was lit up by headlights, and I heard the squealing of tires.

The SUV's windows must have already been down. The broadside of submachinegun and shotgun fire they vomited out, lighting up the Subaru all over again, came too quickly for them not to have been.

Then the SUV leaped forward and out of my way, as if I had brushed it aside with my hands. I heard it sideswiping cars behind me as it rocketed from the lot.

I reached the Subaru. It looked stepped on, the whole side of it crushed in by gunfire. The air was filled with glass dust and the smells of cordite and blood.

The door came off in my hands. Magdalena's head lolled as I pulled her out and spun with her to the ground.

Her right cheekbone was caved in, smashed like the side of the car and filled with blood. Both eyes were completely red, the left one with a seam across it that oozed perfectly clear jelly all the way down the side of her head.

When I grabbed her face up to mine, I felt bones I couldn't see shift beneath her skin.

When God is truly angry, He will not send vengeful angels.

He will send Magdalena.

Then take her away.

23

I wake up. It's difficult. It takes a couple of tries. I'm so incredibly cold that staying asleep seems preferable to finding out why.

Eventually, though, I try to turn over, and the fact that my dick is stuck to the floor wakes me all the way up immediately. At first I think my dick has been nailed there, since it's so numb it feels like a piece of leather that's tethering me in place. Then I touch it and decide it's been glued there. Then I realize it's frozen to the steel floor.

I spit into my left hand—I'm rolled over on my right arm, and I don't want to lie on my stomach again, even for a moment, to free it—and use the spit to de-ice my dick. It takes a couple of applications. It's kind of like whacking off.

As I'm doing it, though, the blindness-panic sets in. Because I cannot see *anything*. Between spit applications I grind the knuckles of my free hand into my eyes. Those weird pixilated multicolored blossoms appear, which I decide means that my retinal nerves are still functioning. Also that, since my eyes themselves feel fine to the touch, it's just completely dark in here.

Which is where, exactly? The moment my dick is loose I jump to my feet. My hospital gown, which has been bunched up around my chest, falls back down to cover the quarter of my body it's supposed to. The bandages from my hand and neck, though, are gone.

I reach forward. Touch a steel wall a couple of feet in front of me. Step toward it and bash my front teeth on something hard and metal. The pain and surprise make me jump back, and I hit another bunch of metal things. Shelves. I move my hands over them like they're a large-print version of Braille. Find dozens of bags of ice in the shape of blood units for transfusion.

I try the other side, then the back. Same thing. The front is a metal door, the handle of which doesn't move at all.

I'm in a walk-in freezer about the size of a jail cell. A blood freezer.

Why?

Obviously I could die in here. I could also get brain damaged, like a sous-chef I once treated who had spent a full night locked in the deep-freeze of the restaurant he worked at. But for someone to use a deep-freeze to try to do either of those things intentionally seems absurd. It's like the Joker leaving Batman in a sno-cone machine, then not sticking around to watch.

Though injecting feces into someone's butt cheek seems a little odd too, when you think about it.

I do think about it for a moment, because it's so disgusting. Then I move on. If I was going to die from toxic shock I already would have.* And in terms of long-term consequences, should I live to find them out, I'm already on every kind of antibiotic there is. Thank you, Assman: I have no idea what's wrong with you, but I do stand by your treatment protocol.

Then I realize why I'm here.

They're not trying to kill me. They're trying to weaken me, like the six different kinds of assholes in *Ferdinand* who stab the bull half to death before the matador even enters the arena.

So that Skinflick can come in and kill me himself.

With his knife fighting, presumably. Where was it Squillante said Skinflick had been training? Brazil? Argentina? I try to remember if I've heard anything about the styles of knife fighting in either of those places. I can't.

I do know that there are really just two underlying philosophies of knife fighting: the Realist School, which holds that any time you fight someone who knows what he's doing you *are*

---

* Toxic shock is an immune response set off by contaminants in your blood such as bacteria—which make up 20 percent by weight of human feces, all grown within your intestines. (Cows can survive on this bacteria, "eating" grass just so the bacteria, their real food, will grow on it.) During shock your veins open up to let white blood cells into your tissues to fight the infection, and the fluid that leaks out with them causes your blood pressure to crash.

going to be cut, so you should prepare for it (these are the guys you see wrapping their leather jackets around their left forearms before a fight), and the Idealist School, which believes you should devote as much energy as it takes to keeping yourself from being cut at all. By never, for example, having a nonstriking part of your body be forward of your blade.

Both schools follow a couple of basic rules. You have to remember to kick and punch if you get the opportunity, because knives are so scary people forget about the rest of you. And as long as you have a knife with an edge on it, you should never try to stab someone. Stabbing is a sucker move. It exposes too much of your body for too little possibility of damage. Slashing, meanwhile, should be done to any target that presents itself (such as the knuckles of your opponent's knife hand), but ideally to the insides of his arms or thighs, where the larger blood vessels run. So your opponent bleeds to death, like animals attacked by sharks in the wild.

On principle—and because I have a tiny hospital gown instead of a leather jacket—I lean toward the Idealist School. Of course, I also lean toward having a knife, which at the moment I don't. So I set about trying to change that.

First I explore the freezer. Naked socket, no bulb, in the ceiling. A lot of shelves of blood products.

Maybe I can build a blood-product snowman, and nauseate Skinflick to death.

The shelves themselves are useless. They're welded to their framework, which is made of thick iron L-bars that are in turn welded to square iron plates, about the size of coasters, which are bolted onto the floor and the ceiling. The bolts are all too tight to fuck with, particularly since I'm quickly losing sensation in my fingertips, even the ones I didn't spit on, and my hand that got cut is starting to stiffen at the palm. Hammering on the shelves, which is hard to do because there's barely any room to raise my fist above them, makes more noise than is probably wise and doesn't even dent them. The door handle doesn't break off even when I put both feet on the door and pull.

I consider what it would be like fighting with just my hands and feet, both of which are starting to feel like steaks tied to the ends of my limbs. I think about strategy: whether I should stay near the door or not and so on.

But thinking without moving starts to shut me down again. I do another sweep of the room. It's hard to be sure I've checked all of every shelf when I can't see and my sense of touch is so bad, so I start using my forearm to feel with. The nerve density is lower, but the better circulation makes up for it.

Eventually I discover that the plate at the base of one of the bars has a sharp edge. The plate's about six inches square and a quarter inch thick. If I could pry it loose with the bar still attached to it, I'd be holding a fairly awesome weapon. I try the trick with the feet against the wall again. No dice. Just a reminder that I'm weaker than I was half an hour ago.

I lean against the shelves to catch my breath. Fuck the fact that the metal is leaching heat out of me. I need to figure out what to do.

Or whether to do anything.

What difference does it make? If I get out of this, David Locano will just find me again, and kill me. And it'll be while I'm working as a gas station attendant in Nevada. Standing around all day because nobody uses gas station attendants anymore, they just swipe their credit cards at the pump.

Whereas if I die here, there's always a chance that Magdalena was right about there being an afterlife. Then a chance someone fucks up and lets me in, and I see her again.

I'm starting to get both loopy and morose. Things are starting to seem abstract, and to not matter. I'm losing it.

I must stop losing it.

I must think of a plan.

I bang my head against the edge of a shelf. The pain wakes me up. Enables me to think, at least, of *something*.

Something so crazy and stupid, so incredibly unlikely to work, that I would never even try it except for one small promise that it makes.

That the attempt will make me suffer magnificently.

So much so that, if it works and I survive, I may even deserve to.

If you keep your heel on the ground and lift your foot toward the ceiling, then spread your toes apart (not that easy, I know—it makes you admit you're a primate), you create a distinct channel along the outside of your lower leg, between the muscles of your shin and the muscles of your calf. This is the channel I'm hoping to cut into.

I drop to my knees by the floor plate, and press my right shin onto it so that the plate's sharp corner jabs into the skin just below my knee. I would prefer to be doing this to my left shin, but that would be too hard to get to with my right hand. So it's my right shin I push down and forward against the corner.

It doesn't work. I've barely scratched myself. I must have let up on the pressure at the last moment, subconsciously preventing myself from raking the skin open.

I numb my shin out with an ice pack of blood, and this time when I run it over the sharpened corner I push down on my calf with my right hand, to keep the leg from bucking. Yeah, the leg *tries* to buck. But this time it's too weak, and the skin rips.

The pain makes me roll over onto my back and grab my knee up to my chest while doing everything I can to keep from screaming through my eyes. But with my foot in that position I can feel that the top of it has turned instantly, completely numb except for the webbing between my big toe and the next one over. Which is great news: I've cut so deep I've severed the nerve that runs just above the muscle.

I wait a minute or so to see if I've also severed the artery that runs alongside the nerve—i.e., whether I've just killed myself, and can relax for the last few moments of my life—then I gingerly feel along the gash to make sure it's long enough. It is: it runs about three-quarters of the way down to my foot. So I roll and press it against the icy floor to kill the pain a bit, and slow the bleeding. I can't really tell if that works.

Anyway, there's no time like the present. I sit back on my ass. My scrotum, which was already tight, yanks tighter so fast it feels like it's going to sling my testicles up into my skull. I sink the fingers of both hands into my leg wound.

A whole new type of pain rips into me, this one reaching up

into my hip, and I realize: I will not be able to try this again. So I force my fingertips down between the hot and ropy muscles.

Which, as slippery as they are, contract like steel cables, almost breaking my fingers. "Fuck you!" I shout, and pull them apart by force, working the fingers of my right hand in deeper. I can feel the pulsation of the artery against my knuckles.

Then it happens: I touch my left fibula.

The fibula and tibia, as I believe I've mentioned, are the equivalent of the two parallel bones of your forearm. But, unlike in the forearm, the smaller of the two—the fibula—doesn't do nearly as much as the larger one. Its upper end forms a minor part of the knee, and its lower end is your outer ankle bone. The rest of it is totally useless. It doesn't even bear weight.

So I shove my fingers through the membrane that runs between the fibula and the tibia, and grab hold of the bone. It's about three times the thickness of a pencil, but it isn't cylindrical. It has sharp edges.

And now I need to break it. Ideally without wrecking my ankle or knee. The very thought makes me turn my head away and vomit down the left side of my chest. Not much comes out, but hey—it's warm. And no way do I let go of my fibula.

How the fuck am I supposed to break it, though? It's essentially made of stone. Any hit strong enough to break it might also shatter it. I think of kicking it into the sharp edge of the lowest shelf, but that's more likely to hurt the tibia, which forms most of the shin.

Then it comes to me. I scoot forward and put my shin up against the edge of the shelf as gently as possible, as close to the ankle as possible. I work my grip higher toward my knee. Then I yank the bone forward, snapping the lower part off just above the ankle and wrenching the upper part free of the tangle of ligaments that hold the knee together.

O Pain.

O Pain.

You know when you're entirely greasy with sweat even though you're in a deep-freeze that you may have taken things too far.

Or when you're holding a knife you've just made out of your own shinbone.

Eventually the door unlocks, then opens, and someone says, "Come on out."

I don't move. I'm backed up against the rear shelf, trying to keep my streaming eyes open to acclimate them as quickly as possible to the light, which right now is a roaring wall of pure white. I'm holding the knife hidden behind its cousins in my right forearm.

A man with a gun appears in silhouette and says "I said, Come . . . Jesus *Christ!*" Then he says, "He's back there. But he's covered in blood, Mr. Locano."

A crowd of other men with guns appears behind him to look in. "Oh, fuck," one of them says.

Then Skinflick speaks. I recognize his voice, though it's rougher than it used to be. Both deeper and with a strange new whistle to it.

"Get him out of there," Skinflick says.

No one does anything.

"It's just hepatitis," I say. "You probably won't catch it from touching me."

Everyone backs away from the doorway.

"Fuck all of you," Skinflick says.

He steps into sight. I can't see him too well because he's silhouetted and my eyes are still freaking out. But he doesn't look good. In fact he looks like someone gave an Adam Locano kit to a four-year-old, when it's recommended for ages nine and up. His entire head is potluck.

I should talk. I'm naked, except for the blood. My own and the extra bag I needlessly smeared all over myself to draw attention away from my right leg, and the tourniquet there that I made out of my hospital gown. There's blood all over the room.

I can't tell if it bothers Skinflick. He comes in waving his knife, held backhand. The blade is serpentine, with a pattern on the side, so it's probably Indonesian.

Skinflick's not bad. He keeps the knife going constantly, in a kind of electron cloud of defense. Idealist School all the way. But the moment he sees *my* knife—proud product of my own flesh and blood—he stops and flinches away in fear and surprise, exposing his entire right side to me.

"Jesus, Skinflick," I say.

I stab him just below the right side of his ribcage, angling upwards through the natural hole in his diaphragm, so that the jagged end of my fibula punctures his aorta before coming to rest inside his beating heart.

Beating till that moment, I mean.

24

The next thing I remember is waking up. The thing I remember after that is thinking that *For a guy who complains all the time about never getting any sleep, I sure wake up a lot.*

I'm in a hospital bed. Prof. Marmoset is sitting in the La-Z-Boy by the head, reading and marking up what looks like a journal article.

I'm struck, as always, by how young he looks. Prof. Marmoset has a kind of agelessness that comes from being smarter and better informed than, say, I will ever be, and having really thick hair. But he can't be that much older than I am.

"Professor Marmoset!" I say.

"Ishmael! You're awake," he says. "Good. I need to get out of here."

I sit up. I feel dizzy but stay up on one arm anyway. "How long have I been out?" I say.

"Not as long as you think. A few hours. I caught a flight right after we talked. You should lie down."

I lie down. Pull the blanket aside. My right leg is heavily bandaged. I still have patches of dried blood all over me. "What happened?" I say.

"You're better at surgery than I remembered," Prof. Marmoset says. "That bit with the girl who turned out not to have osteosarcoma was impressive. We discussed a case like that once, I think. But the autofibulectomy was *very* impressive. You may have to write that up for the *New England Journal*. For the Federal Witness Edition, at least."

"What happened with those guys?"

"The mob guys?"

I nod.

"David Locano's son, you stabbed in the heart. The rest of them you shot with David Locano's son's gun. Except for one of them, whose head you slammed in the fridge door a bunch of times. He's not going to make it either."

"Jesus. I don't remember any of that."

"You'll be wanting to stick to that story."

"Why? Am I under arrest?"

"Not yet. Keep your fingers crossed." He gathers up his papers. "It's great to see you're all right. I really wish I could stay longer."

I force myself to ask. "Are they going to throw me out?"

"Of Manhattan Catholic? Definitely."

"Of medicine."

Prof. Marmoset looks right at me, for what I realize might be the first time in my life. His eyes are a lighter shade of brown than I'd thought.

"That depends," he says. "Do you feel your work as a physician is done?"

I think about it.

"Not even close," I have to say. "I wish it was."

"So we'll figure something out," he says. "In the meantime, you may need to get a grant to go do research for a while. Somewhere far away. I recommend UC Davis. Call me about it." He stands.

"Wait," I say. "What about Squillante?"

"Still dead."

"Who killed him?"

"Your med students."

"What?" I say. "Why?"

"He went into ventricular fibrillation. They tried to stop it by giving him potassium. They thought they were doing him a favor."

"That's my fault. I gave them way too much responsibility."

"That's what they're off claiming now."

"I was asleep when it happened."

He looks at his watch. "*They* weren't. And they knew better than to try to handle a code on their own. Anyway, it's not our problem: they'll either get thrown out or they won't."

"How did you find out it was them?"

Prof. Marmoset looks uncomfortable. "It . . . seemed kind of obvious. Anything else?"

"Just one more thing," I tell him. "I had a patient with multiple abscesses. I got an anonymous call claiming he was bitten by a bat—"

"The man from your needlestick."

"Right. How's he doing?"

Prof. Marmoset shrugs. "His insurance company wouldn't pay for him to stay another day, so he got transferred to a state facility."

"But what was wrong with him?"

"Who knows? *You* can try calling them if you want. Odds are we'll never hear anything else about it. Your own blood work is clear. It's just one more thing that's not our problem."

He pats me on the noninjured knee. "It's like the alcoholics say. Any time you can tell the difference between something you can do something about and something you can't, you should thank God. Particularly if it turns out to be something you can't."

I shift, and the pain in my leg ignites, then fades weirdly. My head and my stomach are both light from painkillers. "Thank you for coming," I say.

"I wouldn't miss it. Call me."

"I will."

He leaves. I doze.

It's cool: he's got shit to do.

I don't.

WARNING

All parts of this book except this paragraph, the acknowledgments, and the dedication are fiction. Even the epigraph is fiction. Believing otherwise, particularly regarding medical information, would be a very bad idea.

ACKNOWLEDGMENTS

TEACHERS Stanley and Doris Tanz, Marvin Terban, Gilbert and Barbara Millstein, Martin Martel, Wendi Dragonfire, Arnold Weinstein, Michael Wilkes

MOVERS Susan Dominus, Markus Hoffmann, Reagan Arthur, Michael Pietsch

SOURCES DESERVING SPECIAL MENTION FOR INFORMATION NOT FOUND ELSEWHERE *Cause of Death: A Leading Forensic Expert Sets the Record Straight*, by Cyril H. Wecht, Mark Curriden, and Benjamin Wecht; Guy Shochat; Office of the Chief Medical Examiner, City of New York; New York Aquarium; *WITSEC: Inside the Federal Witness Protection Program*, by Pete Earley and Gerald Shur

SUPPORT IN NEW YORK   The Bazell family, Benjamin Dattner, Joanna Fried, the Fried family, Eric Grode, Marc Leonardo, Linda Lewis, C-Lo and the Gang, Marcia Lux, Elizabeth O'Neill, Joseph Rhinewine, Scott Small, David Sugar, Susan Turner, Jason White, Jesse Zanger, Sam Zanger

SUPPORT IN SAN FRANCISCO   Joseph Caston, Robert Daroff, Ellen Haller, Cassis Henry, Tamar Hurwitz, Marc Jacobs, Yunnie Lee, Peri Soyugenc, Kim Stopak, my co-residents at UCSF

SUPPORT ELSEWHERE   Michael Bennett, Edward Goljan, the Gordon family, Mary Victoria Robbins, Lawrence Stern

CANINE SUPPORT   Lottie

SUPPORT ALL OVER THE PLACE, SINCE BIRTH   my sister Rebecca Bazell